KNIGHT'S MOVE

Margaret held her own at chess with the infamous Lord Dade—but here in the darkness of Vauxhall Gardens she was a novice facing a master in a far different game.

"I only wish to please you by saying good-bye," he said. But he made no move away from her.

"Why should it please me?" she demanded. "Do you want me to despise you, as others do? You have been a hero to me, my white knight. You saved me from the attack of a mad dog, and then from my own folly and the advances of Creighton Soames."

"The only one your white knight would seem incapable of saving you from, my dear . . ." he rasped, "is me." He pulled her into his arms and lowered his lips to hers. She could feel the rise and fall of his chest against her breast. Startled by the magic of his touch, her mouth opened to his. And like the fireworks lighting the sky above the Gardens, something exploded inside Margaret, showering her with the sensation of light, heat, and color.

Margaret had done the most dangerous thing in the world. She had awoken the dormant desires of a lord who could not want her as a wife but only as a woman. . . .

Miss Dornton's Hero

by

Elisabeth Fairchild

A SIGNET BOOK

SIGNET

Published by the Penguin Group
Penguin Books USA Inc., 375 Hudson Street,
New York, New York 10014, U.S.A.
Penguin Books Ltd, 27 Wrights Lane,
London W8 5TZ, England
Penguin Books Australia Ltd, Ringwood, Victoria, Australia
Penguin Books Canada Ltd, 10 Alcorn Avenue,
Toronto, Ontario, Canada M4V 3B2
Penguin Books (N.Z.) Ltd, 182-190 Wairau Road, Auckland 10, New Zealand

Penguin Books Ltd, Registered Offices:
Harmondsworth, Middlesex, England

First published by Signet,
an imprint of Dutton Signet,
a division of Penguin Books USA Inc.

First Printing, February, 1995
1 3 5 7 9 10 8 6 4 2

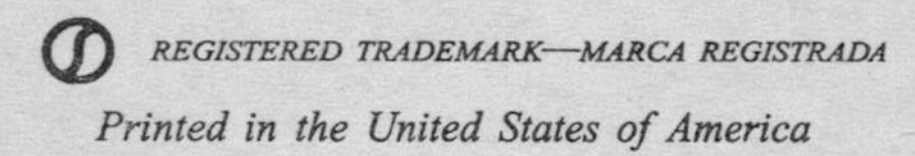

Printed in the United States of America

To my parents, who are still haunted by war—and to those who helped me understand that we must open our hearts to the lessons of our losses—my husband, George, my sisters, Debbie and Susan, and my dear friends: Kalin, Melissa, Julie, Paula and Anna.

Prologue

The Waterloo Battlefield, Belgium
June 19, 1815

THE first thing Captain Evelyn Dade heard as his consciousness swam up out of the dark weight of oblivion was the voice of an Englishman and the groans of the injured and dying. The noises seemed oddly out of place. The last thing he remembered was his uncontrollable horse fairly wrenching his arms out of their sockets as he charged into the midst of a raging battle, his men on all sides. His ears still rang with their cries.

"Royals on!" they had roared. Ahead of them, just as fierce, the Scots had been shouting, "Scotland forever!" There were no more shouts—no more cracking gunfire, no thundering cannon, no shouted orders, no rattle of ball on shield, no shriek of rockets echoing the screams of those hit. There was only the weighty voice of this Englishman, the whisper of wind through the rye into which he had fallen, weak calls for water and the stomach-turning stench of death that hung like a heavy blanket all around him.

Death figured strongly in his memory. Was this death? He had seen it coming on all sides, treading on all that stood in its path. Cannon fire and smoking musket ball, rearing horses and flashing bayonets—all the tools of death. In front of him, like ghosts in the thick fog of gunfire, the double rank of three hundred Scots Greys mounted on their trademark grey horses had plunged and tumbled under the assault.

The Blues, on either side of him, had been flung from the saddle by it. Young men he had known for a lifetime, young men he had known only days, young men in foreign colors whom he would never know—all had been cut down in the midst of the deafening roar of death's approach. The screams of his men and their horses still rang in his ears, all going down in the waving field of rye, mouths working, blood spouting, eyes wide in the horror of confrontation.

Was he down too? He could not remember. All he had to give him a clue was the insistent English voice and a dark, panicky weight in his gut that filled him with the sensation that no matter how dark his memories, reality was bleaker, blacker and completely in keeping with the heavy, bloody stench that imbued every pore of his being.

"Here, lad, give us a smile," the voice grunted, "you've no need of it anymore." Then there was a crack, crack, crack, as if bone were snapping as the voice went on. "There, that's a start. I do thank you for the pearlies. They've good company in this barrel. Scots Greys have gone in before you, and those of the Royals who went down beside you. Inniskillings too, and Frog infantry by the score. Brave lads all." The cracking sound again. "You may not have lived to see England again, sir, but rest assured, your grin shall go on charming the ladies, if only from some other man's mouth." A grunt and a crack. "Some Bond Street beau, I'll be bound, who has rotted out his own pegs with too much wine and sweetmeats, shall be most happy to inherit these lovely teeth of yours. Now, I shall just gently close up your mouth, lad, and mum's the word all the way around. No chance you'll bite your tongue."

The one-sided conversation seemed a bit of madness. Could this be Hell? Dade's throat was thick with thirst, but he had not the strength to cry out for water. His eyes seemed glued shut. He could not pull them open. His legs were numb, immobile from the waist down, as though the great, dark, weighty smell of death pinned them in place.

A second voice grumbled. "Whyever do you go about talking to them in that cloth-headed fashion, Jess? There's none as will hear you, much less answer. Just get cracking and be done with the bloody job. 'Ere's another one." Like the voice of a beautifully human angel, the remark came from directly overhead. "Gone down under 'is poor 'orse, he has. Blimey, the animal's got a great stinking hole in 'im."

Dade felt a hand on his face. He was not dead. This hand reeked of sweat and dirt and blood. Surely one did not recognize the odors of the living when one was dead.

Rough fingers fumbled with his lips.

"Cor! This un's got an effing good set of chompers 'ere, 'e does. But I'll not be asking 'im to smile. 'is face is caked in blood, and a gruesome sight it would be were he to oblige me."

There was a laugh. The rude fingers pried open his mouth. They tasted of blood and gore and dirt. Offended by their liberty, Dade found within himself the required strength to bite down on the intrusive digits.

"Argh!" The hand backed away.

Dade managed to open one eye. A grimy face hung like a round-eyed moon above his. The man was not an angel at all. He was a corpse harvester, come to relieve him of his teeth. He held a tooth extractor, poised to plunge.

"I've still need of them," Dade whispered hoarsely.

A grin cracked the grimy face. "Well, scarper me. He's a live one, Jess, under all this blood, and an Englishman. Just come and see if he's not. Bit me hand, he did, rather than let me take his gnashers. Has need of them, 'e said. Has need of them. Ha-hah!"

Chapter 1

London, England
February 14, 1816

MARGARET Dornton always rose at dawn. It was a custom she had adopted in childhood, in the country. Now, though she spent the Season in London with her elder sisters, the twins, and stayed up until an unseemly hour enjoying what was to be seen and done there, she could not shake the habit. Miss Dornton liked the early morning hours. There was a youthful promise to mornings, all dew and gray mist. It was the only time the house was at all still. Even then Cook was rattling about in the kitchen, and the stable lads were whistling cheerfully in the mews. No, London was not really quiet at this hour, but it was as fresh as it could be. It rained almost every night this time of year, and the precipitation served to kindly damp down the acrid pall of coal smoke that hung perpetually upon the breeze.

It was to St. James's Park or the Green Park Margaret went so early, for a taste of the country, though the trees were still largely bare, the sky usually gray and no flowers yet to be seen other than an occasional snowdrop or daisy.

St. James's was not particularly popular these days, so she had it largely to herself. The park had once been the grounds of a hospice for fourteen leprous maidens, but it was not this ancient bit of history that presently made the park unpopular. Nor was it the ruined Chinese pagoda on the mirrored bridge that had accidentally blown up, killing a poor spectator at the Prince Regent's Centennial Celebration two years past. No, St. James's was simply unfortunate enough to be laid out in the French fashion, with straight-arrow walkways, straight-lined beds of plants and flowers and a straight, narrow, man-made channel sparkling in the middle. Nothing French was the vogue right now. The prince himself was displeased with St. James's. It was said he had plans for redesigning it.

But Margaret could not be disappointed. The promise of spring was to be seen in the park. Soon the cherry trees would be white with blooms. Starlings, robins, finches and tits were busy in the trees. Everywhere there were hints of the coming explosion of growth. Trees and shrubbery were pregnant with buds, the ground soft with a hint of green as the first tender shoots poked out their heads.

Her dogs must be walked. She would not allow anyone else the task, for then she would miss the brisk, almost frosty chill of morning in the first light of the rising sun as it touched the burgeoning trees with magic and glazed the canal with silver. The honking of ducks and geese upon the fog-shrouded water appealed to the romance of her soul. There was something about this time of day that lent itself to the imagination. Anything seemed possible in these early hours, even the implausible prospect of meeting her true love.

"You must not look at any of the gentlemen you encounter this morning, miss," the maid who had tended her fire this morning had warned her.

"Why not?" Margaret had asked.

"The first unattached gentleman a maid sets her eyes on, be it Valentine's Day, is destined to be her true love."

Margaret had laughed at such a quaint notion. She was quite consumed by the romantic ideal of heroes, but not at all by the notion of falling in love. That was the business of the twins this Season. Her sisters were the ones who meant to find husbands, not she.

Margaret would be content merely to meet a hero, someone courageous and brave. She had read about heroes in the daily news throughout the duration of the grueling confrontation with Napoleon and had been introduced to several uniformed gentlemen as they returned from the conflict. They were, she had decided, vaguely disappointing. Could these tired, weather-beaten men truly be heroes? They spoke of conflict, of battles lost and battles won, of brave lads killed and brave lads come home with missing bits. But they lacked a certain spark Margaret was sure must gleam in a true hero's eyes. These were but fighting men, she decided, not heroes. These men—she blushed to think it—seemed ordinary. It occurred to her that perhaps she had as yet met only the garden-variety type of hero.

Margaret felt herself a qualified judge on this particular subject. Courage was a matter of deep interest to her. She had reveled in heroes long before Napoleon spawned the more recent ones in the reading of history and mythology. She had collected dozens of books on the subject, each lavishly illustrated with detailed, hand-tinted plates depicting heroes throughout the ages. These resources offered an excellent idea of what a hero might look like. His demeanor and carriage, the very set of his head, was sure to reveal the courage within him.

One might easily imagine bygone heroes in the park this morning with no one about: Greek heroes with perfect bodies and close-cropped hair or knights in shining armor, their lances fluttering with bright standards. One need not be limited to the heroes of the present in their crisp red or blue military colors, epaulets gleaming, horses at the gallop, swords raised to fight the French. Imagine them Margaret did, for she was certain she was meant to meet some sort of hero in a place the size of London. Fate and St. Valentine could not deny her such an encounter.

Her aunt and uncle could not imagine why she should care to be about so early, but they allowed her to go to St. James's or the Green as long as she dressed warmly and took Ludd with her. The deaf and gouty old footman took an interminable amount of time getting her there, but Margaret could not complain. She enjoyed imagining him her minion ready to fight off brigands with drawn sword, or a wizard with a magic staff in place of his ordinary cane. Ludd rarely interrupted her daydreams with unwanted conversation, and once the park was reached, she and the dogs were allowed to roam freely, as long as they kept within visual range of the old gent. It was as much freedom as a girl who had not yet come out might hope for in London.

"Go, lads," she ordered the waiting dogs. Away they shot across the greening sward. "Come" was all she had to call when the graceful little whippets strayed too far, "Come!" Ever obedient, they raced back to her, like four-legged streaks of life, their breath pluming in the crisp air. Margaret was never so happy in London as when she was out walking the dogs. She was indulgent with her lads, Lapith and Centaur, named after a valiant Greek tribe and their fearsome enemies. Her graceful, galloping dogs always played at mock battle, snapping at each other's ears and tails. She allowed them to range some distance from her. Just as she liked to feel a taste of freedom from the orbit she must maintain around old Ludd, while he sat muffled and cloaked on a bench and read yesterday's news, so too did she allow her precious companions a taste of freedom from their orbit around her.

"Do not go too far, Miss Dornton. I pray you," old Ludd admonished this morning, as he did every morning.

"Of course, Mr Ludd," she replied.

"A horse? I'm sure you do wish you had a horse," he said with a smile as he unfolded the paper.

She returned the smile. Because of the loss of his hearing, which Mr. Ludd steadfastly denied as being a problem at all, the old gent had the most interesting way of turning any conversation into a puzzle. "Of course" became "a horse." It was like a sophisticated word game, she thought, with no clear winner.

It was not a winner Evelyn Dade sought when he arrived at the Cock Pit Royal, his rangy, rough-haired wolfhound hard on his heel, a link-boy to light the way. It was precisely half past five in the chilly darkness just before dawn. The first five-guinea battle was about to begin, but he came not in hopes of winning gold. Dade came to stir the embers of feeling within him that threatened to go out. The blood-racing anticipation in guessing which bird was destined to live and which to die was not an emotion he admired, but surely anything was better than the heavy, muffling numbness that locked him in lethargy by day and roused him in a sweat of agitation and fear every dream-troubled night.

"The Bird Cage is just the thing to stir your sluggish blood," Creighton Soames had assured him. "Come. It will be a treat to see Wally's reaction to the row. I have persuaded the greenhead he must come."

It was this reference to young Wallis Eckhart that convinced Evelyn he must end an already long night with a visit to the cockpit. Creighton seemed in an awful hurry to divest Wallis of all the tenderer emotions and sensibilities that Dade admired in the lad. Empathy, enthusiasm, compassion, pity and the very joie de vivre that made the blood run so fast in youth—that was what Dade witnessed in Wallis. It was this joy in life that pushed young men to their limits, testing their own mortality. Evelyn wished to understand that joy again. He felt he had grasped it once, when just such impulses, such a belief in immortality and invincibility, had led him into the military, with all its color and brash bravado. He had gone in with the intention of seizing glory by the throat. He would, he had believed, throttle it into complete submission. Reality had knocked him down and stood on his chest instead of the other way around.

Glory was a thing he knew not how to define now. It was not to be found on the battlefield. Sorrow, pain, despair, death—these were the dark companions of war. There was some essence to be seen of the most basic good and evil to be found in all men's hearts and souls. But death, when it came in all its explosive, bloody fury, or in the more subtle, bowel-weakening guise of diarrhea, made no distinction between glory and that which was inglorious. It smote down without discrimination.

He came to this place of more death and destruction, if only for birds, in order that he might judge its effect on a young man who had yet to experience the bloodthirsty rapaciousness of mankind. He came too, to see if there was some manner in which he might protect in Wallis that which was lost in himself.

Passing through the crowd, Dade studied, with blank-faced interest, that group of humanity who found a battle to the death suitable spectator sport. They were most of them lowborn, low-minded and male. Blood sports were not generally attended by the fairer sex. Those women who did come were a coarse and slatternly lot, their eyes heavy with too much rum, their manners free. Clutched in every spectator's hand was an ethically dubious bit of hope: the five-guinea bets they cast on which of the glossy gamecocks would peck, spur and claw the other into a motionless pile of bloody feathers. The gong was sounded. Voices were stilled for a moment. The birds were released into the pit.

In that lull, Dade heard the whispered awareness that followed his passage everywhere, like the ill wind that had blown through a field of rye in the stillness of the morning before the battle of Waterloo began.

"Look, it is Captain Dead! Captain Dead!" the sound rippled and swam.

"Look, it is the captain of the dead. See, there with the dog."

Elbows nudged and necks were craned to catch a glimpse of "Captain Dead," a nickname based on the unhappy fact that out of his entire regiment, Evelyn Dade was the only man to have survived. He was no longer a captain. He had sold his colors immediately upon his return, but the nickname persisted, perpetuated, he was sure, by bad luck, his own bad habits and the unfortunately easy correlation to be drawn between Dade and dead.

"Dade!" It was a shout this time, loud and brisk and meant to draw his attention. Creighton called, small, darkly handsome, ruddy-cheeked Creighton who made women swoon with the wicked persistence of his smile and laughing green eyes. Never failing to make an excellent first impression, Cray knew how to dress and talk and carry himself to advantage when he was not drinking his fellows under the table. He rushed at life full tilt. There was nothing subtle, subdued or understated about him. Evelyn Dade and Creighton Soames were polar opposites. Their differences drew them together.

Dade's dark, cocooned emotions left him hungry for light, energy and expression. Many found Creighton brash and wearing. Dade found himself praying that some of Creighton's raw energy might rub off on him. Dade was sure

Creighton possessed the secret to some part of what had been missing within him since Waterloo. He was equally sure that a missing piece what lay dormant and untouched within his soul resided in Wallis Eckhart as well. Eckhart sat beside Creighton, a tall, fair-haired angel beside the diminutive devil. When he was with these two, Evelyn Dade felt complete.

"We're up here, my lord. The view is splendid." It was Wallis who called. Dade nodded and made his way through the crowd without obstacle. There was that advantage to bearing both terrible reputation and menacing moniker. No one stood in his way. Captain Dead and his fearsome wolfhound were considered a force to be reckoned with, a danger to lightly step around. Most men did so without ever doubting their own manhood.

"You're up early, my lord." Wallis had the dewy-eyed, fresh-shaven look of youth just risen. "Did they give you any trouble about letting Hero in? I would not have thought dogs were allowed." He reached out fearlessly to tug the wolfhound's ears.

"Dogs are not allowed," Soames informed Wallis with a raucous laugh and a punch on the shoulder. "None but Hero, anyway." He winked at Dade, who ordered the dog to sit, removed his hat and sat down beside Wallis.

Dade's eyes felt heavy. His body and spirit felt heavy. His left leg ached. The bone cracked at Waterloo had knitted, but the leg still pained him when the weather was damp. It had been drizzling half the night. He was only just turned seven and twenty, yet he felt ancient faced with Creighton's cheerful exuberance and Eckhart's youth. "I regret to say this dawn is the end of my day, and not its beginning, Wallis."

"Really, sir?" Wallis's earnest blue-eyed gaze strayed from the test of fowl will that had ensued with a squawk in the pit below them. "Whatever has kept you out all night?"

Dade shrugged and studied Wallis as the young man's gaze flicked back to the activity in the pit with horrified fascination. There, Dade thought, that was what Creighton had promised he would see. Not cocks ripping each other with barbed heels, but this, the wide-eyed disgust and pity in Wallis's expression. He had felt that way himself once, he was sure of it—the first time he had witnessed a cockfight, the first time he had witnessed the casualties of war. It had been too long since he had felt that peculiar blend of emotion: horror, disgust, pity, fascination and, last but not least, a guilty sort of relief that one's own limbs were all of a piece and not shattered, twisted and mangled like these. He existed somewhere just outside of life, untouched by these emotions. The distance with which he regarded everything, the dark, heavy stillness of his heart, had begun to bother him.

Somewhere on the battlefield he had lost the look and feeling of an innocent man who knew who he was. The world had ceased to make sense. Why? It was an all-consuming and unanswerable question that touched upon every element of his life. Why had so many men died such brutal deaths? Why had he alone among them survived? Why had death followed him with such pernicious greed, taking his brother from him in his hour of darkness? Why had God forsaken him? He had gone numb asking. He was still numb, and like a severed nerve, he could not resist poking and prodding at the whys, and at the absence of his feelings in the hope that some answer was forthcoming, that some sensation might return.

Wallis seemed dazed by the spectacle that so completely captured the attention of everyone around them. "You were telling me what you did all night," he prodded, frowning, trying not to look back into the pit yet drawn to look against his better intentions.

Dade had no keen desire to explain to the lad what he had been about. Explanation would only shock Wallis anew.

Creighton knew no such self-control. "Been watching the dissection, haven't you, Ev?" He prodded Dade's shoulder and waggled his eyebrows in ghoulish glee.

"Dissection, my lord?" Wallis repeated the word as if it scalded his mouth. His look of disgust was now fully focused on Dade.

"He will have been at Newgate beforehand, to witness the corpse's progress, lad." Creighton's hands made a descriptive motion at his throat, as if a noose were being tightened. With comic talent he hung himself with the imaginary rope, rolling back his eyes and sticking out his tongue with a gagging sound.

Wallis's mouth twisted. "Then it is true what is said about you? I thought all of those vile remarks about death in connection with your name were no more than vicious gossip."

Dade could see by Creighton's expression that Wallis's naivete amused him. "What have you heard, Wally, me lad?" Creighton asked in an exaggerated stage whisper. "I can verify the truth or falsehood of any of it."

"As can I, Cray," Dade reminded him quietly. He was too busy watching Wallis to spare Creighton more than a glance. He knew where he stood in Creighton's estimation, always had. He and Creighton knew each other too well. Wallis was different. Wallis liked to believe him a whole man. Dade enjoyed seeing that belief in the boy's eyes. It gave him hope that what he was missing might yet be found.

The crowd roared as one of the cocks went in for the kill, and a wave of dark memories swept over Evelyn Dade. Like a wall, the images and voices from Waterloo fell on him, echoing the roar of the crowd.

"Tell me." Wallis unwittingly recalled Dade from beneath the weight of his memories. The young man's earnest intensity cut through the darkness and let in a brief ray of light. "Is it true that you witness every public execution to be seen?"

The darkness receded. Dade took a deep breath, regarding Wallis steadily, as though the bright young face before him was a beacon that would see him through the cloud of his past. "I do not deny that I go to executions."

Wallis frowned, displeased with his reply. "Do you then make a point of attending each gory aftermath and observe the mutilating dissections of the unclaimed bodies?"

Dade's lips thinned as the crowd roared again. The dark, rich smell of death assailed his nostrils. There was no need for him to look into the pit. One of the birds was dead. He knew it. The dark wave promised to sweep over him again. "I do."

Wallis's color had risen. His eyes had a wounded look. "And do you go to these awful cockfights and bull baitings and dog fights without ever exhibiting the slightest hint of emotion because you enjoy the tide of death that swells in your wake?"

Dade's eyebrows rose. He took no joy in death. He took no joy in anything! Was it true that he exhibited no emotion? Not even distaste, horror or his desire to comprehend the phenomena that ended life? How strange! These events tended to excite the only feelings he was conscious of anymore. He was reminded of his own living state only in witnessing life's extinction.

"I cannot answer that question, Wallis," he said, the words heavy on his tongue. "I go to observe others' reactions, not my own."

Wallis's chin was rigid. "Tell me, sir, why do you honor me with your friendship? We have not the slightest interests in common. Do you mean to tease me? Or am I merely an element in some sort of nightmarish experiment, to see how long a young man survives in proximity to the Captain of the Dead?"

This last remark triggered a rare smile. It took courage, Dade thought, for Wallis to insult him to his face.

Wallis misread the reason for the movement of his lips. He stood abruptly, knocking into Creighton, who was enjoying the argument immensely.

Wallis shook him off, cheeks flaming with indignation. "Enough fun at my expense, gentlemen. I bid you good day." Heatedly, the young man pushed his way through the crowd.

"Nodcock!" Creighton laughed, as though he expected Dade to agree.

There was menace in the look Dade threw Creighton. Soames backed uneasily away from it. "It would be best did you choose to leave the boy be," Dade said gruffly. He tipped his head at the wolfhound, which rose to follow him. The crowd fell away. Captain Dead and his dog, Hero, passed without hindrance.

Dade followed young Eckhart into the park. Wallis whirled upon him with a show of bravado that could not completely disguise a trace of genuine fear. "Why do you hound me, my lord?"

Dade responded in the gentlest of voices, "I felt the

strongest desire that you should hear the last of your questions answered, Wallis."

It was evident from his baffled look that Wallis had forgotten just what that last question had been. Dade indicated the pathway that led north into the heart of St. James's. "Will you walk with me?"

Wallis lifted his chin, nodded stiffly and fell into step beside Dade and the dog.

"You were wondering why I befriended you—" Dade held up his hand when Wallis might have interrupted. "Hear me, and then you may take me to task should you desire. I singled you out because in you I see the best of what I once was. I see compassion, honor and idealism. I miss that."

Wallis stopped in his tracks. "Do you, sir?"

Dade kept walking. His leg felt best if he kept it moving. Wallis fell into step with him.

"I suppose in many ways I deserve to be called Captain Dead," Dade admitted, his voice heavy with regret. "For some time now death has followed me, pursuing me even into my dreams. But a man grows weary of being chased. I have turned to follow death. That is why I go to public executions and to the dissections afterward. I chase death, you see, at a safe distance, not because I relish such company, but with a desire to understand the beast that shadows my every step. Such a pursuit has tempered my soul in dark, humorless ways." Dade gazed intently at the younger man, wondering if he even began to understand what it was he tried to express.

Wallis looked thoughtful.

The Captain of the Dead sighed. How could he explain the dark to one who saw nothing but light?

Wallis surprised him, saying with the gentleness that was characteristic of him, " 'Think not thou canst sigh a sigh, and thy Maker is not by / Think not thou canst weap a tear, and thy Maker is not near.' "

Dade's piercing look caused Wallis to smile and shake his head. "William Blake, from his poem 'On Another Man's Sorrow!' "

Hero interrupted the poignant tension of the moment with a low growl. Hackles raised, he took an alerted stance and woofed low in the depths of his throat.

"Come!" The men heard a young woman's terrified voice calling urgently. "Come, lads, come."

Hero danced uneasily on feet eager to take him away. Please, his caramel brown eyes pled. Let me be off.

"Trouble again" was all Dade had time to say. Then the loud, aggravated barking of a dog ripped Hero from all semblance of obedience, and the wolfhound was off, running toward the shrubbery.

The female voice rose in panic. "Go away! Bad dog. You must go away. I am not afraid of you."

Dade was fast in pursuit of Hero, Wallis right beside him. When the path led them out of the shrubbery, they were met by the striking sight of a young woman backed against a tree, two slender whippets huddled in her skirts. There was something eternal in this image of the woman, with her dogs cowering in the billow of fabric about her legs. There was something misty and hand-tinted, a fragile beauty in her stance as she held off the advance of an enormous mangy cur with a dainty parasol, which she flapped open and closed as she thrust it in his direction.

"Go!" she insisted. "Bad dog! You don't scare me." She seemed a child's storybook creature come to life.

The stray cur too was storybook fierce. A gaunt, rough-looking creature, with a hair-raising growl and a rope of saliva dripping from rolled-back lips. Dade wondered if it was rabid. He wondered too, why? Why was he here in this place and time, confronted by the threat of death yet again? Even as the thought crossed his mind, he called forcefully to Hero, who was almost on top of the beast. "Heel, Hero. Heel!"

All eyes were on the dogs. They stood motionless but for their tails, which beat faster time than usual. Tightly wound bundles of potential fury frozen, hackles raised, the animals were ready to whirl into a disastrous dervish at the slightest provocation. Dade had seen the stance before. These swiftly wagging tails were harbingers of danger.

Before disaster could unfold and death claim its prize, he drew two objects from his pocket, firing them off at the head and flank of the growling stray. Both missiles found their mark. With a howl the animal tucked tail and ran.

The tension that held them all motionless dissolved.

"Good shot!" Wallis crowed as he fell out of a statue-like pose. "What was that you threw at him?"

The shade of a smile lifted Dade's lips. "A white knight and a black pawn to the rescue," he said.

As he bent to pick up the ebony wood chess pawn, a wave of anguish squeezed his heart. To the rescue his men had charged. To their deaths they had gallantly gone.

Wallis frowned as he retrieved the ivory knight. "This man's lost his head."

Dade fought back the dark wave of images that pressed in on his head and chest and gut. Images of young men on horseback being gunned down. "The price of charging to the rescue," he said through clenched teeth.

Wallis laughed as he tossed the headless knight to Dade, unaware of the private anguish he dispelled in saying, "Tell me, do you go everywhere armed to the teeth with chess pieces?"

Dade managed a smile. He carried the chess pieces for sentimental reasons he would rather not discuss. They served as strangely comforting token memories of Gavin. How did one explain? How did one stop the bad memories and hold onto the good when everything one touched or saw or tasted triggered the darkness?

He focused on Hero. Hero was safe. The dog did not provoke memories good or bad. His great, shaggy head was caught up in the embrace of the kneeling young woman who cooed, "Good dog! What a brave creature you are," while her slender canine companions leapt playfully after Hero's tail.

Hero did not usually allow his head to be so accosted by a stranger, and yet before this female he sank down like a great puppy and rolled over to have his belly scratched.

"Have you no self-respect, Hero?" Dade inquired of the animal. As he did, the young woman lifted shining eyes to regard him for the first time.

"So, this is my hero!" She made no effort to restrain a captivating chuckle. "How delightfully apropos."

Dade stopped breathing for an instant.

He could not remember the last time he had laid eyes upon a creature more delicate, a face more fair, honest and open, than that he witnessed in the girl at his feet, his great ugly dog's head cradled in her lap. He was not at all accustomed to such a physical reaction to the face of any female, no matter how beautiful. Beauty alone did not move him. This was quite a separate thing, a sensation he had not been in touch with since some time before the war. Here was his sense of awe revived. It touched him, heart and gut and soul, if only for an instant and made him weak. He felt himself the equivalent of a dog's head standing before her: rough and ugly, dark and worldly, the tainted before the untouched. He darted a look at Wallis. The engaging puppy stood beaming at the girl, as captivated as he.

A gray hood framed the oval of her face like an opening shell. The morning chill touched pink to her cheeks. Her face, pale and as perfect as if an artist had rendered it, had the timeless, symmetrical flawlessness of a cameo. Her hair was an airy ash blond, her complexion translucent with youth. It was, however, her eyes that caught and held Dade's attention. These were aged eyes. Not wizened by wrinkles or any other imperfection, their shining depths were imbued with a deep, boundless wisdom; an inner peace that made them appear deeper than wells, clearer than a cloudless sky and more beautiful, despite their lack of distinct color, than blue or green or brown eyes ever might have been. He could not look away.

These lustrous pearl gray eyes were too wise for the girl's tender years. Because of them, emotion passed over each sweet feature as the shadow of a single cloud passes over a sunlit meadow. These eyes, this face, were beautiful to behold, not because of perfectly molded lips or an elegantly turned nose. No, this creature was undeniably captivating because her thoughts and feelings, her very soul, high-minded and pure, gazed unflinchingly from these remarkable eyes.

Time slowed as Dade searched their depths. He was reminded of the look he usually met in Hero's gaze, or Wallis's. It was trust he witnessed—blind trust. Here was an all-encompassing belief in life and humanity and God. Dade had no such trust left in him, but he was drawn in completely by that blindingly beautiful level of conviction that the best qualities were to be discovered in every man's soul. This young lady's probing look weighed him and, despite his failings, found what was worthy and admirable within him to focus on. Her soul, her beautiful, gentle soul, reached out and touched his wounded, guarded self.

Evelyn Dade was devastated. He fell hopelessly, irredeemably, into a pair of translucent gray eyes.

Chapter 2

MARGARET Dornton looked up into the face of a complete stranger and was surprised that she should be assailed by the feeling that she knew this man whom she had never before met. The gentleman whose wolfhound lolled in her lap was handsome, not in a head-turning sort of way, but in a shuttered manner that drew the eye and then would not let it go. It was as if the best of this gentleman was guarded, hidden behind eyelids held at half mast, hidden behind the screen of a lock of seal brown hair that fell down over his forehead, hidden behind the sleek mustache, beard, side whiskers and the tightness of a pair of lips that had almost forgotten how to smile. There were walls here, walls to keep one out, or to keep him in. She could not be certain which. There was something in the shadowed brown eyes, as he gazed at her, that made her long to tear down the walls, to see what lay behind them.

This was the hero she had been longing to meet. She knew it in an instant. She imagined him a knight for the breath of a moment. Yes, he would be a knight, she decided, this man whose courage and quick thinking had saved her from a mad dog. He looked at her through the visor of his armor.

He held out his hand to help her up. For a moment she imagined the hand encased in mail. With a blink it was but a hand again, wrapped in nothing more exotic than buff leather. "You have named your dog well, sir," she said. "He has indeed this day proved a hero. As have you. I thank you for frightening away that dreadful creature."

With the grace worthy of a damsel rescued from a dragon, she accepted his assistance in rising. His hand, clasping hers, was a powerful thing, a force unexpected. For a moment the same uneasy sensation she had suffered when the frightful, bristling dog had lunged at the tip of her parasol gripped Margaret. In this man's touch she met with a wildness, an energy, an element over which she had no control. It might consume her did she not flee.

He let go of her hand. The feeling vanished.

He opened his mouth as if to speak, but while no words were forthcoming, a window in the blankness of his deep brown eyes opened up to her and communicated a message of great moment. He was drawn to her. He liked her. She could see it as clearly as if he had thrown himself at her feet to pledge undying fealty. She could see too that the dark brown eyes were not entirely brown. There were flecks of gold starring out from the blackness of their centers. The gentleman said nothing and yet told her much in his very silence. It was up to his companion to fill the void.

"One of the Misses Dornton, is it not? You are sister to the twins I met at Lady Hinchingham's drum? Do you recall? I am Wallis Eckhart."

Her hero's dark gaze flickered intently from Wallis Eckhart's face to her own and back again.

"I remember," Margaret said sweetly, for indeed she did remember tall, fresh-faced Mr. Eckhart. She had, on first meeting him, imagined in this young man the embodiment of what her brother Todd might have been, had he survived childhood. At the time she had not known whether to love or hate him for giving rise to such bittersweet possibility. Her sister Celeste had noticed the similarity as well.

"Only look at that tall, fair fellow," she had said. "Does he not remind you of the painting of Father when he was a young man? Why, so similar is he to us in feature and coloring—one might almost assume he was of blood relation, were he not so very tall. There is surely none so blessed in inches in our family."

Just as she noted now the intensity with which her dark hero regarded her every word to Mr. Eckhart, so too had Mr. Eckhart noted their attention that evening. He had stared back at them a moment and then crossed the room to ask Celeste if she would care to dance. He had, for the remainder of the evening, seemed more than commonly interested in Celeste. Margaret had watched the two together and imagined them in love. She looked upon the very tall and fair-haired Mr. Eckhart now with an almost familial delight. This embodiment of her long-lost brother might, with a little luck, become brother in fact.

"Will you be so good, Mr. Eckhart"—she turned her sweetest smile on Wallis—"as to introduce my rescuer?"

"Of course, Miss Dornton," he smiled. "This is Evelyn, Viscount Dade, and his constant companion, Hero." Wallis chose his words with care. "I am pleased to claim both Lord Dade and Hero as friends," he said formally.

Margaret could see by the sudden arching of one seal brown eyebrow that the viscount was surprised.

"How do you do, my lord? I am Margaret Dornton." She held out her gloved hand.

Dade took it in his. Again the knight stood before her, courteous but distant. Again a sense of this man's compelling presence gripped her. Lightly, he kissed her hand.

"Pearl." The word fell strange and exotic from the lips of her hero. "Greek for Margaret, is it not?" His voice was low and even—emotionless. In any other tone his remark might have seemed presumptuous, or off-color. As it was, Margaret found him nothing but polite and vastly interesting for his very subtlety of expression. Pearl had far more luster than plain Margaret. She felt as if she shone a little more brightly given the privilege of such a name. As Pearl, she was a fit heroine for any knight.

"Do you care for the pet name Pearl, Miss Dornton?"

It seemed odd to her that he should care enough to ask. But she could see he did care and that he would never call her Pearl unless she gave her approval.

"Yes. How clever of you. My grandpapa called me Pearl,

but no one has bothered to do so since his demise. It is indeed Greek, and rather pretty. I have always thought so."

Lord Dade's hooded gaze flitted over her face. The hint of a smile lifted one corner of his mustache and touched the tight line of a mouth she wanted to see soften. "Very pretty," he agreed.

She blushed. It was as if he complimented her and not the name.

"And are you called something else, my lord?" she said, daring to respond to his informality in kind.

He went very still. A shadow passed over his features. The gold flecks in his eyes seemed to dim.

Margaret was distracted by the dogs. "I do not understand why," she went on comfortably, "but I have never known a gentleman who bore the name Evelyn without he must divest himself of it in favor of something more masculine."

Her knight had encased himself in armor again. There was remoteness to Lord Dade's expression, a stillness to his mouth that made her wonder if she had offended him. Loath that he should shield himself from her, she struggled to clarify her tactlessness. "My own name lends itself to no end of heartless nicknames."

"Such as?" There was a hint of a challenge in his voice.

"My sisters call me Maggie, or Maggs," Margaret readily revealed to this stranger without ever wondering why. Her chin rose defensively. "My cousin has the effrontery to refer to me only as the Magpie. And when one has pale and elegant swans as sisters, who are blessed with names like Celia and Celeste and born into the ability to fascinate simply by being twins, it is quite appalling to be thought of as no more than a magpie."

Her hero's expression softened. "I see." The breeze lifted the dark forelock away from the pale expanse of his forehead. For a moment the sun glinted on gold flecks in dark eyes and the guarded look was gone.

Before the viscount's guarded mouth could open up to her as well, they were interrupted by old Ludd, who had at last removed himself from the comfort of his bench and limped into their midst. "Who is this, then? Are these chaps bothering you, Miss Margaret?"

"No, no, Mr. Ludd." She blushed as she took his wrinkled, palsied hands in hers. "This is Viscount Dade and Mr. Eckhart, whom I have met once before. These kind gentlemen have saved me from a bad dog."

"Fog? But the fog's all dried out, miss."

"Bad dog." Wallis tried to set him straight by panting and holding his hands above his head like dog's ears.

Ludd frowned at Margaret and then scowled at Dade. "Is the young man nobbed in the dick then, sir?"

For the first time Margaret saw Evelyn Dade smile. It was no more than a whisper of amusement that touched his lips, and yet both mouth and eyes were for a moment engaged. Her hero was very handsome when he smiled. She would like to tease that smile from his lips again.

Dade tipped his head toward Ludd as King Arthur might have tipped his head to Merlin. The forelock swayed across his forehead. She longed to comb it back with her fingers as he spoke with careful clarity and volume.

"There's no harm in the lad. He does but pretend to be a dog on occasion. Do you mind if we walk back with you? I should be pleased to have you lean upon my arm." He articulated beautifully, his voice deep and resonant. Ludd seemed to understand him perfectly.

"Very kind of you to offer, sir. It is time we returned. My leg troubles me in this chill."

And that is how it came to pass that the youngest of the Misses Dornton, who longed to hear herself referred to as Pearl again, was to be seen in the company of the infamous Captain Dead, perambulating away from the canal in St. James's Park, past St. James's Palace, across the Mall and into St. James's Street before she had even come out, much less been approved by the patronesses of Almack's. Within hours she was labeled not "Pearl" by polite society, as she might have wished, but as a fast and coming girl, through no fault of her own and completely without merit. She strolled into St. James's Street quite oblivious to her peril, her arm held safely in young Mr. Eckhart's, while her intriguing rescuer walked ahead, with Mr. Ludd leaning gratefully upon his arm, Hero trailing behind like a great, misshapen shadow.

At her leisure Margaret examined her darkly handsome hero. He was unlike any other gentleman of her acquaintance. There was an air of mystery about him, a cloaked inscrutability that was reflected in the unfashionable cut of hair and clothing and in the colors he favored. Lord Dade had the look, she thought, of a man misplaced in time. His glossy hair was left long and straight and clubbed at the back rather than clipped short and curled upon the brow as was all the rage among younger men these days. His clothing too ran quite contrary to the current vogue of pastel blues and yellows and tans. His coat was deep wine in color, the inside of his furred black cloak a slightly darker hue. His facial hair, unusual in itself—most of the Bond Street beaus followed the classical Greek style of clean-shaven faces—was cut into a chiseled Vandyke beard, with long, dangerous side whiskers. He would have looked quite natural in a painting by any of the Dutch masters, or in the uniform of some long-dead musketeer. He was more swashbuckling than polite, conjuring up within Margaret's romantic imagination the image of a pirate run aground. He certainly carried a sword as though he might be called upon to use it at any moment and seemed always poised to pounce, as if he might lithely jump out of his skin if need be. It was this readiness for action that had saved her from the attack of the dog earlier, she was certain. It gave the viscount an edge, a level of danger she was unaccustomed to. Men stepped out of their path. Women stopped to stare, mesmerized like birds before the swaying head of a cobra.

She was herself mesmerized and could not concentrate either her eyes or her thoughts on anything or anyone else.

Sweet Mr. Eckhart engaged her with pleasantries throughout the snail's pace of their walk back to her aunt's, but though she answered him readily enough, she could not recall a word of their conversation when later asked by her sisters what they had discussed.

Too slow, and yet too soon, they stood upon her aunt's doorstep, the door opened to them by the butler, Centaur and Lapith racing up the familiar steps with happy speed. She bade Mr. Eckhart a pleasant good day, and knelt down again to give Hero's ears a scratching, but it was not until Lord Dade offered his hand a second time that she might rise, and then adroitly lifted her hand to his lips, that Margaret experienced the feeling that her life had been changed this morning by this man. He had not only saved her skin, he had transformed it. The salute to her hand took on new and sensuous importance when it was this man's lips that did the kissing. The barrier of her glove was compromised by the heat of his lips and the gentle friction of his beard.

Time too seemed to have been compromised, for there was a marvelous, minute-slowing sense of eternity in every instant that their eyes were locked upon each other. She was Pearl when he looked at her, not Margaret or Maggie or Magpie. Something in his look declared her rare and precious and valued—a pearl in something other than name. More than that, in his dark, knowing eyes there was a jaded bleakness, an impression of a soul disguised in the misery of having seen too much to be dazzled anew. Yet he found her interesting. She was sure it was so. Some sign of that interest was evident in the penetrating looks that probed so deep within her being she feared he might find some part of her she did not know herself—the Pearl part perhaps.

She might have gone on forever, gazing deep into the mysteries of gold-flecked brown, her hand held in his, had not her aunt come to the door to insist, her voice unnaturally high, "Captain Dade, whatever are you doing here with my niece?"

The unmistakable censure in her question took on greater menace as Mr. Ludd turned on the steps to look at Dade, his mouth agape. "You are Captain Dead?" he demanded in the too loud voice of one who cannot hear his own volume. "I have allowed Miss Dornton to be seen in your company? Oh, dear, I am sorry, marm. I mistook him for a gentleman."

Burning with embarrassed dismay, Margaret looked from the footman to her aunt to the shuttered face of Lord Dade. Captain Dead? What was Ludd on about? "But he is a gentleman, Aunt," she blurted. "Lord Dade and his companion, Mr. Eckhart, have been exceptionally kind to me this morning, even heroic."

Her aunt's back was stiff as a poker. Her mouth was as unyielding as Lord Dade's. "Go inside, Margaret," she said. "I shall attend to the gentlemen. They will be leaving soon, you may be sure."

"Aunt Charlotte!"

"Come away, my dear," Charlotte insisted, reaching out to take her hand, as if to forcibly drag her into the house.

Gently, Margaret disengaged her aunt's hold. Gentler still she replied, "I see you have the mistaken impression that these gentlemen have in some improper way imposed themselves upon my attentions, Auntie, but they have just saved my life and the lives of both of my dogs from a most vicious creature in the park. I will not allow either of these kind gentlemen to go away without my proper gratitude and my heartfelt desire we should meet again soon. It would be rude to do anything less, and I know you would scold me severely for rude behavior."

Lord Dade bowed formally before them, a knight doing homage to the fairer sex, as her aunt struggled for a reply.

"Your aunt does but wish to protect you, Miss Dornton, from the evils of a reputation so foul that you must be sullied merely to be seen in the presence of it."

"Whose reputation?"

He bowed again. There was a strange gleam in his eyes as he said simply, "Mine."

"But, my lord—Captain"—she touched his sleeve to stop him. He appeared to be on the point of leaving. "I would thank you nonetheless. I cannot judge you by reputation, having never heard of yours. My only source of reference is in your actions, and they were most welcome this morning. I should not have come so happily home had you not happened upon me when you did. I am pleased we have met."

His gaze fixed on her hand as it rested briefly on his sleeve, as though he found something unusual in her touch. There was a pleasant heat to this look as his eyes rose to meet hers. Margaret made no effort to disguise her curiosity. In all that she read in this walled-off man, she had no sense of danger, or easy explanation why he should be referred to as Captain Dead.

"I am neither captain nor hero," he said. All warmth and

light seemed extinguished from his expression. "It would please me if you refrained from addressing me as such. I am happy the dog did you no harm this morning, *Pearl*. There are those who would imagine my very presence did incite the animal to violence. It is gratifying to be connected with an incident where my actions gave cause for life's preservation rather than its extinction." He delved deep into her with the intensity of his regard, the pirate studying his captive. When she tried to study him in return, the fathomless, gold-flecked shadow shut her out. "I am sure we shall meet again, Miss Margaret Dornton, for fate has brought us together with happy purpose today." With a bow he turned and walked away, his great, shaggy wolfhound at his heel.

Tipping his hat, Wallis Eckhart said with an engaging grin, "Do give my best to your sisters," before setting off after the man he called friend.

Chapter 3

"Of all the men in London, Margaret, why must you befriend that one?" Aunt Charlotte sighed as the door was closed upon the morning's adventure.

"No other man thought to save me, Auntie," Margaret chuckled, slipping her arm around her aunt's waist.

"Why does he have the effrontery to call you a pearl?"

Pearl, Margaret would have liked to have boldly said, is an heroic and beautiful name, far more heroic than mere Margaret, far more evocative of the romance and beauty she felt deep within than Maggie, Magpie, or Maggs. But there was not enough of the Pearl yet instilled in her to stand up to her aunt twice in one morning, so Margaret strove to placate rather than irritate.

"Margaret is Greek for pearl, Auntie. My mother's father always called me Pearl while he lived. I like it. I could but wish you all might call me Pearl."

"Pish!" Her desire was dismissed as nonsense.

Margaret laughed, Pearl enough—the fearless child of yesteryear born anew—to blithely give her aunt's firmly corseted waist a squeeze. "Now tell me what terror this man is guilty of that he should be called Captain Dead? Is he a murderer by chance? Did he dispatch some poor lover in a duel, or steal another man's wife? Does he drink to excess, or gamble away all of his family's wealth? Or is it perhaps some atrocity he is guilty of in connection with the war? Come, you cannot shock me, Aunt Charlotte. I am well aware of the sins that men abandon themselves to here in London. My mother did warn us, you know, to beware of scoundrels and rakes."

Charlotte Dornton was not to be coaxed out of her distemper. "Your imagination runs away with you, Margaret. Only think what damage you may have done to your chances of success here in London if this morning's folly gets about. Gossip never keeps the story straight, you know. There are scandals to be brewed from the most innocent of encounters. Were you seen by many on your walk home, my dear? Was the street very crowded?"

Margaret laughed, naive in her lack of concern. "The street is always crowded in London. I would suppose it was no less so than usual."

"Dear, oh dear. I have been terribly lax to allow you to go out in the mornings with no one but Ludd."

"You must not hold Mr. Ludd accountable, Aunt Charlotte," Margaret begged. But hold him accountable she did. Margaret could wring no more from her with regard to Lord Dade's mysterious reputation.

It was instead her cousin Allan who filled in the background of her rescuer, and he was not as severe on the gentleman as her aunt might have been. Sharp, fit, bright-eyed Allan, who reminded Margaret of her father's favorite hunting dog, his ears always at the prick, did, in fact, seem to regard Evelyn Dade as quarry worth chasing.

"Magpie!" He burst in upon the sitting room, where Margaret was regaling Celia and Celeste, looking cool and collected in frothy white morning dresses, with the tale of her adventure. "I am told you have met Captain Dead. My mother will speak of nothing else. Is it true? What did you think of him? He is the handiest man I know with a sword. I have seen him fence, and wished I might have opportunity to face down such a master of the sport. He strips to great advantage, you may be sure."

"Allan!" Shocked by such freedom of speech, Celeste tapped his knee reprovingly with her delicate bone fan.

Celia, on the other hand, smiled the special smile she reserved for her fair-haired cousin. As the elder of the twins, if only by a few moments, she had always been the more assertive. "Only think, Allan, he has saved Maggie from the jaws of a mad dog. Is it not romantic?"

Celeste, gentler and sometimes more insightful than Celia, said, "Fencing cannot be reason for the blackness of this Captain Dead's reputation, so tell us why Aunt Charlotte is in such a dither over Margaret's having been seen in his company. Is the man a notorious philanderer or fortune hunter? Must we avoid speaking to him should we meet again? He keeps unobjectionable company, for surely there is nothing to despise in Mr. Eckhart. He is the nicest young man one could ask to meet."

"Why refer to him as Captain Dead?" Margaret asked. "Your mother would not tell me."

"As to that, Magpie, I shall not tell you. 'Tisn't proper for a gentleman to discuss such things with ladies."

Celia flicked open her fan and yawned, as if quite bored with the whole discussion. She knew just how to go about teasing a confession from Allan. "We must discover the secret from some other source, then."

Allan sank down next to her with a sigh. "I would not have you gossip mongering, Celia. Promise me my mother shall never know whence you garnered this information, and I will satisfy your curiosity."

Three ash blond heads tipped forward, eager to hear, none of them more eager than Margaret. Yet she made a point to keep her mind objective. Allan spoke of gossip and rumor and reputation. As her aunt had pointed out, gossip never got the story straight.

"Lord Dade is as odd a character as you could ever hope to meet," her cousin began with relish. "It is said, since his return from Waterloo—"

"He is a war hero, then?" Margaret was breathless with delight. She tried to picture Lord Dade in uniform.

"Yes." Allan frowned at her dubiously. "I suppose one must think so. Dade was a captain of the Royals until his entire regiment was wiped out at Waterloo. He alone survived. So, you see, he became, in a single afternoon, Captain of the Dead, or Captain Dead."

Sweet, kind, thoughtful Celeste said softly, "It is a cruel trick of Fate that his name should be Dade. Only think, if his name had been Peabody or Smythe, he would never have been troubled by the awful nickname."

"There is more." Allan paused significantly.

"Go on, then," Margaret said.

"It is said that the physician who set Dade's leg on the field in France died of a mysterious fever."

"Yes, but what has that to do with Dade?" Margaret insisted.

"Probably nothing," her cousin admitted readily, before leading them on with ghoulish delight, "had not a pattern of death followed the man wherever he went. The captain of the boat that brought him back across the channel died in the middle of the voyage."

"People do die," Celeste said sensibly.

"Yes, they do." It was clear from Allan's expression that he was holding the best of the tale until last. "Perhaps that explains why Captain Dade's elder brother, Gavin, the former Lord Dade, stuck his spoon in the wall at the very instant he heard of his brother's return."

"He simply stopped breathing?" Margaret could not believe such nonsense any more than she really believed her own wild imaginings. This was the stuff myths and fairy tales were made up of.

"So I am told," Allan nodded. "The messenger came in while he was at dinner, bent to inform Lord Dade of his brother's safe return, and with a sudden gasp, it is said the first viscount began to turn blue about the lips, clawed at his throat, and then keeled face first into his roast beef and potatoes."

"How awful!" Celia said, her eyes very round. "Has anyone else connected to Lord Dade died?"

"I shall get to that presently. The story takes a turn here. Dade sold his commission even as he was mourning the loss of his brother and mending the leg that had been broken in Belgium. He remained in London rather than remove to the family estate. It was rumored that the servants feared he would bring death into the house. Even those who had been with the family for years were prepared to give notice."

"Poor man," Celeste said. "He has suffered awfully."

"He has suffered awfully?" Celia protested. "What of the poor souls who have died? I should think their suffering was to be pitied far more than his."

Celeste shrugged. "Yes, but their suffering ended with death. I find it difficult to waste pity on a corpse."

Allan waggled his eyebrows. "There is more, cousins. This poor man you speak of, still dressed in full mourning for his brother, began to frequent the public executions at Newgate, as well as every cockfight, dogfight or bear baiting to be seen."

"No!" the twins gasped in unison, their mouths forming identical Os.

"The latter I can personally attest to as fact. I have seen him myself."

Margaret frowned. This was not at all what she had expected to hear—not at all the image she carried in her head of Lord Dade. Surely a hero did not go to dogfights.

"There is more," Allan persisted. "You will not like to hear this, I am sure." He glanced uneasily behind him.

"If you know beforehand we shall not like it, cousin, then you must show restraint, and forbear mentioning it," Margaret advised him, loath to have the pleasing image of her hero so tarnished.

Her sisters would not hear of such reticence. "No, no! Tell us. Do. Margaret has but to cover her ears if she would not hear."

Allan looked at her. "Well, Magpie? Do you mean to cover your ears?"

Margaret sighed. "Out with it! I can see you are nigh bursting to tell us. Does the man eat babies?"

"No," he laughed at her. "Nothing so terrible as that. It is just that I hear it is his practice to attend the dissection of the bodies after all of the hangings."

All three of the girls went pale. Margaret's breath seemed to stop up in her throat. Could this be true? Was this intriguing man to whom she was now indebted for her very life really so bizarre? How could the man who saw in her a Pearl be so morbid?

Celeste was the one who brought up the matter that they

were all contemplating but none dared broach. "What I want to know is if our Margaret is in danger of dying due to her having been exposed to Lord Dade's person."

They all turned to stare with concern at Margaret.

"I cannot think the Magpie is in any real danger," Allan said without true conviction.

Margaret bravely lifted her chin. "Of course there is not," she said. "Lord Dade saved my life. He has not, in any way, threatened it."

Evelyn Dade had stopped believing in the power of goodness until he met Wallis. Now, having encountered the Pearl as well, he was convinced there were creatures who yet roamed the earth, rare and exquisite, in which great good resided—creatures of the light, whom the dark, crushing wave of death's memories could not touch. He had saved such a creature from harm. Yet how did one life measure against the many? Could one slip of a girl make up for an entire regiment of brawny young men? Could she begin to fill the void left by his brother's death?

He could not turn away from thoughts of the young lady with her slender gray whippets any more than he could turn away from his own potential, captured in the trusting looks Pearl had turned upon him. The young woman's amazing gray eyes had seemed to see only the good in him. He knew such a viewpoint was no more accurate than the belief of many that he somehow marshalled death's dark forces, but Dade could not but prefer the manner in which he was reflected in Margaret Dornton's wise and innocent gaze. Too long had he looked upon his fellow man's fear of him.

He required Wallis to tell him everything he knew of the Dorntons. Wallis complied with enthusiasm and thoroughness. Young Eckhart would appear to have done his own investigating into Miss Dornton's connections. He introduced to Dade a young man named Allan Dornton at the studio where they went to fence. With a strangely unfamiliar feeling of hopefulness, Lord Dade instigated a conversation. He meant to learn more of the Pearl if he could.

"You show excellent form in the lunges, Mr. Dornton," he said when names and cards had been exchanged.

Allan Dornton's hair was a much darker shade of ash blond than his cousin's, but his eyes were almost an identical gray. They blinked twice at the compliment, as if in dismay.

"You are too kind, my lord." His words were gentle enough, but the look that went with them was dagger sharp.

Dade was of the immediate opinion that Mr. Dornton did not care for him in the least. He dared to test the waters. "I trust your young cousin is none the worse for her encounter with a mad dog?"

"The dog left no lingering mark, my lord," Dornton said with thinly disguised disgust. "Unfortunately, the Magpie—I mean, Margaret's encounter with you may have scarred her for life."

Dade was surprised and troubled that he had left such a lasting impression. "How so?" he inquired icily.

Allan Dornton exhaled heavily. "Surely you are not so out of touch, sir. You must be aware that my cousin's character has been placed in question merely for her having been seen in your company. There are those who wonder she has not succumbed to some strange illness, or been run down by a carriage. There are others who are extremely curious as to why you chose to preserve her life rather than end it. Either way, our family's name figures strongly in every whispered conversation in London. Are you so divorced from polite society that you do not know all three of my cousins have been denied entry to Almack's because of Margaret's meager connection with you?"

Wallis leaned in close to whisper, "I'm sorry to say he is quite right, sir. Queen Sarah herself has ruled harshly against the Misses Dornton."

Dade laughed dryly, disappointment bitter on his tongue. "Lady Sarah Jersey should not throw mud when she is all over dirt herself from her run to Gretna Green that she might get herself a husband. If hers is what you define as polite society, your cousins are well free of it, Dornton." The clash of swords behind them, Dade thought, was no more dangerous than the clash of wills between him and the young man who belligerently faced him. Allan Dornton reminded him of himself in an odd way. He had expressed himself with just such belligerent bad manners when his superior officer had argued with him over the missing curb chains. He shook away the memory, his mood in no way improved by this subtle invasion of the past. "You'd best tell your cousins they do not miss a thing in being denied access to Almack's."

"Is that all you have to say in reference to this matter, sir?" Allan Dornton sounded personally affronted.

Dade's eyes narrowed as he regarded the pugnacious young sprout before him. "Can it be you wait for me to apologize for rescuing your cousin from a vicious dog, Mr. Dornton? If so, you'll wait forever. I do not regret in the least saving Pearl from a certain mauling."

"Her name is Margaret."

"Or Magpie?" Dade's eyebrows lifted with satirical contempt. "She was good enough to inform me she preferred Pearl, and if you hope to clear her name, whatever it may be, you would do best in similarly rescuing her from that rabid animal, gossip."

"And how, sir, does one stop such a dog?" Allan Dornton had a short rein on his anger. "Perhaps I err in asking," he snapped, nostrils flaring. "You would seem to have just such a beast nipping at your heels most of the time these days."

"Touché." Dade touched fist to forehead, as if in salute with an imaginary fencing sword. Taking Allan's arm, he spoke so that none but Mr. Dornton might hear their exchange. "Perhaps it would be best if we were seen as friends rather than enemies, Dornton. Then gossip might work to our advantage in the assumption that your cousin did meet me under your auspices."

"Next you will suggest that Pearl, as you insist on referring to her, should make a daily practice of walking with you in the park, as if it were nothing out of the ordinary." Allan's reply was as stiff as his arm.

Dade nodded at a knot of acquaintances as they passed, hoping it looked as if he and Dornton were exchanging some pleasantry. "An excellent suggestion."

Allan spoke through gritted teeth, which smiled with equal intent at those who passed. "I would rather meet you in the park alone some morning, if you catch my meaning."

Wallis cleared his throat nervously.

Dade closed his eyes. Here it was again, standing before

him in the body of a young man. The heavy darkness of blood lust! The belief in the invincibility of youth.

"A duel?" Wearily he looked upon the face of foolish bravado and shrugged. "You no more than egg on the raving beast you wish to carry through with such a challenge, sir. Your lunges are excellent, but your overall form is far too hasty. You would get yourself killed or badly wounded in a blade-to-blade confrontation with me. I have no thirst at all for your claret to be spilled."

"You surprise me, sir."

"What?" Dade said bitterly. "My behavior does not conform after all to its deadly, bloodthirsty reputation? Imagine that!" Out of patience, he turned to go.

"You would not grant me satisfaction, then, my lord?" Allan Dornton dogged his heel, in tandem with Hero.

Dade sighed, his heart heavy. "You wish to fight me still?" His lips compressed. Why must the young and hale taunt death? "Would a mock battle satisfy? Here, rather than in a royal park at dawn? Foils first, with masks and guards, for a single hit and then épées stripped to the waist, another single hit to decide the winner?"

Allan studied him a moment, weighing his offer. Wallis studied the two of them, frowning, awaiting the outcome to this unsettling confrontation. Épées were considered dueling swords, with which one settled matters of honor. A green young swordsman like Dornton was not often offered the chance to cross blades with a master like Captain Evelyn Dade, who was used to handling his sword on a daily basis. An inexperienced swordsman was far more apt to be injured in an épée exchange. Touches to the hands, arms, legs and feet were accepted in such a confrontation, no holds barred, unlike the more gentlemanly exchanges one might expect from the foil, with touches to the torso only, and all done without the added protection of face mask or body guard. Dade could see his idea both intrigued and gave pause, as he had hoped.

At last Allan's head bobbed sharply in agreement. "I have always wanted to test my mettle against yours."

Dade was not completely pleased his offer had been accepted. "I feel compelled to point out to you that your selfish need for satisfaction will do nothing more than feed the ugly dog of gossip," he said. "A fed beast may soon become man's most faithful companion. Would you make society's stray a pet? Can you live with gossip always yapping at your heel, Mr. Dornton? There are moments when you will wish yourself free of the animal, let me warn you." The warning came from the heart.

Allan smiled in a way that reminded Dade afresh of his fair cousin. "If you lose, my lord, do you agree to give up the habits that keep the mad dog of gossip panting at your heels? Will you agree never again be seen at a hanging or a dissection, a cockfight or a bear baiting, and will you agree never again to have anything to do with either myself or my gentle cousins?"

Wallis stiffened.

Dade shrugged. "As I have no intention of losing, Mr. Dornton, I am far more interested in what you intend to forfeit at the conclusion of this match than in any wishful thinking on your part."

Allan's chin shot up. "If you win, I will continue to pretend we are the best of friends and ingratiate you with all of my acquaintances. In addition, you and I and my cousin shall parade in the park together as you suggest."

Dade graciously bowed his head. "I agree to such terms," he said. "Does Wednesday morning suit?"

Margaret and her dogs circled Aunt Charlotte's tiny garden with impatient peevishness and far more haste than was either sensible or ladylike. Margaret did not understand in the least why she must be confined to the garden unless her cousin Allan or her uncle accompanied her. All this over a mad dog. It was the height of stupidity! She had done nothing wrong and nothing wrong had been done to her. Yet her passage was observed everywhere these past few days that polite society might turn its head to stare. Polite society! She kicked at the ribbon-trimmed edge of her skirt and she kicked at the grass, neither of which deserved such abuse. It was not the lawn which questioned her suitability among the high-stepping, nose-in-the-air gudgeons who found her behavior worthy of censure.

Now, Princess Caroline was worthy of gossip. She was reputed to have gone bare-breasted (as Venus) to a ball in Geneva, and to another gathering in Baden with half a pumpkin around her head like some sort of helmet. There were even rumors that she was so enamored of Napoleon she had seduced his brother-in-law! Such behavior deserved scandalized whispers most assuredly. That a walk in the park should elicit so much as a lifted eyebrow baffled Margaret. She had committed no crime, yet there were those who were ready to believe the worst of her, and her sisters as well merely by their relation to her. Even more ridiculous, she was expected to drop instantly dead merely for having come into contact with Lord Dade! It was monstrous! It was most inconvenient. It might even have been hilarious had Margaret had contact with anyone else as willing to see the humor in such foolishness.

But her sisters were not at all amused that they had been cast out of polite society before they were ever really in. Margaret sighed and slowed her walking long enough to throw the leather ball she kept in her pocket for the whippets to fetch. No more than seen in the company of a man, no more than a dozen words exchanged, and she was suspected of what? A liaison with the devil himself? Ye gods! Lord Dade had saved her from a raving dog. No more, no less. For this she was considered an oddity, unworthy of polite company! The whippets scampered back to her, the ball found. She wrested it from Centaur's jaw and threw it again.

Margaret felt like a rubber ball caught in the jaws of gossip and innuendo. Truth was far less interesting than what might be imagined, she supposed. Yet what a great waste of one's time and energy. There was something insidiously corruptive about subtle doubts with regard to one's character when they were wholly unfounded. There was no outright accusation one might refute, only irrefutable suspicion and unanswerable innuendo. Such poison littered one's mind, even when one was innocent of any wrongdoing. It preyed upon one's better sense and ate away the unshakeable faith and self-confidence of the innocent. She who had done nothing to be ashamed of yet imagined that she had. Ideas and imaginings that had never sullied her mind left a stain in her thoughts.

The dogs waited expectantly at her feet again, the ball returned to her. Margaret bent to scoop up the toy. Centaur danced with anticipation, but Margaret was lost in thought and did not immediately relinquish it. What would it be like, she wondered, to be guilty of an illicit connection with a man like Lord Dade? The ball spilled from her hand. What would it be like to engage in secret assignations, whispered unholiness and forbidden kisses in the moonlight? What was it like to be held in the arms of a man who was reputed to marshal the forces of life and death?

"Pearl!" the Captain of the Dead would whisper in her ear. She shivered and wrapped her arms across her chest, imagining they were Lord Dade's arms. Yes, he would call her Pearl in that deep, unemotional voice of his, and pin her with his dark, gold-flecked eyes, and . . . and then what? The romance novels she enjoyed skipped rather obliquely over that aspect of a seduction, and she had no personal experience with such things. She had never before considered so thoroughly the details of such an encounter. Now her mind played with no other idea and her memory with no other man. The world would make a monster of her hero, but how could she believe him dangerous when she herself was regarded as somehow more worldly, more guilty than she really was, merely because she had been seen in the company of Captain Dead?

Celia's voice brought Margaret out of her reverie. Her sister spoke, in the urgent half-whispered tone of someone engaged in desperate business, as Margaret passed the open window to the little drawing room, where the twins went to practice music. The only music in this moment was a chorus of almost identical voices. Margaret would have paid no attention had not her own name figured in the tune.

Celia was ranting with no thought as to who might hear her. "It is Maggs and her dogs that have gotten us into this fix. Had she but stayed at home, we would both have invitations to Almack's, and cousin Allan would never have felt obligated to make such an impetuous challenge. I am sure of it. Do you know Allan tells me Captain Dead refers to Margaret as Pearl?"

"No!" Celeste sounded shocked. "How terribly forward!"

"I wish, above all else, that we might go and see this challenge acted out. After all, it is conducted on our behalf, and I could not stand it if anything dreadful should happen to cousin Allan and I was not there."

Celeste's voice softened. "I have half begun to think you are falling in love with our cousin, Celia."

"Celeste!"

"Well, I do not blame you. Allan is a handsome fellow, and it is clear he adores you. Always has. But as to our appearing at Monsieur Benadotte's salon to watch a fencing match, I have never heard a more ridiculous notion pass your lips. They do not allow ladies in the doors of such an establishment."

Margaret was unable to walk away from such an interesting discussion, no matter that it was not meant for her ears. She was in need of some distraction from the tendency of her thoughts to dwell on the memory of a certain bearded gentleman. Celia and Celeste were always bending their heads together over something. It would not be the first time she had thrust herself in the middle of their whisperings. Margaret did not think her twin sisters vicious in their intention to leave her out of their confidences. It was only natural that, as twins, they were much closer to each other. Age, temperament and identical birthdays made them as close as two sisters could be, but now and again Margaret tired of playing odd man out.

She squeezed the leather ball she still clutched, thinking of her younger brother. How wretched it was that Todd had died. Had he lived, it was possible she would not have grown up feeling quite so separate—so alone.

With some hope that conversation might distract her thoughts from what could be nothing other than regrets in connection with Todd, Margaret tossed the ball over the windowsill. The dogs leapt in after it.

"What is it you should wish to watch?" she asked as she hiked up the hem of her skirt and stepped in over the low sill after the dogs.

Her sisters looked up guiltily as she parted the curtains and advanced on them.

"Have you been eavesdropping?" Celia was indignant. "And what do you mean bringing the dogs in that way?"

Celeste twitched her skirt away from Lapith's questing nose. "We might as well tell her," she sighed. "She is, in some way, involved. She should know that Allan is defending her honor as much as ours."

"In a fencing match?" Margaret's interest rose as she smoothed her skirts. "I do not understand."

Celia glared at the dogs as they scuffled over the ball. "Dear, brave Allan means to defend our shattered honor by crossing swords with your Lord Dade, though he believes himself far inferior in skill."

"But what has Lord Dade done to shatter your honor?" Genuinely confused, Margaret sat herself down across from her sisters and accepted the slobbered ball from Centaur.

"Yours as well, in our having been denied vouchers to Almack's," Celeste reminded her.

"Lady Jersey said to Aunt Charlotte that any decent female would recognize Captain Dead for a dangerous fellow the instant she saw him. She called us silly chits!"

"What utter nonsense!" Margaret laughed and pitched the ball back out the window. The whippets dashed after it, nails skittering on the polished wood flooring. "Lord Dade looks the perfect gentleman at first glance. He is a trifle dark, but he was politeness itself in his behavior toward me. He saved me and the dogs from certain peril. I think him a hero rather than a dangerous fellow, and I do not see why Allan should feel obliged to challenge him. I would much rather he crossed verbal swords with this ridiculous Lady Jersey than metal ones with Lord Dade."

"You are unbelievably naive, Maggie," Celeste scolded. "You should never have taken a strange man's arm up the High Street. You have ruined us!"

Margaret laughed. "I did not take his arm! Ludd did, while I accepted Mr. Eckhart's escort, and surely you can find nothing to object to in Wallis Eckhart. A more mannerly young man never lived. Do not even begin to contradict me, Celeste. I have seen the sheep's eyes you cast his way whenever we chance to speak to him. No, I will not hear this nonsense about ruin. None of this really matters."

Celia stood abruptly, pale muslin and lace swirling around her like the ruffled feathers of a great white bird.

"Whatever do you mean, it does not matter? Your reputation is ruined and ours dragged down along with it, and all you can do is say it does not matter!"

"Reputation does not matter." Margaret was adamant. "Actions and deeds are what matter. In the grand scheme of things, what a bunch of blue-nosed old dames have to say about me, about any of us, matters not one whit. Destiny does not ride the back of gossip, Celia. History does not hinge on what is thought or not thought about me. Wars are not won, blood is not spilled, lives are not lost. It does not matter."

"It does matter," Celeste protested. She shot an angry glance at Margaret. "If we had brothers to look out for our financial well-being as Mother and Father get older, it would be different. But as it is, we have been raised with no other goal in mind than to marry well, and have little hope of accomplishing as much if we cannot circulate."

Margaret knew Celia meant to goad her in the way she mentioned brothers. Todd again, like a knife in the stomach!

Celeste leaned over to touch Margaret's knee gently. "I know you do not consider reputation a thing of great value, Maggs, but as your elders it is perhaps more of a worry for us than you, for we shall soon be deemed even more of a curiosity than our identical faces merit. The bookend old maids they will call us, two more miserable castoffs relegated to the shelf. It may not matter to you, Maggs, but it is a matter of vital interest to both of us and evidently to our cousin Allan as well. He is willing to fight a superior swordsman for our honor, and your reputation."

"Excellent proof that we need not marry at all," Margaret said defiantly, unwilling to give ground no matter how sensible Celeste sounded. "If Allan fights for our reputations on such slim provocation, he certainly is looking after us as well as any brother might." Her vehemence began to overwhelm her. "I defy you to say he is not."

Her sisters looked at each other. It was a special look of such complete understanding and agreement that the two seemed to communicate volumes without ever saying a word. Margaret shut her eyes on that look. It never failed to remind her of her separateness from them, of the thread of loneliness that bound up her life in so many ways.

"I will not waste my life worrying over gossip," she said. "Who are these people whose good opinion we so earnestly seek? They are nobody, nothing. Their breath does not stir the ocean, the sun does not shine, nor the rain fall upon their whim."

Celia sniffed. "Well, we must hope Allan does not become the latest victim to this notorious Captain Dead of yours."

"Must you refer to him by that dreadful name?"

Margaret asked, "Allan has not challenged him to an outright duel over this nonsense, has he?"

"Nonsense." Celeste patted Celia's hand in a consoling manner. "There is no real risk that our cousin will bleed for our honor. Their swords will be buttoned, Celia, never fear. Take courage. Be of brave heart."

Celia sighed. "It does almost make one wish at times that one might have been born a man. No fuss at all would come of such events if we wore breeches."

Chapter 4

MARGARET had to agree. Had she been born a Dornton son, *if she wore breeches*, things would have been different indeed. The idea fixed itself in her imagination. So fixed that she now kept her eyes on her cousin Allan's boots and followed two other late arrivals walking into Monsieur Benadotte's crowded fencing salon, a place that smelled strongly of cigar smoke, resin, sandalwood cologne and the musky tang of sweat. Margaret felt the hair at the nape of her neck rise in reaction to that smell. She told herself she must not panic, and she must not trip over the boots which were too big for her feet and slid about enough to give her the almost irrepressible urge to giggle. The release of such a sound would not do at all.

Margaret was wicked to have donned men's clothes, but her wickedness would be magnified a hundredfold was she discovered a girl by no more than a laugh. She was, she decided, either supremely foolish or incredibly brave. Margaret liked to think of herself as brave. She wanted very much to show courage, to be brave. She wanted to live up to the promise of the beautiful name Lord Dade had used to address her. Pearl would be heroic where Margaret was not.

Margaret's favorite books depicted brave men and women. The opera and theater, both of which she adored, were peopled by courageous characters. Her cousin Allan was brave to challenge a renowned swordsman to fence. Lord Dade had been brave in saving her from a mad dog. She was surrounded by brave examples. How could her own behavior follow any less a pattern now that she had begun to think of herself as Pearl rather than merely Margaret? She must show courage.

The hooded cloak into which she ducked her head was one of Allan's castoffs, dug from a wardrobe full of outgrown clothes her aunt had not seen fit to sell or give away. It smelled faintly of her aunt's lavender pomanders. The cloak was long enough that the edges almost swallowed all traces of the boots that slid up and down on her feet. The cloak was, in point of fact, in danger of dragging in the dust were she not clutching its folds with both shaking hands. Beggars and borrowers could not too choosy be. Pearl—she had in fact begun to think of herself as Pearl—hoped Allan did not spot her. He could not fail to recognize his own cloak. Be brave, she remonstrated with herself. Have courage!

She came late so as to be noticed less. The fencing match was in progress. There was no danger her cousin would spot her with any immediacy. His attention was focused on parrying the blade that came darting into his field of play.

Despite the masks that covered their heads and the matching chest guards they wore, Margaret immediately recognized the men for who they were. Lord Dade was not so tall as her cousin. He was more muscular, more tightly knit. His blade seemed a natural extension of his arm. On the balls of his feet, Dade moved with the muscular balance and grace of a man who rode as much as he walked. There was something in the splendid play of spring-like muscle that reminded Margaret of her whippets when they ran.

Feint, parry and thrust: she knew those were the moves these two masked and vested gentlemen engaged in, but she could not understand any more than that, other than the fact that Lord Dade seemed more casual about the whole encounter than she would have thought advisable. He seemed relaxed almost to the point of lethargy, his wrist moving in casual, effortless flicks as he diverted Allan's more energetic thrusts. Left arms raised, right arms extended, the length of their blades catching the light, the two graceful figures seemed engaged in a curiously evocative ballet. Pearl found the light footwork, the lunging stance, beautiful, even erotic. And yet Lord Dade, for all his lithe grace and emotionless poise, did not seem fully engaged in the dance until with a lightning-quick movement, his whole body invested itself in the advance of the sword. Like a striking snake, he made a clean thrust with the buttoned tip to Allan's exposed heart. The foil bowed upward with the graceful power of impact.

"Hit," the man assigned to judge announced flatly.

Allan fell back, breathing hard. Wrenching his mask from sweat-pearled face, he bowed in acknowledgment of having been bested. Lord Dade merely nodded. Without the slightest sign of fatigue he went to the corner of the room where his dog sat patiently waiting and Wallis Eckhart stood ready to divest him of foil, padded vest and shirt.

Margaret had not realized the gentlemen were to strip to the waist for this, the second and more dangerous part of the contest. She inhaled sharply as the fabric fell away from Lord Dade's shoulders, revealing skin almost as white as a woman's, marred only by the pink streaks of two recently healed scars, one across the shoulder, the second, more dangerous, glancing along the left rib beneath his heart. A fraction of an inch higher or lower, and the blade that had left such a mark would have plunged between the ribs. This body wore marks of courage. God, or the Devil, had seen fit to spare Lord Dade the finality of death.

Margaret had heretofore seen the male physique depicted only in Roman marble. There were unexpected bulges to Lord Dade's chest and arms, unexpected curling hair where she had never realized hair might grow, across his chest and in a provocative line leading down into his breeches. Such detail she had never seen represented on any statue. Her cheeks burned to see it now. Uncomfortably hot, she longed to throw off the confinement of the borrowed cloak.

Lord Dade's exposed shoulders seemed larger than she would have supposed. His arms and neck as well. They rolled with muscle under the pale skin that covered them, with the same satin smooth tension one witnessed in horses of excellent conformation. Such a display was feral, dangerous and tempting. There was, when Lord Dade wore no civilizing covering across his chest and back, the sense of a pirate persona unleashed. His shoulders, his torso, every movement he made, seemed deliberate, self-assured and liquid in its limberness.

Margaret bit her lower lip and wondered what it would be like to touch those bulging arms. There was a spot just beneath the ball of Lord Dade's shoulder that dipped inward, a hollow just large enough for her hand to fit. That hollow moved as her cousin's opponent took up the épée he meant to use. The depression in his arm glided and rolled as the blade was tested, just as every bulge in his arms and shoulders glided beneath the sheath of his skin. She was transfixed by the sight of him, mesmerized by the ebb and swell of the tides of his flesh. It crossed Margaret's mind that Satan was supposed to be the most beautiful of God's angels. Was there a bit of Satan, perhaps, in the allure of Lord Dade's physique?

As she wondered, the fencers returned to the rectangle designated as their field of action. Dade's chest was most interestingly divided by a line that separated the pectoral muscles. The line was faint, splitting the architectural solidity of him in perfectly symmetrical halves from vaulted neck and jawline to where it almost faded out in the slightly concave flatness at the boundary of skin-tight breeches.

Dade's gaze raked the spectators, passed over her and returned. There was a dreadful narrowing of his eyes, a frown, one archly raised brow, and he lifted his sword and saluted her, hilt to forehead.

He had recognized her! There was no other explanation for such a gesture. Cheeks aflame, Pearl's gaze fled his, to see if her cousin had noted the exchange. Allan was striding toward her, a murderous look on his face.

Head downcast, she awaited his ire, feeling less and less pearl-like and more and more plain Margaret.

He crouched to glare in at her under the shadow of the hood. "Magpie! What in God's name are you doing here?" he hissed, his lips thinned with anger. "No, don't answer. Don't look up," he warned her. "We have become an object of interest." With more force than was necessary for ordinary good humor he pounded her on the shoulder, as if he had met a friend. "You are the last person I expected to see here today!"

he said loudly for the benefit of those who listened to their conversation, and then he bent low again, to whisper, "You may be sure I shall deal with you later."

Margaret nodded, her courage flagging. She was afraid to speak, to so much as look up, lest she give herself away. Allan strode back to the field of play and raised his sword in salute, his anger evident in the briskness of every move.

All interest in Margaret diminished as blades were crossed with a ferocity that surprised her. She had been led to believe that épée matches proceeded at a slower, more deliberate pace than those with the foil.

"Fool," the man beside her muttered. "Anger guides him, not skill."

"All the better for Dade," his companion replied. "The second touch will be over in a trice."

Margaret peeped at the gentlemen around the edge of her hood. A darkly handsome fellow whom she did not recognize stared back at her. She turned quickly away, unnerved.

The clash of swords returned her attention to the match, but she was distracted almost immediately when something pelted against the hood of her cloak and then dropped to the floor at her awkwardly oversized feet with a clink. Someone had lost a button. Her attention returned to the swordsmen, whose exchange had slowed, as she had been led to expect. But there was something wrong, something to do with the button at her feet, something to do with the laws of gravity. Why should a button hit her in the head?

Margaret knew, even as she crouched to pick it up, that this was no ordinary button. One of the swords had this protective covering and not some gentleman's jacket. The image of Lord Dade's foil striking her cousin's chest galvanized her into motion. She was not about to lose her kinsman. Her brave cousin might be confronting the captain of the dead in earnest if the master swordsman fought with a naked blade! Her arms catapulted out before her to push the dark-haired gentleman and his companion out of the way. She blundered toward the fencing duo, shouting, "Stop!"

The men before her fell away, eyes wide. Past them, skidding and tripping in too big boots over too long a cloak on a highly polished wood floor, Margaret fell in the midst of flashing blades before she could be sure either of the combatants heard her. "Stop! You will kill him!"

Dade was detached enough from his confrontation with Allan Dornton to respond to the word stop as one of the spectators blundered wildly into the line of swordplay. His reflexes automatic, he smoothly insinuated his body between the cloaked intruder and his opponent's flashing blade. In wrapping himself around the intruder, he was beset by two immediate impressions and a third that took a moment to sink in. He was pierced in the leg by the burn of a naked blade, and in the gut by the feeling that he was falling, falling from his horse to the sound of his own voice yelling stop, while horses pounded past him and shots rang in his ears. The moment washed over him with its familiar dark intensity. It took him a moment to recover, to return to the present, to realize that the youth he clutched so fiercely to his chest, was sweetly scented and gloriously rounded. Dade had not held the yielding softness of a woman to his chest in over a year. There was no mistaking the sensation.

It was Pearl who looked up at him, round-eyed. She had tripped over the enveloping cloak that hid her features in falling into his arms, so that even as he shielded her from the danger of naked blades, the cape slid in a rush from her shoulders, to the floor, unveiling her pale hair. There was a gasp from the onlookers as it became patently evident that the foolhardy soul who thrust herself between armed men was a woman.

"Look to your sword tip, Mr. Dornton. It is naked," Dade snapped in his agitation as he drew Miss Margaret Dornton face first tight against the wall of his bared chest. With a flourish of his buttoned blade he caught up her fallen cape so that she might be as swiftly veiled as she had been unveiled. Swirling the heavy cloth about her shoulders, he sought out the panicked gray eyes that would not look him in the face and inquired with very real curiosity, "Whatever are you doing here? Did you come to see that the Captain of the Dead did not kill your cousin?"

She pulled away from him, to duck her head into the dubious anonymity of the cloak, but the pointed sting of his question lifted her gaze. He read the truth of his assumption in the open book of her flushed face.

"I came that I might live up to the brave promise of the name you call me," she said softly, chin trembling.

He was sure at first he had misheard her. Not foolish bravado again! "So that you might live up to a name? That is why you felt it incumbent upon you to risk life and limb in casting yourself between us just now?"

Damn bravado!

She hung her head, face hidden in the folds of the hood. "I did not think . . ." she faltered. "A button hit me." She looked up at him, "I did not know whose sword . . ."

Her cousin Allan was beside them then, briskly tugging down the hood of her cloak so that the earnest beauty of her expression was hidden. "Come," he insisted. "Best get you out of here before the rest of London sees your face. I do apologize, my lord, both for this unforeseen interruption to our competition and for not recognizing the state of my exposed blade sooner. Shall we call the match forfeit?"

"If you wish," Dade agreed, wincing. The slash to his thigh, which he had yet to examine, was beginning to smart. With a bow he turned away from Allan Dornton and the downcast, hooded figure beside him. This day's work had done nothing to improve the young lady's status among the *ton,* that was certain, but she had indelibly stamped herself upon his imagination. Dade felt within him the almost forgotten pull of his earlier curiosity to learn more of the young woman he had called Pearl. It was good to feel the sing of it in his veins. Pearl had said she wished to live up to the name he had called her. Dade shook his head. Damn bravado. Damn him for calling her Pearl. Margaret Dornton would need a good dose of bravado to deal satisfactorily with the aftermath of this morning's folly. The gossip mill was sure to make a seven-day wonder of it.

"Who was that?" Creighton demanded of him as Wallis helped him into his shirt. "And how did you manage to begin the undressing of her even as you continued to fence?" He slapped Dade's bare shoulder with an appreciative guffaw.

"You give new meaning to the term derobement, Ev, I do assure you. It was a most remarkable sight."

Dade offered no answer. He wished to play no further part in exposing his pearl of innocence to the world.

Wallis Eckhart was not yet so wise. "That was Pearl, and she is far too nice for the likes of you, Crey."

Dade closed his eyes and winced. Wallis was careless with his choice of words. Creighton Soames loved nothing more than a challenge. Tell him he could not do or win something, and he would pursue nothing else. With an elegance of movement, despite his pain, Dade reached up to finger the spotted silk Belcher tie knotted loosely about Creighton's neck. He would prefer Soames did not know too much about Margaret Dornton. The man might be diverted yet.

"Nice tie, Cray," he murmured.

Creighton withdrew his contemptuous look from young Wallis, pleased. "Do you like it, Ev?"

"Indeed. So much so that I would borrow it." Adroitly Dade slipped the Belcher from Creighton's throat before Soames could grasp what he was about, and bound up his leaking leg. Blood had begun to fill his boot.

"I say! You are bloody well bleeding all over my silk tie," Creighton groaned, but blood was not enough to distract him. "Too nice, is she?" He turned back to Wallis. "A female who would wear men's clothing? We shall see about that, lad. There is a naughty streak in any female if one knows how to go about tickling her fancy."

Dade tried to stem the damage, both to his leg and to Miss Dornton's freedom from Creighton's advances. "You will not find her good sport, Cray. She is too innocent and trusting by far not to fall easy prey to your lures."

"You cannot believe that, sir!" Wallis protested. "The lady is far too intelligent to easily fall under Creighton's spell. Like her sisters, she is pure, pristine, perfection! Surely you recognized as much? She is inviolate, despite the recklessness of today's appearance. Creighton will never get near enough to sully her."

Dade's lips twisted. Wallis sounded as if he was completely infatuated with the girl. Such an ardent defense, coupled with open insult, was sure to secure Soames's interest.

Creighton laughed. "I shall pry open the shell this pearl hides herself within so that I might mount her on my pinkie ring. Just wait and see. I shall have her wrapped around my little finger before the month is out. Care to place a wager on it, gentlemen?"

"Fie on you, Creighton," Wallis spat. "I will not wager on the downfall of innocence, for to do so would only encourage its annihilation."

Dade nodded. "The boy is right, Cray. There is no glory to be found in destroying the delicacies of character either in oneself or in another. You will bring yourself down along with your intended victim."

Creighton laughed. "Preach such stuff to any but me, Ev. Your milquetoast pulpiting sways me not."

Dade allowed none of the pique he was feeling to evidence itself in his countenance. "Will you be so good as to put off your pursuit of innocence long enough to see to the fetching of my carriage, Cray?" When Creighton had taken himself off on the errand, Dade could no longer restrain his frustration. "Creighton loves a challenge, Wallis, and while the Pearl poses none, for her defenses are negligible, you have thrown down the gauntlet and Creighton would slap your cheek with it."

Wallis scowled and began to object, but Dade was in no mood for argument. His leg was hurting far more than he would have expected for a scratch, and he was immensely irritated that Wallis was enmeshing himself so foolishly in Margaret Dornton's affairs. "I would be vastly obliged if you would refrain from protesting too much until we are safely ensconced in my carriage, Mr. Eckhart. My leg is troubling me, and the walls have ears."

Wallis was not at all used to Dade calling him Mr. Eckhart. He clapped his mouth shut—far too late to do much good in Dade's estimation.

Chapter 5

ALLAN blew in the door of his mother's house like a gale of harsh wind, hard on the heels of his disastrous sword fight. "I have come to take the Magpie and her dogs for a walk in the Green," he announced between gritted teeth, his eyes on the stairs as if he expected Margaret to stand waiting for him.

His mother was unruffled by his tone. "How thoughtful of you, Allan," she said. "Margaret slept late this morning. She is a little miffed, I think, that I do not allow her to walk her dogs in St. James's Park without you or your father to accompany her. It is very good of you to think of her. She is certain to enjoy the exercise."

Allan did not bother to inform her that his cousin had not been in her room at all, or that he had just dropped her off from his carriage near the back garden gate so that she might climb through the same window she had climbed out of to avoid being seen in his attire. He was in no mood to be scolded for foolish behavior until he had had his fill of scolding the Magpie for hers.

Celia took her cousin aside. "Why should you be so keen to honor Margaret with such a treat when she has sulked all morning behind a locked door? Have you not come to tell us of your encounter with Lord Dade?"

He frowned. "No. You will hear too much, all too soon, concerning the entire incident."

Margaret appeared in the doorway, hastily tying on her bonnet, both whippets dancing about her feet in anticipation of an outing. Allan broke away, his expression grim, saying brusquely, "Come on, then. We are wasting time standing about here."

Margaret was not at all surprised that her cousin had asked for her company, and hers alone, for a walk in Green Park. He had told her he meant to arrange it just so in his carriage as he raced her back to her aunt's house. This walk with Allan was not so much an honor as an opportunity for her cousin to give her a tongue-lashing in private. He had begun the job in his carriage, but had nowhere begun to run out of breath, or invective, in the short journey to his mother's. She could not blame him. It had been excessively foolish of her to dress as a boy and go to a place where no decent female had ever set foot. She had been even more foolish to dash between two armed men.

She berated herself assiduously for her folly. She had really done it this time! The gossips had been offered a worthy topic in her behavior. There was no explaining this away. Who would have thought that she, Margaret Dornton, of all people, might shock a man called Captain Dead?

Allan began his tirade as soon as they reached the wooded slopes of the Green, into which they and the dogs might safely place themselves out of hearing of any who passed. His castigation was of shorter duration than Margaret had expected. Beyond the initial "Whatever were you about, going into such a place, dressed in such a manner?" and "How could you even think of dashing into the midst of two armed men? You might have been killed!" Allan said very little to reprimand her. He was too concerned with his own lack of discretion to bother much over hers.

"How could you fight him with a buttonless sword?" she asked in turn. He seemed to have been waiting for the question. A look, as if of panic and deep remorse, swept his features.

"I was angry!" He tried to defend himself by drawing

her in again. "I was furious to find you there. And as a result I may be forced to flee the country."

"Flee the country? Surely not. Your honor is not so damaged as that. Everyone thought you fought on unaware."

He tousled his fair hair with agitated fingers. "It is not that, cousin."

"What then?" She bent to stroke the dogs and calm her hammering heart.

Allan rubbed his brow and sighed. "I actually pinked the viscount. I am sure I did, though he did not say a word in mention of it. I am sure that I stabbed him in the leg even as you were falling at our feet."

"Was he hit in protecting me?" she exclaimed. "I thought he flinched. Is the wound severe?"

"I don't know. It might be no more than a scratch."

Margaret's head rose abruptly. The dogs shied from the hand she still held out to them. "Call on him. Go and see for yourself. The worst he can do is turn you away."

"No! You do not seem to understand. The worst he can do is to die on me. I fear such an end would be the ruination of my entire family."

"Not to mention Lord Dade," she said wryly.

"I know! I know. I have made the situation far worse instead of better, just as he predicted."

"He? Lord Dade did not want to fight you, then?"

"No. Said it would only fire up the gossipmongers more than they already were."

"Well, he was right, and my own foolishness put the seal on it. The only reason I leapt between the two of you, the reason I convinced myself I must go to the stupid match, was because I thought he might injure you fatally on account of me. If he is injured, it is as much my own doing as yours. We must call on him, that we may see the truth of his condition for ourselves."

"You? You cannot go with me."

"Why not? My reputation is already in tatters, and after this morning's work gets around I shall surely be sent home. What further harm can be done in visiting a man I may have had a part in murdering?"

"Murdering! That's a bit harsh."

Margaret shrugged and set off at a brisk walk with the dogs. "Are you coming?"

He stood watching her as if anchored to the spot. "Stop!" he called. "Really, Magpie. This will not do."

She kept on walking as if she had a very good idea of where she was going when she had none, the dogs scampering in her wake.

Allan trotted up behind her and caught her by the shoulder. "Margaret, stop."

She shrugged off his hold on her. "I mean to go, Allan," she said firmly.

He laughed. "Where? You've no idea, have you?"

Her chin rose. He had called her bluff. Of course she had no idea where Lord Dade lived.

"Admit it." He chucked her under the chin.

She glowered at him. "No, but I'm sure I can find out. I shall just ask until I find someone who can tell me where the viscount has rooms."

He raked his hand through already tousled locks. "God, Magpie, really. You cannot mean to stop just any stranger and ask where a bachelor lives!"

He was right, of course, but her mind was made up. She shrugged and pinned him with her most self-assured stare. "Which way are we going, then, cousin?"

He sighed heavily and eyed the sprinkling of people who were traversing the park, weighing her threat. "This way," he said, turning on his heel to lead her where she would go.

Lord Dade's bachelor's quarters were just north and east of Green Park. There the Dornton cousins went, the whippets following. They were met at the unpreposessing, brass-fitted door by a slender, close-faced gentleman's gentleman who informed them that his master was not at home to visitors and would they mind coming back some other time. Allan nodded gravely and formally handed over his card, which was accepted with equally formal grace. The solemnity of the moment was diluted, however, by an indignant shout that came from the dark recesses of the apartment.

"You shall not leech me, so you might as well stick those nasty black creatures back in your bag!"

Wishing them a crisp good day, the manservant closed the door on whatever reply might have been made.

Allan's back was very stiff as he and Margaret and the dogs made their way down the steps. Headed once more toward the Green, he squeezed Margaret's arm and said through gritted teeth, "You heard. He is attended by a physician. There is no other conclusion to be drawn than that I have in fact injured the man."

"Agreed," Margaret said shakily, striving to remain calm. "What does one usually do under such circumstances?"

"Such circumstances have never been mine to contend with. I haven't a clue." Allan laughed uneasily. There was no time for further reply. He was hailed from the steps of the dwelling they had just been turned away from by the same darkly handsome young man Margaret recognized from the fencing match.

"Hallo! Mr. Dornton. Wait a minute!" With little regard for traffic, the gentleman leapt across the road after them. "Creighton Soames," he introduced himself, producing his card. "Friend of Dade's." Allan shook his hand, but Margaret was disconcerted to find the gentleman's amused green eyes fastened on her. "Come to assess the damage, have you?"

Allan blinked in surprise. Creighton laughed and gave him a playful shove. "I know that's what I would do were I walking about in those shoes." He pointed at Allan's feet. "Which way were they headed, then?"

"The Green," Allan replied, his expression one of puzzlement. It was not the normal method of introduction to approach strangers in the street and thrust one's card at them.

"I shall walk along with you for a bit. I am going that way myself." Soames started off up the walkway. Allan, always polite, took Margaret's arm and followed. "Best thing you was turned away at the door by Lord Dade's man, you know," Creighton said. "Ev is suffering no more than a good slash across the thigh, but leeches, large and small, put him in the foulest of moods. The man with him now is pouring foul droughts down his throat and rebinding the leg. Ev was a bit peeved to hear that a perfectly good pair of his breeches had been ruined by the cut you gave him. He would most likely have received you ill had you shown your face in his rooms."

"When you say Ev, you are referring to Lord Dade?" Allan inquired uncertainly.

"Of course, man. Didn't think you were interested in anyone else's injuries."

"The wound is not serious, then?" Margaret's voice was soft. She felt intimidated by Creighton Soames, to whom she had not yet been officially introduced.

"Oh, I do beg your pardon!" Mr. Soames stopped their passage to reach for her hand. "You must do the pretty"—he bobbed his head in Allan's direction. "What is the name of this lovely young creature whose arm you are so fortunate to possess?" He winked audaciously at Margaret as he bent his head to kiss her hand.

Allan looked nonplussed and Margaret knew her cousin hated to introduce her without himself knowing the gentleman he presented her to. He did his best to maintain a sense of decorum. "Margaret, this is Mr. Creighton Soames."

Mr. Soames held up one elegantly gloved hand to put a stop to such formality. "Tut, tut! You must call me Cray, Dornton. Everybody does."

Allan was not used to such casual manners with a new acquaintance. "Yes, well, this is my cousin, Margaret Dornton, ah, uh, Cray. She will address you as Mr. Soames."

"Of course, and unless I am much mistaken, your lovely cousin Margaret is none other than the daring young Pearl who briefly was unveiled at the fencing match this morning," Creighton Soames said with a pleasant smile, as if he had no more than asked Allan to agree with him on a matter of the weather.

Allan's mouth fell open. Margaret gasped.

"Never fear." Creighton took Margaret's arm without raising an intelligible word of objection from the speechless Allan. "I shall not tell a soul I have found you out, but you must not deny me getting to know you both better, for I cannot remember when I have met a more entertaining and courageous pair of cousins." He clapped his hand on Allan's shoulder. "Challenging Ev, of all people, to a fencing match . . ." His attractive green eyes crinkled with delight.

"Dashing into the midst of flashing blades, all kitted out in men's attire." Possessively he patted Margaret's arm, as if they were friends of long standing and he was due certain privileges. "Tell me," he chuckled, "are there more daring Torntons to amaze me?"

Margaret was in a sweat that Creighton Soames would consider it no more than an amusing afternoon's work to spread the word of her folly throughout London. She did not trust the devil-may-care joviality of the handsome stranger who captivated the affections of both her sisters from the moment they were introduced. Unsure why she did not trust him, Margaret determined to observe him very closely, in order that her suspicions might be either verified or calmed by what he did rather than by what he chanced to say.

Creighton did his utmost to win her over, to win them all over, in fact. He called every day to inform them of Lord Dade's progress. His smiles were never so bright as when Margaret entered a room. His conversation aimed to entertain, his flashing green eyes sought her out with friendly purpose. He seemed quite infatuated with her hand whenever he took leave of her, for it remained clasped by his fingertips a fraction of a moment longer in his salute to it than any other hand he took possession of. Margaret was somewhat taken aback. Generally the twins won the lion's share of people's attention. Mr. Soames's attentions were undeniably flattering, and noticed and remarked upon by Margaret's sisters. Both set aside their pique that their younger sister was receiving so much attention because they were immensely pleased Mr. Soames chose not to scorn them along with the rest of the *ton.* Margaret dared not tell them Creighton Soames reveled in their scandal as much, if not more, than the rest of the world reviled it.

Aunt Charlotte adored him. "He is very pleasant, Margaret," she said, "so lavish with praise and pretty compliments. I would never have imagined you might be endowed with a suitor before either of your sisters, but it is not to them Mr. Soames brings flowers and chocolates. He professes an especial fondness for your pets, niece, but I am certain he likes the animals' mistress even more than he does the dogs."

Margaret's uncle allowed that Mr. Soames was an easy conversationalist, as long as one did not broach politics or the military, both subjects of which the young man laughingly professed complete ignorance. Even Allan unbent and began to call their visitor Cray, as requested.

It was only Wallis, who had become as permanent a fixture as Cray, in whom Margaret found a reservation equal to her own with regard to Creighton. Not voiced openly, Wallis made evident his feelings by way of certain expressions he cast about when Creighton's compliments seemed unusually thick.

"How now, Creighton, doing it up a bit brown," he would mutter, his mouth tightening as he steered conversation in a new direction.

Margaret watched and listened carefully to the charming Mr. Soames. Every time he smiled at her, or kissed her hand, she tried to dismiss from her very active imagination the image he provoked—that of a snake—not the poisonous kind but a more exotic variety she had read about. It hugged its prey to death.

While Wallis was pleasant, well spoken and engaging, he could not compete with Creighton's boisterous style. All too often he fell into the background of theDerntons' attentions. All save Celeste's. This worked out rather well for all concerned, for Wallis found Celeste as interesting as she found him. He made it clear, however, that he was concerned lest any of the Dornton sisters be wholly taken in by Creighton. His brow furrowed when Creighton's manner elicited too enthusiastic a response.

Margaret was astonished to find that no hint of her involvement in the much talked-about fencing match seemed to sully the sparkling gossip that surrounded that event. While it was widely known that a fair-haired female had jumped between the fencers, no one seemed to be able to identify her. She was, of course, all the more interesting for this omission.

"It is assumed," Creighton passed on to her, with a twinkle in his eye, "that the woman must have been a soiled dove, a back-stairs hoyden favored either by Lord Dade or, heaven forbid, your cousin Allan."

Despite this show of faith that Creighton Soames had no

intention of revealing her identity, Margaret's fears did not begin to fade with regard to that handsome and all too charming gentleman until the afternoon he stopped Allan on the street to inform him, "Ev is fallen into a fever. The doctor has voiced some concern about an inflammation of the wound. I know you meant to call on him." Cray had a worried look that made Margaret's heart sink with concern. "Would you care to go with me?" Creighton made the offer without his usual smooth self-assurance. So unusual was this unexpected pathos in Mr. Soames that Margaret lost sight of how unusual it was that she should be asked along on such a visit.

"It would not make him angry to see me?" Allan's concern troubled his usually genial features.

"He is too weak to throw you out, and if you would care to make your peace with him, perhaps sooner rather than later would be advisable."

Allan blanched to hear such fatalistic advice. "Is his life in danger?" he insisted.

"That would be ironic, would it not?" Creighton said with a sigh, a shrug and a sliding glance in Margaret's direction. "To survive Waterloo only to be laid low by no more than the prick of a fencing sword?"

Chapter 6

CREIGHTON Soames had no qualms about letting himself in the door to Lord Dade's town house when there was no response to his knock.

"Come," he said with a wink of devil-may-care nonchalance as he held the door open for them. "Gimble must have his hands full, and"—he hooked arms with Margaret—"we must not keep you standing here, exposed to all the world on the stoop of a bachelor's abode."

Margaret, who had been stewing over the prudence of that very issue, did not feel in the least relieved when they were safely inside. She should not have come. To do so placed her imperiled reputation in further danger. She knew better and yet had been unable to resist the lure of seeing for herself if Captain Dead would live.

"Hold them, lads. Steady!" came a shout from above as Mr. Soames shut the door and slipped off his coat.

"Dreaming of Waterloo again, are we?" Creighton muttered, his voice echoing in the stairwell as he made his way familiarly across the marble entry and up the stairs, theBorntons trailing after him.

"Steady on, don't let them get away from you." The voice rang out again from above their heads. A low rumbling followed as other voices attempted to stop the outburst.

Up the stairs the unheralded guests trotted, Margaret tugging on Allan's arm, whispering, "Is this right, cousin? Surely we must not simply barge in this way."

"Stay here on the landing," Allan whispered over his shoulder, something desperate in his tone. "I shall just go up and see for myself how he gets on."

Margaret nodded and remained on the stairway landing as the gentlemen proceeded. There was a gallery at the head of the stairs. Her companions turned left on reaching it and disappeared from view.

The shouting, which Margaret was certain must be Lord Dade calling out in delirium, rang in the stairwell. "Hold your positions. Hold those horses, damn you!"

She had the feeling she had stepped into the midst of a battle.

"Here we are, Gimble," Creighton called briskly, as if in announcement that the cavalry had arrived. "What may we do to help?"

"Welcome, gentlemen." The manservant's voice was very faint. "I require assistance in holding him."

There was a brief period of mumbling. Margaret crept two risers higher than the landing, straining to make out the words. The voices quieted. She listened harder, holding her breath, closing her eyes with the effort.

"Gavin!" The terrible shout flung her against the wall, so unexpected was the volume of its sound, so deep the level of its anguish. That single word, drawn out as if ripped unwillingly from the very bowels of a man in extreme pain, rang around her in the stairwell. Gavin. She knew the name. Lord Dade was crying out for the ghost of his late brother in his delirium. To hear such anguish over the deceased could not but move her. She understood all too well the depths of such feeling for a lost brother. How many times had her own shouts for Todd lifted her out of a fitful slumber?

"Gavin! Why?" The cry battered her again, as if the dead might be raised were it wrenching enough.

Margaret clapped her hands to her ears and retreated to the landing, where the awful image that she strove so hard to forget appeared in her mind's eye.

"No!" she whispered hoarsely, biting her lower lip in hopes that pain might drive away the painful image that plagued her memory, the image of the woolen blanket that sturdy, flailing baby legs kicked over the edge of the cradle and into the fireplace. It was an image that smoldered and smoked in her memory just as the blanket had, until pretty, dancing yellow flames seized it and raced up into the crib to make the baby cry. She, not yet three, had watched from her little bed, fascinated by the flame. She was frightened by the screams from the cradle, yet uncertain of their meaning. She did not cry out until the baby wailed with such terror she could not but shriek along with him. Her imagination was a curse and not a blessing in moments such as this.

Nanny had come running too late. The housekeeper and her father too late—too late to save the baby, but in good time to stop the fire before it spread. Margaret had screamed and wept and thrashed in Nanny's arms and wakened half the household as many as four times a night in the months that followed, while the house was shrouded in black and her mother could not set eyes on her, or anything to do with little Todd.

"No!" The shouting above seemed to echo the unvoiced scream in her head. "No, no." Lord Dade's voice weakened. Margaret felt like sinking to the floor, weeping, with her skirt up over her head, to hide her overwhelming sorrow from the world. She felt like running down the stairs and out into the street to escape the heaviness in her heart. But there was no heroism in flight, no courage in tears.

Unable to remain in the stairwell alone with the awful memories and the shouts of a man in pain, Margaret resolutely dashed a tear from her cheek, lifted her skirts and advanced on the source of the sound. She was determined to face her demons, determined to ease suffering in her fellow man now that she could.

To the top of the stairs she rushed headlong and turned left. Her breath came hard and fast. Her walk slowed. There was no mistaking the direction. A great deal of movement and discussion came from the room in which everyone was gathered.

Margaret took a deep breath. She trod lightly as she approached the open door. It was a gentleman's private sanctum she dared to invade. She could see bared flesh and linens. The room was dominated by an enormous posted and draped bed of a dark wood. The bed had swallowed Lord Dade. The man-servant she had seen for the first time only days earlier at the door looked slightly less collected than she remembered him as he fought to hold onto his master's flailing arms. Creighton Soames bent over the opposite side of the bed, pinning in place Lord Dade's ankle. A black-clad gentleman stood over the patient, manfully maintaining his professional dignity while folding back the tossing bedclothes with one hand and holding high in his other a tray of leeches.

"Light!" he shouted imperiously. "Will someone please bring me more light? I have dropped the blasted creature and cannot see what I am about, to save my soul. You must hold him still, men, or we shall have the bed full of leeches and none of them on him."

Shadows swung across the ceiling, across the figures by the bed, as her cousin altered the stage set before her with the pool of light he brought with him in the form of a lamp.

The man in the bed wanted none of it. "No! Must not take the leg," he muttered hoarsely, his eyes staring at some unseen horror in the shifting light on the bed hangings. He was winning in the struggle with Gimble as he thrashed about, his free leg flailing in and out of the bedclothes with enough vigor to cast himself completely free from sheets and counterpane. Margaret blinked, not so much in amazement at seeing a man's night-shirted nakedness, but because the pale, thrashing leg reminded her too much of smaller flailing legs and blankets on the floor.

"Dear God, Magpie! What are you doing here?" Allan breathed, cutting into the nightmare of her past. He turned. The light turned with him.

Margaret blinked in the glare.

"Be still with that light," howled the physician.

Allan swung the circle of light once more toward the bed. The doctor had thrown back the bedclothes and lifted Lord Dade's nightshirt. His wounded thigh was completely exposed. Pearl was transfixed by the dark-haired expanse of pale flesh. Her eyes were drawn irresistibly to the angry, swollen redness of Dade's wound.

"You had best trot back down the stairs," Allan ordered.

"Someone grab his other ankle," the doctor complained. "I still do not know where the blasted leech has gone."

Allan grabbed the moving leg with his left hand. The light bobbed and dipped in his right. Margaret crossed to the window and threw back the draperies, that daylight might further illuminate the goings-on.

"Excellent," the doctor crowed. "Found you, you little devil."

"Hands off," the invalid croaked from deep in the pillows as Margaret turned uncertainly back to the bed. The gentleman tangled in the bedclothes twisted energetically away from the ministrations of the frustrated physician, despite the many hands that would hold him still.

"Can you not confine his limbs between the three of you?" the doctor intoned dourly. "We shall never be done with him at this rate."

"Away from me." The voice from the pillow seemed to gather strength and volume. With a burst of renewed energy, the injured limb slipped from Allan's grasp and kicked outward, overturning the physician's tray and unbalancing the doctor himself enough that he fell backward into a wardrobe. His hat went flying as he cracked his head smartly on the door.

"Damn!" the doctor thundered, scrambling to his feet, his hand to his abused head.

"Are you injured?" Gimble was suitably solicitous.

"It is a wonder I have not split open my head." The doctor fingered a tender spot on his crown, scowling ferociously at his still restless patient. "Does he mean to be the death of me?"

Margaret threw a hand over her mouth. In the fracas a leech had landed on the balding forehead of the doctor. With each angry complaint it flopped about.

"Hold still." Gimble politely reached for the leech, no trace of amusement bending his lips.

The physician backed away from his approaching hand, backed right into the door of the wardrobe again, which had swung open upon first encountering that sturdy pate.

"Blast!" the doctor shouted as his reflection met him in the cheval glass set up beside the wardrobe. "Gad!" he shouted with increasing fury as he wrenched the objectionable creature from his thrice-abused cranium. "Enough of this folly, gentlemen," he blustered. "Where is my hat? You must find Lord Dade a more understanding physician. I've less recalcitrant patients yet to be seen." Grabbing up his hat and box of medicines, the humiliated man stalked from the room, tossing the offensive, black bloodsucker to the floor as he went.

Lord Dade, his energy evaporating, still thrashed and banged his head against the headboard. Rather than watch him continue to bruise his head, Margaret leapt in beside Creighton Soames. Cradling the tossing head in both her hands, she leaned in close to the dodging ear. "Shh, shh, shh," she crooned, hoping that where a shout did not work, a whisper might. "Have courage, sir. You are safe and tucked away in your bed."

The mumble in Dade's throat died off. Arms and legs fell still in their attempt to throw off the hands that pinned him to the bed.

"There, that's working." Gimble sounded relieved.

Allan was anything but relieved as he set the lamp on the bedside table. "Whatever are you doing here, Magpie? Did I not ask you to wait downstairs?"

"You did, Allan, but—"

Dade moaned and began to stir.

Across the pillows Gimble whispered urgently. "Keep talking, miss. Whatever it was you said, it calmed him. Perhaps I can catch the doctor before he is gone. At the very least, I shall show him to the door."

"Ech, the bed is all over leeches," Creighton complained. "Here," he suggested to Allan. "I shall hold the stupid tray, while you place the things back in it."

Allan was not ready to fall in with the scheme, but he was distracted from scolding Margaret. "You cannot expect me to pick them up." He voiced his outrage.

"Kindly delay your argument, gentlemen," Margaret said in a stern undertone. "We do not want Lord Dade thrashing about again before the awful things have been removed from the bedclothes."

She might have laughed had she not been so focused on

pouring soothing words into Lord Dade's ear, as the two gentlemen went about locating the scattered leeches, mumbling their disgust.

Gimble returned, disappointed in his errand.

"Never mind the stupid physician," Creighton grumbled. "Help us with these blasted leeches. They are everywhere! The sheets are writhing with them and must be changed."

Margaret continued to murmur soothing words while the sheets were first searched and then the patient himself studied, to be sure the leeches were not making lunch of him. This involved pulling the bedclothes completely off the bed and then rearranging his nightshirt in stages, while Gimble examined him limb by limb and Allan held high the light.

Once again Allan urged Margaret to leave the room, but Creighton laughed, and told him, "Don't be missish, man. She cannot see much, seated as she is, with her back to it all and her nose in Evelyn's ear."

Margaret did not bother to inform him that she saw everything quite clearly, in the tilted cheval glass that had so disturbed the doctor. Based on this shocking display, she was certain that her cousin was right. She should be downstairs at the very least and, in point of fact, probably out of the house altogether, with no other female there, not even a maid, to vouchsafe her reputation. But now that she was here, she could not talk herself into listening to her conscience. She was too caught up in the day's adventure, too caught up in the glimpses of shoulder, back and leg to be seen in the mirror. She was fascinated by the study of her patient's sleeping visage: the heated pink in his cheeks, the set of his chin, the relaxed position of his mouth, the vulnerability of his nose and brow.

She leaned in close to his ear, her head sinking into his pillow, and babbled on, saying nothing of great import. She spoke of the chessboard that was set up on a table just beside the bed, the pieces paused in mid-game. She pretended the two of them were continuing the game. All the while she marveled over the man whose ear she filled.

She marveled at the nearness of him, at the great, muscular size of him, at the texture and coloring of his skin and hair, especially that which covered so much of his face. She wondered over the delicate shaping of his ear, the line of brow and nose and cheekbone. She was fascinated by the fine hue and smoothness of his lips in the midst of the dark danger of mustache and beard. Dade lay fretting, his head ticking erratically in the palms of her hands. She wished him well again. She wished him sound and well and looking at her, Captain Dead or her knight in shining armor, whichever he might be. Even as she wished it, his eyelids fluttered. Dark, fevered eyes looked at or through her—which she could not be certain.

She gave a little gasp, so unexpected was his regard. Courage, she must have courage. "My lord?"

"Water," he whispered and tried to sit up, brow furrowed, the gold flecks in his eyes very bright. "I am too hot." He tried to throw off the fresh bedclothes. "Get the poor horse off my legs," he insisted, glaring at and through Allan.

Allan's mouth fell open. "I beg your pardon!"

"Never mind him, sir. He's delirious again," Gimble said as he poured a glass of water from the pitcher on the bedside table. "Lord Dade was found pinned under his horse at Waterloo. He does but relive the moment."

"Drink, my lord," Margaret said softly as Gimble gently lifted his head and coaxed the liquid through flaccid lips. Her eyes searched the fevered ones before her with concern. "Drink. You must drink. You are injured and feverish, sir, and fretful over the physician. But we have sent the leech away, my lord, and do but seek to make you comfortable again. Lie back while your valet sees to the sheets. Soon you shall be in fresh linen with nothing to do but close your eyes upon us and sleep your way into perfect health again."

She touched her hand to his forehead. He seemed to find some comfort either in the water or the placement of her hand, for he faded back into lethargy, his head sinking into the pillows. Alarmed by the heat of his skin, Margaret requested that Mr. Gimble bring her a bowl of cool vinegar water and some cloths for his forehead. Her gaze passed from Allan's concerned expression to Soames's. "He is burning up with fever," she said. "How long has he been like this?"

Soames shrugged. "No more than a day. He spoke quite rationally to me yesterday."

"Is there no one in his family who will come and stay with him? No sisters who will see to his needs? Gimble cannot manage this on his own. Someone must sit with him until this fever abates."

"Gimble managed alone when he returned from Waterloo. Poor Ev's relations are scattered to the four winds, none of them anywhere near enough to see to his health."

Gimble returned with the vinegar compress. "Actually, sir, there was a woman hired in to help, but my lord sent her away again once he could walk. Said he had been accustomed to doing for himself in the military, and saw no reason to change that just because he had come into his brother's inheritance."

"Well, hire her back again," Soames suggested.

"No!" Allan startled them all by objecting. He flushed. "I mean, I've just the female. You remember my old Nan, cousin?"

Margaret did vaguely remember a practical matronly woman who had coaxed her to eat a bite after her brother's funeral. She nodded.

Allan went on enthusiastically. "She has retired here to London, with her sister. No one could be more comforting or attentive when one is ill. We must fetch her here."

"Capital idea. I shall drive you," Creighton offered. "Let us go at once."

"Excellent!" Allan was always happiest when he had some control over a situation.

"I think it would be best if I remained here with Gimble and Lord Dade until you return," Pearl said calmly as she squeezed out a pungent vinegar compress and placed it on Dade's forehead. She looked up at the two gentlemen, who regarded her as if she suggested something quite scandalous.

"But, Margaret, we cannot leave you here alone in a bachelor's bedchamber! I should not have allowed you to come here in the first place. To leave you alone is out of the question."

"I am not alone," she said sensibly. "As you can see, Mr. Gimble is here to help."

"Magpie, this will not do."

Margaret thought Allan looked very much like his father

when he tried to appear decisive and commanding. She smiled at him. "Is it somehow more acceptable to leave the man you have injured in the care of a single servant than to encourage me to stay and bathe the fever from his forehead? Do not be ridiculous, cousin. You will require the room I would take in the carriage, for if I recall correctly, your Nan was not a slender person. Now please be sensible and go without wasting any more of our time in argument. I shall not be dissuaded by your very proper sensibilities. They make no real sense, you see. This gentleman is weaker than a kitten and certainly no danger to my innocence."

Allan opened and closed his mouth a few times until Creighton grabbed his arm and dragged him toward the door. "C'mon, you great gudgeon. She has the right of it, you know. Only tell me where this old Nanny of yours lives and we shall be back in a trice, no one ever the wiser."

Allan exhaled heavily and went.

Chapter 7

"AND now, Mr. Gimble, you must tell me what you have been doing for Lord Dade's wound," Margaret said firmly when the door had closed on her cousin and the sound of Creighton's phaeton had receded in the distance.

She was surprised that her cousin had given in so easily to the idea of leaving her. Whatever would her aunt say if she heard of this? What would her mother think?

The room in which she stood seemed so very masculine, the man in the bed before her, so very large. But she was no longer merely Margaret, she was the brave, even heroic Pearl, who would never allow a servant to sense her doubts. Resolutely, she lay back the covers to examine the injured leg, carefully tucking the covers about Lord Dade's abdomen so that he was no more exposed to her than was necessary. The wound was in the upper thigh: angry, red, hot, and swollen. Courage, she said to herself, have courage.

"Hot and cold compresses, when he will allow it," Gimble said.

"Excellent. He would appear to be willing to allow them now. Shall we try turpentine and milk?" She leaned down to sniff the wound, as she had seen her mother do any number of times as she waited on injured crofters who worked her father's land. Mother made all of her girls accompany her at least once a week in visiting the sick, but Margaret was the only one with affinity for the task. She had been exposed to all manner of healing ways and knew enough to say with authority, "The wound does not smell putrid."

Gimble regarded her with newfound respect. "Milk and turpentine, miss? In what proportion, if you please?"

He left her alone with his sleeping master when she had given her requirements. She studied her patient now that he was peaceful. She could examine him to her heart's content now, with no one the wiser. He was in some ways very different in repose than when awake. He seemed vulnerable in sleep—in need of protection. He had lost his watchful, ready-to-spring-into-action look in repose. His hands looked somehow less capable and not at all threatening, extending as they did from the arms of a frilled nightshirt. They were curled against the pale linen, like the hands of a child. The lines in his forehead were ironed out. His face, which she had always considered handsome, if a trifle wicked, had lost all trace of devilment now. Odd, that anyone should fear this man as the harbinger of death. He had no more control over such forces than anyone else.

Margaret watched the slow rise and fall of his chest. What a shame it would be if this man's breath ceased life's wonderful rhythm. Leaning closer, to turn the vinegar compress, she inadvertently found her breathing pattern had slowed to match his. They inhaled and exhaled almost as one. Margaret closed her eyes and listened to the faint rushing of air as their chests rose and fell in perfect harmony. Strangely, she felt as if in patterning her breathing after Dade's, she understood him better. In the identical rhythm of their pulses something that had slept within her unwound like a tightly coiled spring.

Her eyes flew open. She understood now, as never before, why it was an uncommon practice to leave young women alone in the company of young men, most especially in their bedchambers. Her mind seemed undone, freed from some constrictive binding she had never even known was there. Unrestrained thoughts coursed through her head: of touching this man, of leaning into the hollow of his neck to better hear the music of his breathing, of being touched by him in turn. As if the loosening of her thoughts released the normal physical restrictions on her extremities, she reached out to touch Dade's beard with trembling fingertips. With trepidation she gave herself permission to stroke the texture of his side whiskers with one hand while the other gently toyed with his mustache, finger and thumb traveling in opposite directions, down the sides of his mouth, coming together again at the carefully clipped point that covered his chin. She wondered what the face beneath looked like, what it would feel like.

She had wondered at the texture of this hair. It was both sleek and wiry, and Margaret felt depraved for having run her fingers through it. She felt even more immoral for wondering what this hair might feel like against a woman's cheek. Surely Lord Dade's kiss must differ from that of other men merely by merit of this extra brush of hair.

On impulse she ran her index finger over the plush heat of his lower lip. His flesh felt so very smooth in contrast. He stirred as she touched him and turned his face more fully toward her, a tiny moan leaking from his thoat. The pattern of his breathing changed. Alarmed, she drew her hands away, but even as she did so his eyes opened.

The keen edge of his look was like the light gleaming on the edge of a sword. With the same lightning reflexes that had flexed a foil against her cousin's chest, he grabbed her wrist in one hand and clasped her waist with the other. The look in his eye made her quake. The level of his strength took her breath away as he pulled her onto the bed before she could so much as let loose a squeak.

"No," she gasped. Did he mean to ravish her? The heated hand that overpowered her waist slid along her torso to cup her breast. "No!" She struggled, but viselike he drew her toward him, until she seemed to drown in the fevered sparkle of dark, gold-flecked eyes.

He meant to kiss her! She was sure of that much. He pulled her so close, the warmth of their breath mingled. A sigh passed from his mouth to hers. Her eyes roved wildly from his nearing mouth, lips slightly parted between the glossy hair of mustache and beard, to the piercing glitter of those eyes. He glared at her, almost cross-eyed so close were their faces.

"Curb chains. The men must have them," he mumbled fiercely.

Their lips came within a hair's breadth of touching as he spoke, but as if in speaking, his objective was met, his eyes shut, his hand loosed its incredible hold on her, and a second sigh passed from his mouth to hers. No more than that. As quickly as he had roused, Evelyn Dade fell into repose again. The grip on her wrist fell away. The hand that cupped her breast slid limply into the rumpled bedclothes.

Her pulse beating erratically, her heart in her throat, Margaret felt both an intense relief that she had not been forced to fight him off and an almost reciprocal regret that this, the most erotic and arousing encounter she had ever faced, should end so tamely. She was quick to roll to her feet, her breathing labored. She was quick to back away from the bed, hand to throat, panicked not so much by what this delirious man had done without full consciousness of his behavior as by the reaction of her own heart and mind. In the split second she had been knocked off her pins—pulled body to body with the viscount—she had felt as if she were come home. His hand, his chest, his rib cage, all of it had felt firm and solid and achingly provocative. She had closed her eyes as his hand ran up to cup the weight of her breast, not out of horror but because his touch pleased her. His arms around her had seemed a nest, and she had flown into them like a bird. That such contentment should assail her, if only for the briefest instant, seemed a wondrous and frightening thing.

Margaret lifted her hand to the breast he had cradled in his palm. It had never before occurred to her that a man might wish to touch her just so, or that such contact might stir her heart into a peltering turmoil and cause her nipples to stand up in hard, aching points.

With no one there to notice, Margaret blushed. She was wrong to have come here today, wrong to insist she be left alone with Lord Dade.

She backed away from the man in the bed, backed almost to the wall, where her foot ran up against something that fell against her ankle with a rattling noise. She looked, breath caught, first at the bed, to see if the sound had roused Dade, who flickered not an eyelid, and then at her foot to see what she had run into.

A stack of elaborately framed paintings and prints were leaned face against the wall. It was their hanging chains she had given cause to rattle. Margaret knelt to replace the one she had knocked up against. Curious, she flipped through the frames to see what had once hung upon these walls and was no longer deemed acceptable.

The pictures were military in nature: prints of battleships and regiments on the march; several oils of proud horses at the gallop, necks arched, their riders armed to the teeth.

Margaret knelt there a moment, wondering about the man in the bed behind her. Why he had sold his commission and stripped his rooms of military memorabilia? He was a hero and yet sought neither recognition nor memories of his heroism. This confused her. She had a simple, idealistic concept of heroics and could not fathom why anyone would shove glory face against the wall.

She rose and stood very still for several minutes beside the bed, reliving in her mind's eye what had just transpired. Never had she been more intrigued by any man than the one who lay sleeping here. Resolutely turning her back on him, she set out to explore his room. She would better understand why she felt at home in this man's arms, of all the arms she might have chosen to fall into.

Lord Dade favored the same colors in his bed hangings and draperies as he did on his person: deep, rich colors, wine red, midnight blue, forest green and burnished gold. There was nothing pale or muted here, nothing soft. There was a crisp regimental order beneath the room's sickbed clutter. Books were neatly shelved against the wall: military tomes and treatises on the history of England and France and the Americas. There were rolls of maps sticking higgledy-piggledy out of a boxy umbrella stand in the corner and a chessboard of carved ivory and ebony wood stopped in mid-game beside the bed. She paused to study the board. The white knight was broken. Poor man was missing his head. She wondered why.

Other than the chessboard, there was little life in the

room, no plants or miniatures of loved ones, no ancestral painting staring at one from the wall, no poetry or prints of animals, plants or birds. Even the furniture, heavy and dark, had twisted arms and legs.

It was in one of the wardrobes that Margaret began to find answers to the question of why Lord Dade shoved his heroism against the wall. It was the same wardrobe into which the hapless physician had crashed. The door hung open, knocked askew in the collision with his balding head. Margaret could not resist a peek within for evidence of the hero she believed she witnessed in Lord Dade.

Here were kept all of the former Captain Dade's uniforms. There were two gleaming crested helmets, a rack of carefully pressed, scarlet-cuffed and -collared blue coats, scarlet-ribbed gray trousers, a row of carefully polished boots and spurs. There were cloaks, leather gauntlets, sword belt and gloves. All was neat and pressed and tidy and gleaming, except for the first thing that met one's eye, a sadly abused coat. Once scarlet-trimmed blue like the rest, it was now so caked with mud and dried blood that it was difficult to decide if its fabric was more blue or brown. At the shoulder seams, where epaulets normally gleamed, ragged holes gaped. Holes too where shining gold buttons should have marched along the front with a froth of gilt trimmings. All that glittered was gone. Pearl found the sad coat a puzzle, and she stood holding the door to the wardrobe staring, trying to imagine one good reason why this tattered specimen had not been given over to a rag collector.

"Dreadful thing, isn't it, miss?" Gimble came in reeking of turpentine, a basin of milky fluid in his hands.

She dropped her hold on the bloodstained garment.

"I have begged his lordship to allow me to throw it out, but he will have none of it," he said, with no hint of reproach for her delving into his master's wardrobe.

She shut the door on the tattered uniform and joined him at the bedside. "Why should he wish to keep such a thing?" she asked in a low voice, unwilling to disturb the sleeping patient no matter how intense her curiosity.

Gimble was equally circumspect. "That was the uniform my lord wore at Waterloo. The corpse harvesters found him in what was left of it, after scavengers had picked him clean of buttons and rank. He was beneath his horse, all covered in mud and blood. They thought he was dead, along with all the rest of his lads, and meant to relieve him of his teeth."

She grimaced. "But why keep such a sad reminder?"

Gimble shrugged. Dipping a clean square of cloth in the basin, he handed it to her so that she might saturate the wound. The patient stirred, but did not cry out or rouse completely from his sleeping state.

"He tells me he would not forget such a day. He says it does all seem a dream sometimes, a very nasty nightmare that never really came to pass, much like any of the other nightmares that trouble his sleep. The coat makes it real."

She nodded and daubed the turpentine concoction on the wound. "Is that the day he shouts about in his delirium?"

"Aye, that day and any of a dozen others. Lord Dade was involved in the fiercest of the fighting. Nightmares trouble him, miss. Almost every night he cries out with them. There is one in particular in which he shouts to me about curb chains for his horses." He shook his head. "I suppose his mind does not let go of such days any more than he will let go of that uniform."

Margaret, who understood nightmares far better than most, looked about the room—at the stack of prints turned face to the wall, at the wardrobe she had just closed, at the man in the bed whose every night was troubled by violent dreams. Was this the life all heroes suffered? It had never before occurred to her that there was a dark side to heroism. And yet with this man as model, she could no longer ignore such a possibility.

Chapter 8

THE darkness weighed heavily on Dade, pressing down on him. The weight of it threatened to crush him flat, to squeeze the life and breath out of him. Images came to him in dark, disjointed flashes, an unending wave of them. These glimpses into his past were painfully vivid, destructively so. They pierced his soul like grapeshot, leaving him full of holes—bleeding, wounded perhaps beyond mending. He was in Belgium, on the battlefield, reliving the bloody charge in which his comrades had fallen on all sides. Ahead of him, a horse was hit by mortar and went down, missing a leg. Beside him, a young man he had known for more than ten years was jerked from the saddle by a barrage of bullets, half of his face missing. A rocket tore through the ranks, hissing and spurting, maddening the animals. His own mount, eyes bulging, took the bit and would not be turned, could not be slowed as it plowed a path between animals that fell and thrashed and reared on all sides.

No curb chains! He could not stop the horse, short of shooting him, without a curb. Up an incline they plunged, into the midst of the Greys, all the while Dade yanking the reins with every ounce of his strength, trying to slow the horse, trying to stop this disastrous race toward death. The Blues were supposed to be guarding the rear, not plunging headlong to the front of the ranks. But the noise, the panic all around him, made it impossible for him to sway his terrified mount. Behind him, following his lead, plunged his entire regiment, brave lads.

Spartan, his horse, did not stop until with a shudder it was mortally hit. Squealing, the gelding went down, taking him along, just as his regiment charged into the heart of the fiercest gunfire. Darkness engulfed him then, an uncertain twilight where gaunt and bloody fingers pulled at his rings, his armaments, his clothes, his hair. The great weight of pain in his soul sat upon his chest, pinning him motionless. Frantically he struggled to be free.

Suddenly, a woman lay her head down beside his and whispered in his ear, "The white knight has lost his head."

So startled was he by this bizarre turn of events that he stopped struggling against the darkness, against the crushing weight, and turned to look at her. It was Pearl whose fair head was sunk upon his pillow. Her wise, knowing eyes looked directly into the heart of him, stilling his panic. Her voice was like a light. He moved toward it. He was in bed. She was telling him he must calm himself. The sheets were being changed. The doctor had gone away. Courage, she said. It would soon be over.

He was soothed by her voice even though he knew the darkness still pinned his legs in place so that he could not move, could not fight, could not run. Pearl wanted to play chess. She seemed not to notice that his pinned legs had begun to burn. He could see the flames, smell the fuel. She seemed unperturbed that part of him should be burning. Her whispers tickled his ear. The nearness of her made the flames in his nether parts rise. He pulled her down beside him in the grass, away from the darkness, away from the fire that would take her too if he let it.

Her voice, her lips, her hands, quenched the heat in him. She smelled of jasmine. The light of her pushed away the darkness. The coolness of her hands, stroking gently across his flaming thigh, put out the fire, only to raise another in his loins. The caress of her softness, the warmth of her body as she came willingly into his arms, filled him with peace and contentment. Was there time to save the lads? Was there a chance he might yet turn back the frightened horses? Curb chains. All would be right again if only he had curb chains! He had to tell her.

He woke, alone in his bed, nothing more clutched to his chest than a pillow. No Pearl. No curb chains. Only dreams and regrets. And yet so real was his imagining that he could have sworn the bedclothes still held a hint of Pearl's perfume. There was a parrot squawking. A woman hummed. He wondered if this too was a dream.

"Pearl?" he called, a seed of hope alive within him like a tiny flame that held off the darkness.

The face of the woman who bent over him was not at all the sweet, youthful Pearl of his imaginings. This matronly, pudding-faced female was an utter stranger.

"I was beginning to wonder when you would wake up," she said cheerfully, as if she knew him.

Dade squeezed his eyes shut, shook his head, and looked at her again. He was not dreaming. This was his room. The chessboard he and Gavin had spent many an evening bent over loomed large beside the bed. The white knight has lost his head. Had Pearl said that? He could neither remember nor reconcile dreams with reality. The space around him was too changed. Clad in wrinkled nightshirt, he was lying in a place transformed. A great many unfamiliar things met his roving gaze, chief among them the woman who adjusted his pillow. There were a number of potted palms and, on the wall beside the bed, a print he had had no hand in choosing. It depicted a knight in full armor rescuing a willowy white-gowned maiden from a fire-breathing dragon.

"Gimble?" The name came out with no strength to it.

The humming stopped. The woman he did not recognize leaned in so close to his face he could smell tea on her breath. "You're hungry, I'll be bound."

"Who are you?" he croaked.

The woman briskly poured him a glass of water from the carafe at his bedside. He swallowed the liquid gratefully.

"That's better," she said. "I am Agnes Boothe. I have been brought here to look after you, my lord. You are looking much better today. How is your poor leg feeling? You will be happy to hear you have received two callers this morning, both of them anxious to hear how you progress."

"Who?" Dade sat up, scowling at the dragon print, flung back the covers, swung the aforementioned leg over the side of the bed with a wince and tried to stand.

"Mr. Eckhart and Mr. Soames, sir. They have been in and out of the house any number of times these past few days."

She did not seem at all surprised when he fell back onto the mattress, legs buckling. He was pleased that this strange woman did not fuss over him. She allowed him to struggle back into an upright position without a word or any sign that she realized how fatigued the effort left him.

"Ah, yes, the leg." It all came back to him now. He had been pinked in his wounded leg by that upstart Allan Dornton, who had dared to fight him with sword unbuttoned. Was it yesterday he had last seen Pearl, done up in men's clothing and trying to save his life?

"Days, Mrs. Boothe? You mentioned days. How long have you been here?" he asked, with an idea that more than one fevered night had passed. Otherwise his room could not have been so thoroughly changed. "And is it Wallis or Creighton who has been messing about in my rooms? Do you know?"

"Well, dearie, it has been four days you have been flat on your back. As to who has brought you all the lovely—"

She was interrupted by a knock upon the door.

"I shall just go and see who that may be." She went briskly from the room, even as Dade called after her.

"Where is Gimble gone? Why does he not get the door?" And then, rather forcefully, "I am not at home to visitors."

He managed to stand tolerably well in her absence, and even made a turn about the room, in which he relied greatly upon the walls for support, dodging the newly placed palms in the corners with an oath or two of impatience. In this manner he was able to examine more closely the new prints that made his room strange to him. There were four of them in all. Other than the dragon, there was a tranquil watercolor landscape with a church spire and a reflecting pool that shimmered in the foreground, with a bridge passing over it on which a pair of lovers walked.

"Hmph!" was his response to it.

Another landscape, in oils, was of a mill, set in the curve of a river. For a moment, in his mind's eye, a mill in France creaked into view. He shut his eyes on the painting, shutting out the memory. He had had enough of memories.

The fourth picture roused no such feelings. It was an understated architectural print of a Roman frieze. In it four draped young women bearing water jars upon their heads were accompanied by a male figure whose legs appeared to be those of a goat. He gazed at it for several moments, chewing all the while upon his lower lip, forbidding himself to look at the painting of the mill. He concentrated on goat legs and the question of who had brought him such a varied collection of artistry.

Allan Dornton, feeling guilty perhaps?

He passed with great care, and the sturdy assistance of the door frame, into his drawing room, where the source of the bird calls he had heard was explained. There were two brilliantly plumaged parrots in a wire cage that hung from a stand at the far end of the room. In front of that cage stood none other than Allan Dornton, whistling and chirping to the exotic creatures within while he passed seeds into their feeding dish from a paper packet.

"Come to finish me, have you?" Dade wheezed, peeved to find his quarters summarily invaded.

"You are up, sir! How splendid." The young man's face lit up. For a brief moment Dade was reminded of his cousin.

"Indeed, I am. Did you think perhaps you had crippled me for life?"

Allan Dornton blushed and clumsily put down the seed, spilling some on the floor in the process. "That was never my intention, sir," he said with a soulfully earnest expression. "I cannot blame you for assuming as much, based on my foolishness in fencing with sword unbuttoned."

Dade was not ready to be mollified. His leg pained him awfully because of this young man. "I ought to run you through for barging in unannounced. How did you manage to get past Gimble and that gorgon, Mrs.—what is her name? I have only just met her."

"Mrs. Boothe," Allan said with an unusual gleam in his eye. "And I will not have you insulting her. She is my old

Nan, you know, and only came because I implored her to. She knows I come every day to feed the birds and clean out their cage. She will have nothing to do with them, and they have pecked at Gimble because he *will* make sudden, uneasy movements. I have brought you a newspaper which you may peruse intact until it comes time to line the bottom, and then I shall require at least half of it. It occurred to me you would be quite out of touch with the world when at last you woke up again."

Out of touch with the world indeed.

"You employed the woman to look after me?"

"Mrs. Boothe? Yes, the doctor your valet had called in was making a dreadful hash of the affair. We dismissed him."

"We?" Dade's casualness belied the interest with which he listened for an answer. It crossed his mind that perhaps Pearl was not just a dream, that she had been here after all. It occurred to him that the prints that graced his walls might be her doing.

Allan bit down on his lip. "Yes, well, I hope you will not judge me too overbearing, but the man would keep trying to leech you when it was clear that you were having none of it. We—I figured you had bled enough already from the awful hole in your leg." He lowered his head, blushing, took a deep breath, scratched his collar, and said, jaw set, "I should not be at all surprised if you did not forgive me for that supremely idiotic lapse in judgment. I do beg your pardon, though, and have done what little I might to see that you remain among the living."

"Meaning Nurse Boothe's able care?"

Allan nodded and dared to look up at him.

"And the pictures in my room, perhaps, and the plants? Perhaps even the birds you are feeding? Whatever possessed you of the notion that these things would please me?"

Allan's neck stiffened. "They were not entirely my idea, sir. If they do not please, you have but to toss them out. But I must warn you that my cousin will be gravely disappointed. She and Wallis spent most of an afternoon selecting the prints and half of another picking out the birds."

"She did, did she?" Dade leaned against the wall in the sitting room, where yet another new vista met his eyes, this one a sunlit park in which couples strolled. "Well, you may tell her . . . and Wallis, I appreciate their kindness."

Allan sighed with relief.

"And"—Dade swung around to face him—"I am touched by your concern for my well-being, after such a callous lack of regard for it when you dared to cross naked blade with me."

"Thank you, my lord."

"Do not waste your breath on thanks when I would have you use it in helping me to the sofa. I shall sink to the rug in a heap if I attempt the course without assistance."

Allan leapt to his side.

"How is your cousin? She looked quite fetching in breeches. Were they yours?" Dade observed the telling rigidness in the arm on which he leaned. "That bad, eh?"

Allan cleared his throat. "She has a way of steeping herself in hot water, Maggs does! But, happily, she was not recognized at the fencing match. You and I are reputed to have been fighting over a mistress as a result of that little escapade, I'll have you know. I beg you will not deny the possibility if you are asked. No, the Magpie is in trouble for defending your honor in public to a number of my mother's friends who dared slander your reputation in her presence. Gave them all a famous set down. Said you should not be referred to as Captain Dead at all, because you had survived against great odds, not once but twice. Claimed you had nothing at all to do with causing anyone else to keel over, that it was all just unhappy coincidence that people who came into contact with you dropped like flies."

What a naive fool the girl was, Dade thought. How wrong in her assumptions as to his character. He was responsible for the deaths of many. He and missing curb chains.

"Like flies?" he muttered as the darkness of memories teetered on the edge of his awareness.

"Well, those were not exactly the words she used . . ."

"I see."

"Anyway, the upshot was that the ladies are more firmly set against her than ever, though they have softened toward Celia and Celeste. The two of them may be given vouchers to Almack's after all. As for poor Magpie, they say she is too opinionated by far. Her name has not been included in any of the invitations we have received the past two weeks, and while she is not officially out, she was always invited to the less formal events in the past. Mother is livid. She wants to send her back home straight away. Father won't hear of it. Says we seal her fate if we send her home so abruptly. Says she will never be able to show her face again in London if we bundle her off into the country."

"Wise man, your father."

"Thank you. I'm inclined to think so. But as it stands, the Magpie has little to do in London. It has been up to Wallis and Soames and me to keep her amused."

Dade took a moment to digest this. "And do you?"

"Do we what?"

"Keep her amused?"

"Tolerably so, I think. She does not complain. We walk every other morning in the park with her, as she so likes to do. Creighton is always lavishing flowers and sweets on her and has even condescended to take the girls shopping on occasion. He was with us the day Maggs picked out your prints. Wallis too. He is a great gun, by the way. Brought the girls the latest musical scores so that they might practice their dancing. He and the Magpie have a bit of a spillikin competition going on. Wallis swears he has never met a female with a steadier hand."

"I am not surprised Wallis takes to your cousin. They are much the same sort of personality," Evelyn said softly. He refrained from telling Allen that he was quite convinced Wallis was well on his way to falling in love with Margaret.

Allan shrugged. "He is a great favorite amongst all the girls. Shouldn't be surprised if he were to end up marrying one of them. They do fall into a bout of giggles and whispering whenever his name is raised."

Dade nodded. It crossed his mind that Wallis and Pearl made the perfect couple, and yet he found no happiness in the promise of such perfection.

"Creighton Soames charms the girls too," Allan went on, "though I should not be quite so happy to call him cousin as Wallis. I know he is a friend of yours, my lord, but the fellow can be a trifle crass at times."

Dade frowned, but not out of any feeling of insult toward his friend. He was imagining, without pleasure, Creighton's vow to wrap Pearl around his little finger.

"Creighton bears watching," he warned. "He is not always the gentleman he pretends to be. You do not allow your cousin to be alone with him, do you?"

Allan reddened. "You must take me for a cheesehead, indeed, if you think I am foolish enough to trust the girls alone with any man—even Wallis, and he is as harmless as they come."

Dade said nothing, only looked at him and thought dour thoughts about Wallis and Creighton engaging Margaret Dornton's affections while he lay trapped by misfortune and delirium in bed.

Allan cleared his throat uneasily, his face now scarlet. "I do keep my cousins out of reach of any man with the strength to bring harm to them, at any rate."

Dade's eyes narrowed as he pondered this remark a moment. The image of Pearl's fair head upon his pillow swam into his consciousness again. "Tell me, Dornton . . ." He paused. He could not come right out and ask Allan if his sister had been left alone with him. He sighed, and because Dornton stood waiting for him to finish his sentence, he said, "Why do you call the poor girl Magpie?"

Allan blinked at him, his face blank. "Why?" he echoed. Unexpectedly, his features seemed suddenly childlike and sad. "I suppose it was the mourning blacks. The first time I saw her, cousin Margaret looked just like a magpie. It was at the funeral for her little brother, Todd. Died before he was more than a few months old, poor little mite. Something about a fire and the nanny being careless." He stopped a moment, remembering, his expression bleak. "Tiniest little coffin. It was my first funeral. I remember how very solemn Margaret looked, all in black, with her pale baby hair fuzzed up all around her face like down on a little bird. She refused to play with her sisters and me when the service was over, refused to so much as say a word. I expect she was dreadfully upset. I heard whispers she had witnessed the fire in which her brother was burned. Anyway, the rest of us tried to get her to smile, or say something. When she wouldn't, we began to tease her, as children will, calling her Maggie Magpie, sure we could provoke some sort of response."

"And did you?" Dade's memories were completely forgotten in this exploration of Allan's.

Allan frowned. "I was six at the time. Even at that age I remember being quite struck by how large and melancholy her eyes looked as the Magpie stared at us, all jeering at her. I remember thinking as great tears welled up, making her eyes seem even larger, that it was mean of me to goad her. She never did talk to me that time."

"And yet you still call her Magpie?"

"Yes." He seemed surprised it was so. "Rather unfeeling of me, come to think of it, but the name stuck. I always thought of it as a sort of endearment." He shook his head. "You said she told you she preferred to be called Pearl?"

"Yes." He wondered if Pearl was plagued by dreams.

"I shall have to try to remember that."

Dade, who had suffered with his own name in more ways than one, hoped he would. "Do you think your father might be convinced to come and see me?" he said, changing the subject.

"My father? Call on you? Whatever for?"

"I think, between us, we might do something to salvage the situation of your cousin's reputation."

Allan grasped at the remark. "Do you? Well, I am all for that. Poor Mag—Pearl. I shall do my best to induce him to call on you if that is your game." He took his leave soon after that, but before he closed the door behind himself he turned to Dade with a puzzled look and said, "Oh! Almost forgot. Magpie asked me to relay a message to you next time we met."

Dade was keenly interested. "Oh?"

"Yes, she said . . . let me get it right now—pawn to queen three. Said you would understand. Do you?"

Dade dropped his gaze to the floor, afraid he would give too much away if he looked at Allan. Pearl had been real in the midst of his dark imaginings. "I do," he said softly. "You may tell her I got the message, and thanks to you both for taking care of me."

* * *

When Gimble returned from walking Hero, who fell upon his master with delight in seeing him risen, Dade directed his valet to help him back to bed. Leaning on his shoulder, he said, "Allan Dornton has been here while you were out. Will you bring the portable secretary to my bedchamber? I must dash off thanks to him and his cousin for their kindnesses while I have been ill."

"As you say, my lord. I shall bring it directly, sir."

"Tell me, Gimble, what has Miss Dornton thought to do with the prints that once hung on these walls?"

His valet never flickered an eyelid. "The young lady thought it would be best if they were locked away in the wardrobe with the rest of your military kit, rather than leaning against the wall where someone might trip over them. I hope you do not mind my taking the liberty, my lord."

All of his memories locked in one closet. "I do not mind," Dade said, his eyes closing as he fell back against freshly plumped pillows. "I do not mind at all." He did not mind anything but that she had been here, alone in this room with him. His light in the middle of darkness. How could her cousin Allan have been so careless as to allow such a thing? It smacked of mischief, the kind at which Creighton excelled. Allan had mentioned Creighton in connection with the physician having been turned out of the house.

"Gimble!" His valet had disappeared into the hallway.

"Yes, my lord?" His head popped around the doorway.

"It was Creighton who brought the Dorntons here the day the doctor attempted to leech me, was it not?"

"Yes, sir. Mrs. Boothe came to us that same day."

"Thank you, Gimble." Dade dismissed him, his thoughts centered quite seriously on how Creighton might intend to use this unfortunate incident to his advantage. He leaned out of the bed to study the untouched chessboard, frozen in the middle of the game he and his brother, Gavin, had begun on the evening before he had left for France. It was a game they would never finish.

He closed his eyes a moment. The pain of losing Gavin was still fresh. Why had God taken his brother on the very day of his return? Was it in retribution for his part in the deaths of all of the men in his regiment? What purpose did one more death serve? The pattern of life was far more confusing than the pattern of a chess game.

"Pawn to queen three," he repeated under his breath, reaching out to shift the position of Gavin's pawn. But when his fingers closed around the piece, he found himself unable to lift it. Moving this insignificant piece of carved ivory was an admission that he and Gavin would never again set up the chessboard in order to test each other's wits, never finish what had been so lightly started. The concept of this friendly, if trivial, exchange between brothers, permanently halted, filled him with anguished rage.

Was there any truth to the suggestion that he had brought an early death to those around him—especially those he cared for? Had he been in any way responsible for Gavin's unexpected demise? Had he in some unknowing way set into motion the course of events that might bring sweet, innocent Miss Margaret Dornton to harm? He prayed it was not so, and his better sense shouted an emphatic *No!* But there was the darker, more primal part of him, the small, weighed down, frightened part of his soul, that held onto doubt.

"No!" he cried out, pushing aside such a thought as vehemently as he dashed the chess piece against the door to his wardrobe. "No!" He swept the back of his hand across the chessboard, flinging ebony and ivory pieces to all corners of the room. Too many memories, too much to regret.

And yet this outburst of destructive anger gave him no real release from the dark seeds of doubt and anger. What if he was, in truth, some evil harbinger of death? Did he endanger the lives of all for whom he cared? Wallis's life perhaps? Gimble's? God help him, not the Pearl?

He slipped his legs out of the bed and knelt with a groan to search for the far-flung chess pieces. So many promising lives wasted, and yet he had survived. He had been flung upon his head like one of these hapless chess pieces, pinned beneath his horse and kept alive by nothing more heroic than his own unconsciousness. And while he slept, the game of war had played on.

Gimble came into the room carrying his portable secretary and accidentally trod on one of the fallen chess men.

"Oh, dear," he said as he bent to pick it up. "What has happened here, milord?"

"Some difficulty in deciding my next move." Dade tried to laugh, though he felt more like weeping as he gathered up all the pieces within reach and carefully set two opposing forces upon the board exactly as they had been before his burst of temper. The forces of good and evil did at times appear to struggle for his soul, as if in a game of chess.

"I see," Gimble said carefully. He placed the secretary on the bed and bent to pick up more of the stray chessmen. "I am afraid this poor white knight is missing a bit off the top, sir." He held up the broken piece.

Dade lifted his chin, thrusting the darkness from him. "Never mind, Gimble. The white knight gave up his head for a very good cause."

The chessboard was reassembled, each piece carefully returned to the spot he had swept it from. Pawn to queen three. Dade deliberately moved the black pawn as Pearl had indicated and fell to studying the board. What must his next move be?

Chapter 9

MARGARET was an outcast. She was stared at and whispered over. Heads shook in judgment wherever she showed her face. Her aunt wished her gone from town. Her sisters were personally affronted that she had threatened their prospects by openly expressing her viewpoint to her elders. She had offended their aunt's most intimate friends, all of whom had a very high opinion of their own conclusions and none at all of hers. Her cousin Allan was too busy keeping secret her appearance at a fencing match, clad in his clothes, to defend her. Ever the optimist, he was of the opinion that the crooked path she walked might yet be straightened out.

She cared for none of it. At least that was what she said to herself, and anyone else who cared to listen. Her happiness in being allowed the opportunity to explore the wonders of London could not be clouded by groundless gossip and mean-spirited strangers. She meant to see the world someday, and London was but one city among many! So she went to the lending library with her sisters for books about faraway places. She accompanied her aunt and uncle to the theater and the opera. She enjoyed the card games Wallis used to divert her, played at the harpsichord with Creighton Soames to turn the music, and took long walks with all three of the gentlemen and both of her sisters, who no longer had a plethora of balls to keep them up all night. Yet with all this to see and do, often were the moments when Margaret fell into reverie, imagining another encounter with the viscount who had become her hero.

There was a part of her, which she would not allow to surface, that was as disturbed by her recent activities as were those around her. She was afraid to face her feelings with regard to Lord Dade. He roused something in her that might best have been left to slumber.

Was he no more than wish fulfillment, she wondered, the unwilling embodiment of her long-awaited hero? He was in some ways not at all what she had expected. There was a grimness to this hero business that she could not ignore.

Was his fascination that of the forbidden? Her only interest could not be love. She had encountered the viscount on only three occasions, and surely one did not fall in love so swiftly. No, she had been lured in by possibilities, and now yearned to know more of this man and his hidden feelings. There was nothing more to it than that, and that was far more confusing than she had ever anticipated.

She went to her cousin, whom she knew meant to continue calling on the intriguing Lord Dade. She tested Providence in asking him to relay a message to her hero in the form of a chess move. It was forward in her to communicate thus, a risk she thought twice about taking, but surely it was a small thing, her reaching out to the man in this manner?

The viscount was on the mend. Wallis, Creighton and Allan brought copious reports. Margaret received no immediate answer to the chess move other than Allan's assurance that the message had been conveyed and apparently understood. On the following evening, her uncle called her to his library.

The summons was a surprise. Uncle Harold was not wont to concentrate his energies on his nieces' affairs. He focused almost exclusively on his responsibilities as a member of the House of Lords at this time of year. Margaret entered the library with a mixture of trepidation and curiosity.

"Sit down, my dear." Her uncle seemed to sense her fears and tried to put her at ease. "Perhaps you would care for a drop of Madeira?"

She nodded, hands knitted together, and hesitantly settled

on the edge of a chair. He pressed a half-filled glass into her nervous fingers.

"I have spent the afternoon closeted with someone who would appear to be as concerned about your future as I am."

"And who would that be?" She took a sip of the wine.

"Lord Dade."

She almost spat her mouthful of spirits on him in her surprise. What could Evelyn Dade have to say to her uncle with regard to her future? Her heart leapt. Did he see himself in some way part of it? Did he not remember that she had been left completely alone with him, and that he had, in his delirium, dragged her onto the bed with him! God help her: it was better he did not remember that.

"I am hoping you will agree to what we have decided."

"Decided?"

"We have decided that it makes a great deal of sense that Lord Dade and his young friend Wallis be seen in our family's company on a regular basis. Both Allan's foolishness in challenging Dade to a mock duel and your own misguided walk with Dade along the Mall, coupled with a rash desire to champion his cause to Charlotte's circle, might eventually be deemed as no more than excessive high spirits should it be thought that all of the parties involved are friends of long standing." He rubbed his forehead in exactly the same way she was accustomed to seeing Allan rub his. "I do not know if we can pull this thing off, but it is the most sensible course as far as I can see. I was never more mortified than to hear Allan had dared challenge a gentleman of Lord Dade's caliber with a sword he knew to be bared."

Margaret squirmed uncomfortably in her chair. How much more shocked would he be if he knew that it was she who had leapt between the fencers, dressed in men's clothing!

He sighed. "As for what you said to your aunt's acquaintances, experience will teach you, my dear, that rare are your elders who care to have their heartfelt beliefs contradicted. These women may be thoroughly foolish in their notions, but you gain nothing in rubbing their noses in it. To the contrary, you make unnecessary enemies of the very women it would be wise to befriend. Diplomacy, my dear, is a concept worthy of close study."

Margaret hung her head. It was all true what he said, and yet this was the last thing she wished to hear him discuss in this moment. Would he not tell her more of his conversation with Lord Dade?

Her uncle sighed. "What is done is done. I am not one to waste tears on spilled milk. We must simply see what can be done to mop it up, child, and take care nothing possesses you to tip the bucket over again."

She nodded.

"So, Margaret, you will spend time happily, even diplomatically, with Dade and Eckhart?"

"Of course, Uncle."

"Good! You relieve my mind. And how do you find him?"

"Sir?"

"I am curious as to what you think of the viscount, niece. I was dubious as to his intentions when he asked me to call on him, but pleasantly surprised by his demeanor when we spoke. I have heard disturbing gossip in connection with his name since his return from the war. Yet now that I am expected to introduce him to my circle as a friend of the family, I do not find the task an arduous one. He was surprisingly affable. Do you know he told me he is quite fed up with the business of making war and would like to go about learning how to unmake it?

"Does he mean to follow a career as a diplomat?" she asked.

"I suppose he might. In any event, I mean to put him in the way of some fellows who follow such a path. I hope they will not embarrass me by snubbing the man. Lord Dade's reputation . . ." He trailed off.

Margaret dared speak. "I think, sir, that it takes very little, sometimes, to ruin a reputation."

Her uncle managed a smile. "I tend to agree. We shall see what we can do to restore yours."

She nodded.

"Now, what of this other chap? Wallis Eckhart?" He watched her carefully from beneath lowered brows.

Without reservation Margaret assured him, "You could

not meet a gentler soul, Uncle, or a more polite young man. He is, as Allan would say, a splendid fellow."

"Excellent! I am pleased to hear as much. Lord Dade spoke very highly of him, but I hoped you would second the opinion before I unleashed him on you."

She stood, and would have left him, feeling much relieved, had he not stopped her in the doorway, saying, "By the by, Dade asked me to tell you his next move was bishop to bishop four. Has this something to do with chess, perchance?"

"Yes, Uncle," she said, breathless both with delight that Dade meant to carry on with the chess, and with fear that her uncle would question her in more detail with regard to this game she played. But her uncle's thoughts had already returned to the papers on his desk.

"A challenging game," he mused, his lack of attention a dismissal of sorts.

Relieved, Margaret escaped her uncle's study and ran to the chessboard she had set up in her room, in a pattern to match the configuration of the board in Lord Dade's own bedroom. She remembered it exactly. She remembered every moment, every minute detail of that afternoon, with crystal clarity. Bishop to bishop four. She moved the piece as she readied herself for bed, then stood studying the board until her toes were chilled. Satisfied with what her next move should be, she tucked herself in and blew out the candle.

Under cover of darkness, she clutched her pillow against her breast and imagined it a man—a half-naked man, delirious with fever, who clasped her in his arms and tried to kiss her. She even went so far as to imagine her hand was his, and ran it slowly up the ridges of her rib cage to cup the familiar softness of her breast. Her nipples stood up hard and sensitive against the crisp linen of her nightshift as she remembered another hand, hard and hot against her yielding flesh.

And yet Margaret was disappointed. The pillow she clutched was not a man after all. It had not the solidly warm and comforting mass of a man. The pillow had no arms with which to reach for her, no lips to press against hers. Margaret sighed, wistful. For the first time since childhood, her imagination failed her. It was not enough, not nearly enough.

* * *

It was Easter Sunday, in St. James's Church of all places, that Margaret next had contact with Lord Dade. He arrived, sans Hero, exactly on time for the beginning of the services, accompanied by the ever faithful Wallis Eckhart. Row upon row of lorgnettes were lifted to take note of this singular event, for Creighton Soames had only the Sunday before intruded himself upon the Dornton pew. Neither gentleman was considered particularly devout. That Captain Dead this Sunday came, of all Sundays, head bowed before the risen Lord, and was as easily welcomed into the pew, proved something of a miracle!

"Perhaps the Dornton sisters have it in mind to convert all the rakes and scoundrels in London with their charming ways," Lady Jersey was heard to quip.

She was not the only one among those gathered to find opportunity for remark. Whispered speculation rose between the Corinthian pillars and bounced off the beautiful, barrel-vaulted ceiling more fervently than prayer, a hissing, snake-like sound silenced only by the overriding noise of the organ as the service began.

Margaret took no notice of the gossips. She was too enthralled by the notion that she was to be granted opportunity to speak to her tragic hero once again, too pleased by the notion that he shared the same bench as she. She was as guilty of sidelong looks during the service as the parishioners were guilty of craning their necks to watch at the conclusion of the service as the Torntons and their entourage passed into the sunshine of the street.

St. James's was within walking distance of her uncle's house. They did not have to wait for a carriage to be brought up to them.

Margaret knew her aunt Charlotte was not yet reconciled to the idea that it was to her brood's benefit that they be seen in public with Captain Dead, but she did her best to appear civil in front of so many curious onlookers.

"Did you care for the service today, my lord?" she asked stiffly.

Lord Dade paused in the walkway. "I was quite moved by the reading of the Psalms," he admitted, his voice heavy. His dark eyes closed, as if to help the concentration of his memory. "'He satisfies the longing soul, and fills the hungry soul with goodness. Such as sit in darkness and in the shadow of death . . .' "

Aunt Charlotte's handkerchief fluttered as much as her voice. "Oh, to be sure, my lord. 'He sent his word, and healed them . . . brought them out of darkness and the shadow of death,' I am sure you may depend upon the Scriptures."

"On that, and the understanding of the kindhearted," Dade agreed, his expression suitably grave.

As Aunt Charlotte made a kind point of introducing the viscount to Margaret's sisters, Margaret was quite certain her aunt might be depended upon to be numbered among the kindhearted where Lord Dade was concerned from that day forth.

"Do you have a longing soul, my lord, a hungry soul?" Margaret asked when Dade at last turned his attention to her, having spoken first to her sisters, her uncle and Allan.

She did not expect much of an answer from him, only meant to provoke further conversation, but he turned to her with an earnest expression and gauged her response when he said softly, "I am well enough but for these, Pearl, well enough but for a strange craving from deep within." He pressed a palm to the spot where his breastbone ended. "This emptiness I would fill," he said, and though she heard and understood each word, it was the look in his eyes that spoke loudest. The walls that ordinarily shut her out were down. The longing he spoke of reached out to her from the darkness of his eyes as if it were a measurable thing.

She was amazed he allowed her to see so much of what went on in his heart and mind.

He blinked. The look was gone. She wondered if she had imagined it as he fell into an uneven sort of step beside her. Margaret could see that the viscount depended on his cane for support, as might be expected of a man with a wounded thigh. She got the feeling he resented his weakness and would have liked the cane to have been no more than fashionable.

"And your injury?" she ventured.

"The wound heals nicely, due in great part"—his lip quirked upward, and his gold-flecked eyes searched hers—"to an excellent milk and turpentine poultice that has proved most efficacious."

Her eyelashes fluttered, her cheeks burned. How much did he remember? She hid her reaction beneath the brim of her pretty Sunday bonnet. She could not meet Lord Dade's regard when his eyes accosted hers with such a penetrating look. Did he know it was she who had recommended the poultice? Did he know she had, with her own hand, applied it the first time it was used? Could it be he meant to thank her personally with his words, without exciting the attention of anyone else in their party who might be listening? His eyes fairly glowed as he observed her reaction. Heat rushed into Margaret's cheeks. Did this gentleman make a point of alluding to his awareness that she had had personal dealings with intimate areas of his thigh on the Sabbath? The mischievous sparkle in his eyes deepened her blush.

"I owe my speedy recovery too," he went on, "to the restorative effect of Mrs. Boothe's care."

"Oh, I say, I am glad to hear you approved of her," Allan leaned back to interrupt. He promenaded just ahead of them, with Celia on his arm. His parents led the gaggle of them, like geese to water, pausing now and again to see that they were followed in good order.

"A capital woman," Dade remarked, but as he said it, his eyes were fastened on Margaret. She could see it was so in the outermost periphery of her vision. Did he find her to be a capital woman? She tipped her head to look past the brim of her hat at him.

He looked away. "Her care, and the positive influence of a number of changes that were wrought in my surroundings by those who were touchingly concerned about my well-being, have served to hasten my recovery substantially."

Celia entered into the discussion. "Changes in your surroundings, sir? You must elaborate. Anything that might assist in the health of an ailing loved one should be made common knowledge."

"Oh yes." Celeste appeared to be listening as well. "Do you know that when we were all quite small, and Celia and I were confined to our beds by the most dreadful colds, that Margaret, then but six or seven, dragged into our room and placed about the bed all of our favorite toys and books and pictures? It was ever so comical, for it took every ounce of her strength to do as much."

Celia was nodding. "I remember. She announced rather stoutly that she did not care to wear black, and so we must, the both of us, get better immediately. She was so very earnest in her entreaty that I was quite consumed with guilt that I did not immediately recover."

Celeste picked up where her twin left off, as was so often the case. "She also brought a great pitcher full of fresh blooms from the garden every day, that we might look at something pretty."

"She made a great fuss over the fire screen—"

Celeste hastily interrupted. "And induced Mama's pug to curl up on the coverlet beside me, by scolding him profoundly in fluent French. It was vastly entertaining."

Margaret was rather distressed by this strange dual recital of her behavior, as if she were not even present. She tilted her head uncertainly to look up at Lord Dade. Was her habit of nursemaiding the ill so very odd?

The warmth of his expression relieved her. The golden glints in his eyes seemed momentarily to blaze.

"If all you say is true"—he did not so much as glance at Celeste and Celia—"I can think of no one I would rather have care for me, were I still bedridden, than your sister." Margaret searched his expression for any traces of amusement or sarcasm. She could not identify the gleam in his eyes.

"As it is," he went on, "I cannot complain. I too have been surrounded by things that lift my spirits and speed the hours away: potted palms, colorful birds, books and papers, games of chess and prints to decorate my walls."

"Much like when we were children," Celeste chortled.

"Very much like," Lord Dade agreed, his eyes still fixed on Margaret as if she were something precious and beautiful to behold. A young lady's heart could not but race, having met with such regard, but even in her happiness Margaret was uneasy. She was sure Lord Dade was completely aware of every single instance in which her behavior had influenced his recovery, though he mentioned not a single, openly damning word to that effect.

"You are fortunate in your friends," Celia said.

"Old and new," the viscount agreed graciously.

As he and Wallis prepared to take their leave of the Dorntons, Lord Dade asked Margaret if she still made a habit of walking her dogs in St. James's Park of a morning.

She nodded. "We have all of us fallen into the habit."

"It is an amazement to us all that Cray gets himself out of bed so early for nothing more than a walk in the park." There was unmistakable sarcasm in Wallis's tone.

Lord Dade, if he was similarly surprised, admirably hid the emotion. "Perhaps you would not mind too much if Hero and I were to join your party on occasion?" he suggested. "My leg requires regular exercise, as does my dog."

"Oh, do come," Margaret encouraged him. "I should love to see Hero again, and perhaps in that way we might continue our game of chess."

"Have you another move to confound me with, Pearl?"

She blushed. Something in the way he looked at her gave double meaning to his words. "I can only hope I am not the one confounded, my lord. Bishop to knight five."

Chapter 10

"KNIGHT to bishop three," Dade said quietly to Margaret Dornton the following morning when he and Hero met her party beside the canal in St. James's. In so doing, he physically maneuvered himself between Creighton and the young woman whose virtue Soames had vowed to take advantage of.

Creighton tapped his shoulder. The arch of one carefully plucked brow evidenced his awareness of Dade's intent. "Word is, you've been converted," he drawled.

"Oh?" Dade frowned. Soames's brash ways had begun to wear on him of late.

Creighton made a point of speaking loud enough that the entire party might be amused by his wit. "Yes, Queen Sarah tells any who will listen that it was on Easter Sunday that Dade did rise from the dead, along with our Lord, at St. James's. I'm sorry to have missed that miracle!"

Dade smiled wryly. "Ah, but Creighton, one must be faithful to witness miracles." Dade knew. He had witnessed a sort of miracle in himself. His memories had not pressed in on him since he had risen from the sickbed. He did not know what to attribute the miracle to, but it was a miracle nonetheless, and he had thanked God for it on Easter Sunday. "Where were you on Sunday morning, pray tell?"

Creighton grinned wickedly. "On my knees in a nunnery, worshiping angels, if you must know."

Wallis turned from the canal, where he had been skimming rocks, jaw dropped, cheeks crimson.

Dade's frown deepened. He glanced hastily at Pearl, who busied herself with throwing a leather ball for her dogs. It would appear she did not understand the vulgar parlance with which Creighton termed his visit to a brothel.

Soames laughed, his gaze passing languidly from his face to Wallis's. "Tell me, my pious friends, do you both mean to go to the Townley collection to study Greek vases rather than do the merry with me on Friday?"

Dade had no idea what he referred to.

Wallis, his blue eyes darting daggers in Creighton's direction, leapt into the conversation, possibly in hopes of stifling Creighton's unruly tongue. "We are to go and see the Elgin marbles, my lord. Care to join us?"

Beautifully pink-cheeked from her exertions with the whippets, Margaret leaned companionably on Wallis's arm and joined in the entreaty. "Please do," she said. "Allan has arranged for a party of seven. With Mr. Soames begging off, we are short one."

Dade could not refuse her, though he had no real interest in Greek vases. "I should be pleased to join your excursion," he said in all seriousness.

Creighton burst out laughing. "You, Ev? Pleased to look at marbles and vases? Really! This is a change of heart." He leaned over to whisper in Pearl's ear.

She ducked her chin and blushed. Dade wondered just what Creighton might have had to say about him. He made a point of finding out later in the morning, when Wallis at last relinquished his hold on Miss Dornton's arm.

Pearl stood alone, looking at the swans that floated in the canal. Concerned that her friendship with Creighton had already dangerously progressed, Dade joined her.

"When first I met you, Miss Dornton, I was not struck by any premonition that you were a foolish young woman," he said bluntly.

Pearl turned to stare at him, eyes wide. "Do you mean to scold me?" she bit out. "You, of all people, would ring a peal over my head? Well, sir, your admonitions come far behind the times. My cousin, uncle, aunt, even my sisters have had a proper go at me already." She plunged on. "I know it was wrong of me to put on my cousin's clothes, and wrong to go to a fencing match. I know it was wrong to jump between two armed men. I hold myself in part responsible for your wound, and I have tried to make amends—"

He laid a hand on her arm, silencing her diatribe in mid-sentence. "Miss Dornton, please. I am aware of all you have done to assist in my recovery. All! It is that which concerns me. That, and your friendship with Creighton."

She blinked in dismay, her gaze consumed by the sight of his hold on her arm. He let go of her and took a deep breath. "Tell me, what was it he whispered to you earlier that brought you to the blush?"

Her cheeks colored again as she lifted her chin and said, "He said I would make an art lover of you." Her lashes swept down. She shifted uneasily. "He then went on to rudely suggest, 'Some sort of lover, anyway.' "

Dade would have liked to read what she was thinking in that moment in her eyes, but she refused to look up at him. "Creighton is a crude fellow," he said.

She nodded.

"He could have said something far more embarrassing. He knows, as I know, that you were left alone in my private chambers."

She glanced swiftly at him in reaction to that remark.

"It does not please me that your cousin could have been so careless. Such a situation, no matter how innocent, lends itself to paltry remarks and innuendo—an arena in which Creighton excels. I would warn you against him. He will most assuredly take advantage, in some way, of his knowledge of your folly."

Her hand rose to her throat.

Dade knew he was not handling this matter in the gentlest or wisest manner, but he was not at all in the habit of couching his words. He was not at all schooled in the art of speaking with the sort of softness with which he was used to hearing Creighton ingratiate himself to women. He went on, knowing he was bungling the conversation, and yet his voice and manner remained as coolly expressionless as ever. The thing must be said. "As a result of my own indiscretion I am prepared—in fact, I am obliged—to offer for your hand in marriage."

Her eyes widened like a horrified child's. Her hand crept up to cover her mouth.

He could see that she was shocked that he should ask such a thing of her, in such a manner! His gaze raked over her. What kind of answer might he expect of this innocent young woman, not yet wise in the ways of the world? He had imagined in his mind both possible responses and could not say which he hoped to hear more. If she said yes, he would not be surprised. His recently acquired title was enough to make many a young female agree to such an arrangement, no matter what her feelings were with regard to his reputation. Yet he had reason to hope there was more than that between them. If she said no—and he began to think, from the expression in her eye, that she intended to refuse him—the response would be perfectly understandable too, even commendable. Surely they did not know each other well enough for a lifelong commitment. Yet he didn't want her to refuse him out of pride alone. That would not be sensible.

"You must realize that any possibility for your future happiness is severely compromised if the fact that you were left alone in my house becomes common knowledge. You have already suffered greatly for no more than having been seen walking upon the high street in my company. There will be no surviving people's opinion of this far more serious contact we have shared, no matter how well-intentioned, no matter how innocent."

"Oh!" she said, and called her dogs to her. He saw that she took comfort in their unqualified affection for her, and took advantage of their diversion to think of how she must answer his unexpected proposal. "I am touched by your concern," she said at last. Her eyes cut quickly to look at him and then away again, almost as if she feared him in some way. "I realize my actions have placed you in a position where you feel compelled by gallantry and honor to offer for my hand. I do apologize. You will understand I mean no offense at all in refusing your kind offer."

She wrung her hands, bit down on her lower lip and took a deep breath. "The very idea offends my sensibilities as much as I am certain it does your own. I would not intentionally force any man to offer for my hand due entirely to my own stupidity." Color warmed her cheeks. "I have, I must admit, flung caution to the wind, but you shall not be made to pay for my mistakes. My reputation is under very narrow-minded scrutiny for nothing more than our walk out of this very park, but surely something so foolish will soon be forgotten now that you are making a point to walk with us again. As to the other circumstance you mention, no one other than you and I, my cousin Allan, Creighton Soames and your servant, Gimble, has any knowledge of it. To date, Creighton has been the soul of discretion. He has proven himself a good friend to you and nothing but honorable in his intentions toward me. I trust, indeed I pray, that you are mistaken in your belief that your friend would abuse me with this sensitive knowledge he possesses. Surely he can be trusted not to speak of it?" There was a fleeting trace of doubt in her eyes.

Lord Dade's doubt was not fleeting. He was not inclined to easily trust in anyone. Certainly Creighton Soames was too much of a loose fish to trust with this young woman's fate. Even the best of men fell down in their judgment on occasion, and Creighton was not the best of men.

She went on refusing him. "Even if he did speak, you are under no obligation—"

"No," Evelyn broke in with a harshness he would have liked to recall once it passed the threshold of his mouth, but he was frustrated in his design and unwilling to stand arguing any woman into burdening herself with his name. "I fear I have not expressed myself with eloquence or tact. We do not know each other at all well. I have a keen understanding of the fact that you win no great prize in me as a husband. My reputation . . . suffice it to say, there is some truth to what is said against me. It may also be said that my circumstances are not without advantage. I can keep you very comfortable on the inheritance left me."

"Dear God!" she moaned. His words stung. Her face, as

she turned away from him, had about it the look of a woman deeply offended.

He tried to mend the breach in their understanding. "I do in no way believe you meant to coerce me—"

"Stop! Please stop!" she insisted, her voice shaking. The dogs sensed her unhappiness and jumped against her skirts to offer sympathy in the only manner they knew how. She cooed to them in fluid French and stooped to stroke each delicate head. The animals lay themselves down when she ordered them to do so, their eyes following her every move with as much concern as might have been witnessed in Dade's gaze had Pearl but lifted her eyes to look at him. She stared instead at the swans, remote and elegant, upon the silvered water of the canal.

"I am immeasurably grateful for your gentlemanly offer, my lord, but I cannot and will not accept either your generosity or your charity," she said at last. "Please refrain from pressing the matter further. I am resolute. Shall we shake hands and speak no more of this?"

She held out a nervous hand and dared to raise her gaze to meet his. There was a bleakness in her expression that surprised him, but before he had decided what to make of it, she disguised it with a brave smile. He took her hand between his own, troubled.

"I cannot promise that I shall never broach this topic again, Pearl, but for now I will bother you no more." He released his grip on her hand, uncomfortable with her rejection of him. The matter between them was anything but settled. Bowing curtly, he strode away.

Margaret's heart ached. How contemptible Lord Dade must find her. He was heir to an immense fortune, and she had placed herself in such a position he was obliged to offer for her. It was desperately humiliating. She had dared hope that the feelings that had begun to stir in her breast whenever he was near, whenever his name was mentioned, whenever she so much as set eyes on the chessboard set up beside her bed, might be shared in some small way by him.

She had hoped his shuttered heart might find genuine affection for her, given time. The thought of marriage had crossed her mind, a union based on the full-grown blossom of their mutual understanding. Not this! She was mortified. The seed of possibility could not grow healthy in the soil of such beginnings.

As Margaret watched Lord Dade walk away that morning, she fully expected it to be the last she would see of him. She was wrong. He joined the morning gathering on the following day and again the day after. He did not make a point to take her aside as before, but nodded to her whenever she happened to look his way and chatted about the weather and other trivialities. In all ways he tried to make himself pleasant and unobtrusive. On three occasions he skillfully diverted Creighton Soames's attentions when it appeared he had the intention of descending on her, and on more occasions than she could count, he seemed, subtly, to recommend her to Wallis.

Margaret was confused and troubled and ill at ease with the obligation which stood between her and Dade like a stone wall. How did one go about broaching conversation that might bring them to a better understanding of each other? she wondered. How was she to interpret his present behavior? Unschooled in the ways of men and women, she had no idea how to be flirtatious or coy, how to use a joking manner to breach the gap in the broken bridge of communication between them. Lord Dade, on the other hand, gave no evidence whatsoever of an inclination to press his suit or a desire to change the way in which matters stood between them. She might have thought herself forgotten did not his gaze focus upon her frequently as she walked about the park on Wallis's arm.

In response to Dade's warning against Creighton's intentions, Margaret tried to make her escort either Wallis or her cousin Allan in hopes of discouraging Mr. Soames's persistent attentions. On more than one occasion, she linked arms in an unwelcome manner with her sisters, Celia and Celeste, who would have much preferred to walk and talk without her tagging along. Creighton observed her retreat with amused nonchalance and attached himself like a limpet to her arm whenever the opportunity arose. Viewing her handsome, smiling escort with reservation, Margaret tried to turn the conversation down another pathway whenever Creighton considered her relationship with his friend Evelyn Dade a matter for discussion. She was not always successful.

"He is looking at us again," Creighton said to her at one point. He was, of course, referring to Lord Dade, who stared at them with dark, brooding intensity. "What spell have you cast on the poor old man?" His question was couched in a most suggestive tone.

"How can you call him old?" she said. "He is no more than a year or two your senior."

A grin spread slowly across Creighton's perfectly molded lips, and he leaned close to whisper slyly, "He is far too old for you, Miss Dornton. Perhaps not in years, but certainly in the age of his experience. I find it immensely interesting that he is drawn to you as much, if not more, than he was once drawn to darkness and death."

"Whatever do you mean?" Margaret quavered, sure Mr. Soames meant to fulfill Dade's dire prediction in bringing up her afternoon alone in the viscount's bedroom.

"You know exactly what I mean, you saucy little minx. Do not think you can fool me. Your eyes give you away. You think you've the power to tame the wildness in him, to paint white the blackness in his soul. I warn you, it is a dangerous undertaking."

Margaret shrank from this suggestiveness and glared at him, offended. "I do not at all care for your tone, Mr. Soames. Do not tease me with innuendo and suggestion. I am not at all acquainted with your meaning."

Creighton laughed. "You do not know, then, that Dade, though he makes a point of walking with you at the crack of dawn every morning, claims himself too exhausted to join his friends for any sport of an evening?"

Her surprise must have been delightfully evident, for he attempted to expand upon it. "You will next swear you have nothing at all to do with his having missed the latest Newgate necktie party."

She was staring at him now, wondering if he was teasing her. "He no longer goes to the hangings?"

"No more cut-caper sauce." He pretended nonchalance,

plucking dog hair from his lapel. "His chair at the academy goes empty as well."

Margaret winced at his casual vulgarity. "I am pleased to hear it." Her eyes could not help but settle on Dade as he chatted with Celia and her cousin Allan. Why in heaven's name had he ever frequented such places?

"He has lately become one of the stars in your uncle's firmament. I wonder why."

Again Margaret held her breath, waiting for mention of her foolishness. When Creighton merely looked at her, waiting for an answer, she said in the steadiest voice she could muster, "Lord Dade has shown interest in the art of diplomacy."

"Has he indeed?" Creighton drawled. "My dear Miss Dornton, the viscount begins to immerse himself in society again, and all on your account, it would seem."

She frowned. He was correct, though not for the reasons he would like to believe. Dade was immersing himself in society again, and with her uncle's assistance, in an attempt to clear her name from stupid gossip, not because he held her in any great esteem.

"You do me credit where none is due," she said with a trace of sadness.

"Come now, you are too modest! He has no other reason to have so suddenly changed his ways. It is naively clever in you to have created such a turnabout in gloomy old Captain Dead. Shall I warn you, I wonder, that the darkness you would conquer may in the end consume you? Or should I be jealous, Miss Margaret Dornton? You have not used your considerable feminine wiles to exert influence over me, and I am sadly in need of reform, let me assure you."

Margaret smiled uneasily, amused by the circuitous route all of Creighton's conversations took. It invariably led back to himself, and lately he had dwelled more often than not on his undying affection for her. So practiced was his attitude in offering up avowals of his love, however, that she could not find room in her heart to believe a word of it. More often than not, she met his declarations with a blush, a laugh and a shake of the head. Never offended, he merely sighed soulfully and told her she would one day come to believe his assertions, for he was as constant and unavoidable as the warming weather.

Margaret cared naught for that. She prayed only that out of his affection for her, Creighton would remain discreet about her afternoon alone in Lord Dade's bedroom.

Chapter 11

IN the newly expanded Townley buildings in Park Street, the enormous and breathtaking Elgin marbles captured the focus of Margaret's attention to the exclusion of all else, even news from Wallis about Lord Dade.

"Dade will arrive late," he told them breathlessly, himself late to their appointment. "If at all. He is regrettably engaged in an important meeting with Lord Castlereagh."

Margaret heard the words and was vaguely disappointed. She had been looking forward to seeing Dade again, even if she did not have any idea what to say to this man now that he had offered for her hand and she had refused him. But her disappointment was very weak in the face of the beauty that was dubbed the Elgins.

Her aunt turned to the guide who had been explaining the arduous process by which the marbles had been removed from the Parthenon and transported to London. "Let us move on. We have wandered among the marbles for a good quarter of an hour, and I wish to see the latest acquisitions in the Egyptian collection."

"Do you mind if I stay here a little longer?" Margaret inquired, her eyes never drifting from the arched neck of a horse, eye bulging and veins working, as it rose from the floor as though breaking through from some nether world. "I have not yet looked my fill."

The others agreed. They would come back for her, along with the guide, once their own interests had been met. Alone she remained, dwarfed and silent, but for her footsteps among the cool, perfect marble gods and goddesses. She was immeasurably awed by the pale, scarred remnants of what must have been a phenomenal sight long ago. They were soul-stirring even now in their fragmented, imperfect, time-worn state.

That man might make god-like enormous blocks of stone gave Margaret the impression she walked amidst greatness. She gazed upon the culmination of an art form. Stone had become a fall of cloth so delicate one could read the curve of breast beneath. The marble robes of Aphrodite leaning on Dione flowed with liquid grace. Stone had become too the bared flesh of a perfect arm and leg and shoulder in the reclining nude of Dionysus.

He was her favorite. This masterpiece of sculpting captivated her imagination. Powerful and vigorous even in his restful position, as he bore most of his weight on one elbow, the god of wine and revelry, exquisitely trapped in stone, drew her gaze and would not relinquish its hold. He reminded her, in a breathless, guilty sort of way, of Lord Dade half risen from his sickbed, reaching for her. This figure, larger than life, matched that larger-than-life moment in her memory. A part of Evelyn Dade seemed trapped in the stone before her. Some element of what they shared was here. If she examined the marble long enough, she might fathom it.

Slowly, her gaze never parting from the articulately rendered stone, she circled the figure. Time had not been kind to the face of this god. He was missing most of his nose. His lips were chipped and worn. But it was not really the face that mirrored her memory of Lord Dade, except perhaps in the noble brow, which was still intact—and in the shape of chin, neck and muscled shoulder. His hands and feet were missing. She filled them in, in her mind's eye. These were undoubtedly Lord Dade's well-muscled legs, that had been shown to such advantage in a fencing match. This too was the chest that had been bared so well. She circled slowly the great statue, admiring the powerfully muscled curve of spine rising up off folds of cloth artfully cut into stone.

Margaret wanted to touch the marble, to smooth her hand over the scored, weather-beaten flatness of Dionysus's belly, to cup her palms around the time-scarred ball of calf, knee and shoulder. And yet she could not. There was an irreverence both in laying hands on a god and in touching a masterpiece of unsurpassed beauty. One could not hold perfection in one's hand any more than one might pluck up a moment from the past.

Round and round she went, slowly, deliberately studying this male form, deliberately matching imagery in her memory. She was glad to have been left alone. To stare with such concentration at the naked male form while others observed was sure to be misinterpreted. On her third circuit of the marble, she was, however, unnerved by the feeling that as examiner she was herself being examined.

She turned. None other than the gentleman who had so filled her thoughts this quarter of an hour and more stood framed in the doorway, a marble god given life and clothing, and a penetrating gaze. Margaret shivered.

"My lord." She dipped her head, blushing to think he should come in to find her staring intently at the naked male form. She wondered how long he had watched her. "I did not expect you," she said, faltering.

"I can see you did not." A tight smile lifted one side of his sleek, dark mustache, lit momentarily the dark, brooding eyes, and was gone. He understood her embarrassment. She could read his awareness, his comprehension, in both look and stance. His perception multiplied her uneasiness.

"Alone again, Pearl?" His words brought her head up and stiffened her shoulders. Did he mean to scold again? She eyed him warily. His eyes held a dark intensity she was not used to seeing in their walks in the park. Creighton's warning ran through her mind. Such thoughts made her wonder if it was not very dangerous to be a young female alone with this gentleman of dubious reputation—when he was not locked in delirium.

"I was sure Wallis meant to accompany you." There was something in his tone that would seem to warn her against him as much as Creighton had. She cleared her throat, nodded and moved away from the overpoweringly male force of

Dionysus to stare at a section of a no less provocative frieze in which a youth who looked somewhat like the oft-mentioned Wallis, wearing only a billowing cape draped from the shoulder, stood amidst a number of restive horses.

"There is a great group of us galloping about in here," she said. "The others have gone on to examine Egyptian artifacts and the upstairs room full of Greek vases."

"You find little fascination in such things? Or in remaining a part of the herd you spoke of?" He seemed possessed of a restless, pacing energy that gave her the feeling he would like to walk on.

She spread her arms, pirouetting slowly. Her gesture encompassed the room. "Dear Wallis cannot hold my interest when I have opportunity to walk among the gods of ancient Greece. Do you not find them truly magnificent?"

He licked his lips uneasily and scanned the room, his eyes darting restlessly among the marbles with a reserved, almost a pained, look. "I do not care for them."

She failed to recognize the source of his discomfort, and turned a disappointed look upon him. "I am immensely sorry to hear you say so. They are my favorite among Townley's collection. How is it man can chip away at stone and find flesh, fabric and hair? As likenesses to nature, you must admit, these renderings of the human and animal form in stone are incomparable."

He nodded, his sleekly bearded jaw rigid. "They are very lifelike. Too lifelike for me to feel comfortable with their shattered appendages. Too many missing heads and limbs for my taste."

"Oh!" She sighed with comprehension and turned to look at him with cleared vision. "I see. I am sorry to have lingered when they cannot but remind you of—"

He interrupted her. "It is of no moment."

But she had to apologize, make him understand. "No, no, it is just that I did tend to see and admire what was there, without ever really considering what was missing." She examined the scarred and broken marble bodies with new awareness, her features mirroring the melancholy thoughts that such a perspective brought. "Was Waterloo really so horrible?" she asked at last.

He cleared his throat, his face expressionless. "I do not like to speak of it."

She nodded and dipped her head, embarrassed. She had thought herself enough in his confidence to discuss a time and place that clearly pained him. Not long subdued by this gentle set down, she made an attempt to lighten the moment. "You do not speak of it unless you are shouting in your sleep?" she dared remark.

He shot her a dark, pained look, one that seemed to increase the distance that separated them without a step taken. His eyes seemed for an instant to glaze over, as if with ice: hard, cold and dark. He was, in an instant, a stranger to her.

It was not Margaret's intention to pain him. His look frightened her. She plucked at his sleeve and said with great feeling, "I do not mean to sound hard or callous, but you see, I do not at all comprehend what you and so many other young men have experienced. Do many of your comrades suffer the nightmares you do?"

His gaze came back to her, as if from a great distance. His mouth was very tight, his tone impatient, the light in his eyes dim. The walls were higher than ever today. "I do not know. As I have said, I do not like to speak of it."

"With no one? Not even a priest?" she could not refrain from asking, so startling was such a concept. She and her sisters discussed everything—most especially their fears. She could not imagine carrying them around with absolutely no one to share their burden.

Margaret could see by Dade's expression and the pulled look of his mouth that indeed he spoke of the matter with no one. "Oh, but sir, I cannot think it a good thing to keep such sorrow locked up inside you. Perhaps your dreams would be less troubling if you found someone sympathetic with whom to discuss the matter."

"Shall we go on to the room where the Egyptian collection is housed?" he asked her stiffly, his arm extended that she might link hers through it. He shut her out and shut up her mouth with both suggestion and gesture as clearly as if he had said to her once again, "I do not wish to speak of it."

She took his arm with the feeling that it was vital she

should have some physical contact with him in that moment, that he might more clearly understand her agitation in having reminded him, quite unwittingly, of the horrors of war. Darkness separated them like a palpable barrier. "Yes, we may go on, my lord." She forced herself to sound cheerful. "I will be happy to discuss chess if you wish to change the subject. My next move is pawn to king's knight three. But please, sir"—her smile faltered—"do not shut me out entirely. I understand your feelings, perhaps more than you realize. If you do not feel comfortable discussing the war with me, then please, I beg of you, find someone who can understand and release some of the burden in your heart."

Her words left no ripples in the dark, blank centers of his eyes. She had never known him to look so cold. It disturbed her.

"I shall cease my teasing of you now," she said bravely, "if you will only tell me . . . are you offended that there are those who would commemorate Waterloo with the Elgin marbles? I have read in the newspaper that London is seen by many as a new Athens in her success over France, which Napoleon himself declared as the new Rome."

He shrugged, still distant. "It would seem a remote connection."

She stopped in the entrance to the Egyptian room. "Not at all. Had Napoleon never invaded Egypt, Lord Elgin's embassy to Constantinople would never have been given permission to remove these sculptures from the Parthenon. They would likely still be baking in the Mediterranean sunlight, losing hands and feet to time and the weather had there been no British response to such an invasion. I should never have had the opportunity to examine them."

He laughed. She had not expected to make him laugh and was pleased that her words so far had relaxed the stern set of his mouth.

"Castlereagh said to me today that some good will come out of even the most evil circumstances. Is that what you are getting at?" His eyes had come back to life again.

She smiled at him, her whole face alight. "Exactly. The part you played at Waterloo was a far greater coup to the art world than you or any of your fallen comrades might have envisioned. Like stones thrown into a pond of time, your actions rippled out to touch lives and forces most would not even recognize."

He stood a moment looking at her with intense, brooding concentration, the gold flecks that radiated from the dark centers of his eyes glowing, as if her words, like pebbles, touched the still depths of his innermost thoughts in some way she herself did not recognize.

Uneasy with his silence, she would have withdrawn her hand from his sleeve had he not grasped it, taking it in haste to the level of his mouth, where he kissed it with a fervor that unsettled her almost as much as his former chill.

"I hope you will always speak your mind to me, Miss Dornton. Your thoughts and actions do sometimes contradict both my comfort and opinion, but like grains of sand in an oyster casing, they offer up pearls of wisdom."

His gaze locked with hers for a moment with an intimacy that surpassed his kiss to her hand. She was moved and flattered and yet strangely frightened all at once. The walls in the depths of his gold-flecked eyes that so often held her at bay were down. There was evidence in the melting warmth of his gaze of the depth of his affection for her. His feelings for her, his strange mood swings, she found confusing. And yet in this moment as they stood framed in the doorway between two ancient worlds, she was sure he wanted to kiss her. She could see no other purpose in the increasing heat of his gaze. She could sense no other intention in the subtle movement of his head toward hers. The air between them seemed fraught with expectation, as the distance separating them shrank. His eyes begged permission, burning with desire held carefully in check. Margaret knew it was wrong of her, but she could not deny her own desire. She did not turn her head, or drop her gaze, or back away from him as she might have done.

The dark centers of his eyes expanded. His breath touched her cheek.

As if in response to a signal, she closed her eyes. Shivering, she swayed toward him, expecting their mouths to meet, wanting such contact, wanting the heat of his lips to warm hers. Her heart throbbed uncomfortably, so foreign, scandalous, even dangerous was her desire.

He did not kiss her, however. There were footsteps on the stairs and then voices. They jerked back from each other with guilty speed. Her face, lips and neck burned with embarrassment and an awareness of what had almost happened. She dared to look at him.

The walls were up again. She could read nothing in the dark void of his eyes. Was he angry with her?

"I think it is best we were interrupted just now," he said tersely. "Shall we be good and join the others?"

Margaret was unused to subterfuge. She could no more than nod and attempt to calm the unruly beat of her heart.

Dade nodded and led her into the room, saying loud enough that any who approached might hear, "Would you care to see the Rosetta Stone? It is quite remarkable, I am told. The key to understanding an otherwise lost language."

Margaret could only nod. Her vocal cords did not want to function. Her lips, disappointed in their own pursuit of a complex foreign language, refused to part.

Chapter 12

"THE hyacinths have broken ground" was what Margaret first said to Dade when next they came together in St. James's Park. "Spring is truly upon us. Only look!"

He did look. The wind tugged merrily at her curls and brought a cheerful blush to her cheeks as she tossed a little leather ball from one gloved hand to the other. Margaret Dornton's gray eyes spoke a language as mysterious and secretive as that Dade had observed carved on the surface of the Rosetta Stone when they were last alone together. She had wanted to kiss him. She thought about it still. He could see evidence of her curiosity in the looks that darted between them like birds searching out a place to nest. Dade looked and looked at Margaret Dornton, mesmerized by the thought that this bright and beautiful young woman was drawn to him, heady with the knowledge of how close they had come to a stolen kiss among the gods. The knowledge lent a mature mystery to the smile Pearl hid artfully from the rest of the world behind the cowl of her hooded cloak, while it quickened Dade's pulse with the rare, sunny heat of a yearning that surprised him. The ghosts of his memory seemed very pale in the light of the sun today, in the light of Margaret Dornton's smile. Evelyn Dade felt as if the weight in the pit of his stomach and in the darkest recesses of his heart had been in some way lifted.

"May I?" Evelyn reached for the ball. When she handed it to him, with a puzzled expression that knitted the pale expanse of her forehead, he succeeded in making it disappear from his palm, through sleight of hand.

She stepped closer, reaching out to turn his hands, searching for the ball. Her approach, her touch, as much as the light in her pearl gray eyes, filled Dade's heart with the certainty that this innocent was as taken with him as he was with her. She had regretted the interruption of their kiss as much as he. The idea warmed him deep within. A part of him that had long lay dormant unwound and began to grow.

"Magic!" she said softly. "Will you do it again, sir?"

Something in the way she said it, in the way she leaned close to him, made Dade wonder if she was asking him if he meant to kiss her again. With a smile that had her blushing, he made the ball reappear from behind her ear. Her cheeks flamed rosier than the brisk weather alone accounted for as he brushed past a lock of her hair and ran his fingers all too familiarly against the silken lobe of her ear. It was a soft, delicate ear on this soft and delicate spring day.

She did not scold him for the liberty he took, only blushed, ducked her head shyly and entreated him to show how the trick was done. He made the ball disappear again from the palm of his hand. From behind her other ear he produced, not the ball this time but a chess pawn.

"My knight takes your pawn," he said very softly, his voice gruff with need of her softness. He would have leaned forward and kissed her right there in the park in broad daylight, and she would have let him, had not a wave of small feathered creatures took flight above their heads with a sudden rush of wings.

"Unfair advantage if your king uses sorcery to take her pawn," Creighton interrupted them with a drawl. It was he who had startled the birds. "What trick are you up to, Ev? The seduction of an innocent?"

Dade made an unhappy noise and turned to face Creighton. "Magic does not come easily to everyone," he said gruffly. This magic could not withstand the hard-edged scrutiny of Creighton Soames's forceful personality. Beneath his piercing gaze the tender bud of their growing relationship seemed sordid and inconsequential.

Creighton winked cheekily. "Depends on the type of magic involved, Ev."

Magic there was between them, Dade had to admit as the days slipped swiftly past. Spring unfurled around them. Gray, foggy London seemed an unexpectedly pretty place, a place of wonder and opportunity. His darkest, most troublesome memories seemed to have fled. Deepening friendships blossomed among all the young people who gathered beneath the lacy white cherry trees of St. James's. Dade took advantage of the private sunlit moments that he shared with Margaret Dornton beneath the swaying trees. The two of them spoke with an increasing freedom about any subject that occurred to them. Any subject save one.

Pearl tried once to touch upon the war. The weather on that morning was crisp, clear and sunny, and as if she had shed some of her inhibitions along with her heavy winter cloak, his bare-headed innocent dared ask, "Tell me, my lord, about the Battle of Waterloo."

Her eyes, her very face, were open and fresh and sweet as the periwinkles she had been pleased to point out to him. Her hair, curled in a riot of tendrils about each temple, *à la grecque,* while the weight of it was braided across the crown of her head, shimmered in the sunlight like a fragile filigree crown. She was completely and naively ignorant of what it was she asked him to put into words on this fair and gentle day, when nothing more raucous than the screech of a jay or the chatter of a squirrel rent the air.

"Tell me about the battles you relive in your sleep." There was something compelling in the way she asked him to open up to her, as if she really was prepared to hear whatever he had to say.

Dade frowned and turned his face entirely away from her to watch the mock battle that had sprung up between two small lads out for a stroll in the park with their nanny; a younger sibling was tucked away in the perambulator she pushed. Two stout sticks served as swords, which the lads cracked together with force enough that bark flew.

Did the male sex prepare for war from the very earliest days? he wondered. Did they have some inherent propensity for violence from their inception, while their sisters did not? One did not often see little girls poking at one another with sticks: while it was one of the favorite pastimes of little boys.

His contemplative silence worried Margaret Dornton. He could see it painted across her features as clearly as if she had voiced the emotion. He managed a smile. Such a face as she presented to him demanded smiles. She bloomed like a newly budded flower in the dappled sunlight. He would not trample something so fragile, so delicate, so pleasing to his heart. He would not darken the brightness of the day.

"Why did I join the military?" he muttered. "The usual reasons. The military gave my life purpose and promise. I sought glory, and medals and rises in rank. I sought my reason for being put on this earth."

"And did you find these things?"

He bowed his head. "I discovered that what I sought was not, after all, what I really wanted."

"No? What do you want, then?"

He looked up, surprised by the question. He had never really asked himself what it was he wanted since his return from France, not since Gavin's death. "I don't think I know."

"Do you know what it is you do not want?"

Dark images filled his mind, images he would rather not recall. He bowed his head and shook them away. "Yes."

She nodded. The hint of a smile touched her lips. "Then you are halfway to finding out what it is you desire."

Desire. The word reached out to him from her mouth and wrapped itself around him. He desired her. Her mouth, her arms, the look she sometimes bent his way without any consciousness of how such a look could twist a man up inside. There was no denying it. He desired her. He wanted to lie in his bed of a night with this beautiful, perfect, shining, sun-dappled Pearl clasped in his arms. Surely, with such innocence in his grasp, the darkness of his dreams could plague him no more. He could never say as much to her, however, as she stared earnestly into his eyes, awaiting his response. Could there be anything right in someone like him winning such a creature? Did he want nothing more than to seduce her, as

Creighton had suggested? She deserved better. Much better. There rested a seed of fear within Dade that Captain Dead might curse the sweet innocence of Miss Margaret Dornton. He did not want that blot on his conscience along with everything else.

"You are right," he said. "In knowing what I do not want, there is a clear map to what I do. I want . . ." He wanted the peace that shone so clearly from the wise depths of her beautiful gray eyes as she waited to hear his response. "I want to make the horrors I have suffered to have meaning, to fit them somehow into the pattern of my life and into the reason for my being," he said, afraid to be more specific, afraid he might jinx the future if he voiced his desires aloud.

Silence fell between them, a comfortable, contemplative silence in which her eyes lingered in their shining, earnest study of his expression, and her lips curved upward in a satisfied, knowing smile. It occurred to Dade, as he stood looking at the young woman who went so easily about the task of uncovering the essence of his soul, that the warmth of the sun and the wafting of a breeze had never so gently kissed a brow as it did now. He could divulge no more of the darkness within him with this creature of light.

"As for battles, the only battle I am interested in discussing with you, Pearl, is that to be had on a chessboard. Have you decided on your next move?"

She nodded. "Yes, I have. Bishop takes queen."

Thus, with as much delicacy and finesse as Dade possessed, the topic that most troubled him was dropped. She politely obliged him in refraining from raising it again. The chess game progressed apace with the progression of the season. Every day brought another move. The hyacinths put forth color, daffodils and narcissus nodded bright heads. His bishop took her pawn in check. Finches, wagtails, starlings and robins finished the work upon their nests and set about filling them with eggs. Her king moved in on his.

A spate of wind and chilling rain chased all from the park save Dade. He came as usual, despite the downpour, Hero trotting wetly at his heel. He had news. His headless knight was checkmating Pearl's queen today. Even more important, Lord Castlereagh had offered him a position. Dade came to inform the Pearl that their game was ended, perhaps forever.

That the park should be deserted surprised him. Rain was too frequent a factor in England's weather to let it keep one indoors. Beneath the dripping brim of his hat, Dade walked the pathways that had become so familiar to him, and he found them unfamiliar. He examined this place that had become dear to him. It seemed forlorn and forbidding without Pearl and her whippets walking with him. The trees glistened and dripped. The birds fluttered wetly in the leaves above him, their song momentarily stilled. Even the flowers turned their faces from him. Colors seemed less bright, shapes less distinct; yet it occurred to Dade that not once in his walks in the park had the dark memories from his past assaulted him.

Hero, sleekly wet, followed Dade with the stiff-legged, high-shouldered, miserable gait of an animal baffled by his master's desire to get out in the middle of so much wetness. Ignoring him, Dade lifted his hat from his head and turned his cheek a moment into the soft fall of droplets. He imagined all of the darkness in his soul washing away with the rain, draining away his pain. He relished the cool wetness, the infinitesimal weight of each droplet as it contacted hair and flesh, purifying him. He stroked his mustache, ran a hand across his damp beard.

Breath pluming in the chill, Dade realized that it was Pearl, and his days with her here in this park, that had made him come to such a crossroads in his awareness that no more than a raindrop might bring him release, relief and joy. He realized too that in accepting the position Lord Castlereagh offered him, his days here with her were numbered. His only comfort for that thought lay in knowing that Creighton Soames would never win his Pearl, never wrap her around his finger, as he had boasted. She was clearly drawn to Eckhart's company, as he had hoped, not Soame's. She was always to be found in conversation with the fair-haired giant. He had fostered the growth of the relationship in any way that lay within his power. Now it brought him nothing but pain, for Evelyn Dade realized, deep in the core of his being, that he was himself hopelessly in love with Miss Margaret Dornton.

Before Dade's thoughts could grow too maudlin, Hero

shook violently, thoroughly pelting him with a stinging spray. He laughed, "C'mon, then, you miserable creature. Let's get out of this wet. I have need of a barber. It is time to put a new face on things."

As the rain ran in rivulets down the windows, the rest of the usual walking party gathered in the Derntons' cozy drawing room for steaming cups of tea and toast while a log crackled on the fire and the whippets contented themselves with chasing after the little ball which Creighton made a game of tossing into difficult places for them to reach.

"It must be someplace bright and lively and sheltered from wind and rain," Celia dictated.

"Vauxhall Gardens," Wallis suggested. "You have yet to see the fireworks."

"Vauxhall?" Creighton groaned. "They are too miserly with the ham. Besides, it is not at all protected from the weather. No, we must go to Astley's. There is no brighter, merrier place in all of London."

Allan bent to free the dog's ball from beneath a lacquered Chinese cabinet. "I second the notion. They've a new playbill going up about town. They mean to reenact the Battle of Waterloo. I should very much like to see that."

"Waterloo?" Margaret echoed. "How interesting."

She looked up self-consciously when Creighton laughed and said with a devilish wink, "Now, why is that, I wonder?"

She blushed.

Wallis studied her from his chair. "I wonder if Evelyn will care to go with us to such a thing."

"Do you think he might find it too painful?" she was moved to ask softly.

Celia had not the good grace to pretend she did not hear her. "He has but to say no to our invitation if it too greatly affects his sensibilities," she pointed out.

The truth of this was self-evident. A date was chosen, Margaret's uncle named as their escort, transportation arranged and the necessity of a box to contain their party agreed upon.

When the rain came to a halt three days later, the trees were much greener, the air sweeter, the flower beds filled with more vibrant color. The cherry trees and the channel were alive with birds on the return to St. James's of the walking party.

"I have missed you," Margaret enthusiastically greeted Hero with an ear ruffling when he appeared with his master. "But who is this stranger you bring with you? I do not believe I recognize the gentleman." She slipped her arm from Wallis's to walk around Dade, considering the unexpected changes in his appearance from all angles.

Wallis's blue eyes were lively with curiosity. "Barber got carried away, did he?"

Dade stroked the unfamiliar smoothness of his chin. "A new face was in order," he said, "to go with my new position." He was still not used to the wind on his face, not used to the clean-shaven stranger who stared from the cheval glass of a morning, not used to the idea that his freedom to take morning walks would soon be curtailed.

"Castlereagh offered for you?" Wallis sounded pleased.

"Yes," Dade smiled. He was looking forward to the prospect of returning to France, not to kill but to help keep the peace. He was strangely self-conscious beneath Margaret Dornton's intense examination. Did she find him too changed without mustache and beard? She said nothing, and yet could not seem to take her eyes from his face.

"I like this new face of yours, Lord Dade." She linked one arm companionably with Eckhart and held out her other hand for Dade to take. "It is as though a door has opened on your face, sir." She smiled up at him as he fell into step beside her. "And now we may come in. I should think the French will be quite taken with you."

There was an earnestness to her expression and the lilt of her voice that convinced Evelyn Dade she found something to concern her in the changes he had so deliberately wrought. She was, he thought, like the rain on his cheek. He felt every drop of her.

She wore, this morning, a dress he had never seen her wear before, a dress in which she seemed to bloom as much as the garden around her. It was edged in a flounce of willow green ribbon crisscrossed like a lattice and headed with a row of embroidered roses in several shades of pink. On this bright, sweet, rain-washed morning Margaret Dornton seemed in some way more beautiful than he had remembered, as changed in appearance as he. There was a distance between them that he did not quite understand. Perhaps it was the sight of her hand tucked so cozily in the crook of Wallis Eckhart's accommodating arm.

"I have missed the sunshine," he said as he studied her countenance, trying to figure out what it was about her that seemed different, not realizing that it was his own perspective that was changed. "The park seems somehow more beautiful for its having been denied me," he said.

As did she.

Margaret smiled and closed her eyes, her lashes fluttering as she breathed in the sweetness of the breeze. Wallis grinned down at her, his affection evident. The gentle blond giant looked content to have Miss Dornton hanging on his arm. It occurred to Dade that Margaret Dornton and Wallis Eckhart would forever be a piece of his mental picture of springtime in St. James's Park. They were, both of them, pale and golden and tender with possibility.

Pearl opened her wise gray eyes. "Sunshine never so warms the heart as when one has suffered several days of rain," she murmured. Dade was not surprised to hear her echo his feelings. Her gaze settled on her sisters, who sat side by side upon a bench, with Allan and Creighton hanging over their shoulders, examining a number of gilded vellum invitations. "Just as a score of invitations are never so appreciated as following a dearth of them."

"Ah! You are welcomed into society again," Dade surmised, strangely disappointed. The strings that bound them together were all at once unraveling.

As if her thoughts echoed his, she said, "Yes, you shall no longer be obliged to walk with us."

He frowned.

She laughed. She meant to tease. "Unless it pleases you, of course. I do hope it will please you. Just as I hope you are willing to join our party to Astley's. Dear Wallis has made arrangements for all of us to go to their newest program before the week is out."

She smiled brilliantly at Wallis. Dade had never known

her smile to pain him, but this smile, directed at another man, did just that. He squared his shoulders and said what he had come to say.

"Regrettably, it is true I shall no longer be able to join you here in the park. My new duties curtail my time and freedom."

Her eyes and mouth registered the impact of his statement. She was disappointed. More so than he might have imagined, given her attachment to Eckhart.

Hoping he might make her smile again, he said, "I should be delighted to join this party to Astley's, though, and you must tell me of the invitations you have received. It sounds as if your time for gambols in the park will soon be limited as much as mine."

She shrugged in the French fashion, her expression still not fully recovered from the awareness that their time together would seem to have come to an end. "Society, it seems, has decided to forgive the MissesSerntons' past transgressions, conveniently forgetting why it chose to snub us in the first place." Mischief played about her mouth as she said, "I believe we are prodigal daughters for no more reason than bald-faced curiosity."

"Curiosity?" It was Wallis who asked.

"Yes." Her eyes sparkled with what looked like anger. Her eyebrows arched upward, birds on the wing. "Society wonders why three virtually unknown young women should have so thoroughly captivated the attentions of several of society's more promising bachelors."

Anyone had only to look at her to know the answer, Dade thought, but what he said was "Am I to be counted among these promising bachelors?"

"Do not flatter him with an answer, for he already knows the answer," Wallis said. "Our Lord Dade is fast becoming the fashion all over London."

"Is he?" Her mouth looked pinched.

"Yes." It was Creighton Soames who answered as he joined them. "A walking, talking mystery cannot but provoke interest so long as it does not pose a danger."

"Yes," Dade agreed dryly. "Without a single dead man to

my credit in months, there is something irresistibly interesting about the cloud that hangs over my past."

"As long," Creighton cut in on him, "as it is in fact a piece of the past."

Dade wondered if Creighton's cynical outlook was accurate. The subtle plan he and Lord Dornton had set into motion was working its gentle magic. The Misses Dornton had walked so often with Evelyn and his compatriots that such activity might be considered ordinary. Margaret's past transgressions were a forgotten piece of the past.

Wallis looked affectionately down from his great height at Pearl's uplifted face. "Do you know that everyone has taken to calling me and Allan and Cray 'Dade's pups'?"

She nodded, her eyes alive with amusement. She patted her hand upon his sleeve. "Celeste says Lady Jersey compared you both in some biting way to Hero, always trailing about in Lord Dade's wake. Allan tells me too"—she slid a glance in Dade's direction—"that the sword fight has been waved aside as nothing above common interest since Lord Dade has not died as a result."

He nodded. His cordial meeting with the Dornton family at St. James's Church and their subsequent walks in St. James's Park had been noted and digested by the guardians of morality among society's upper crust. The purpose of the morning strolls had been met. There was no more real need of them. Was there?

Creighton winked at Pearl. "There is only one question that still hangs unanswered. Who was the audacious young lady who nearly got herself killed in stepping between two sword-wielding gentlemen?"

Wallis tried to keep the matter a light one. He smiled at Margaret. This time it was his hand did the patting. "The knifing question as to the young lady's identity dulls with the passage of time. It will be forgotten entirely before long. Don't you agree, Creighton?"

Creighton shrugged and yawned elaborately. "We shall all be deadly boring soon" was his response.

Chapter 13

THE half-forgotten fear that Creighton might yet reveal Margaret's identity as the mysterious female who had interrupted a fencing match dressed in men's clothing and stayed unchaperoned in a bachelor's bedchamber raised its ugly visage again when he found a remedy for boredom in a brandy bottle. He met the Dornton party, reeking of the stuff, on the night that the group arranged to go together to Astley's.

His inebriation was evident from the moment he clambered into Lord Dornton's town coach with imprudent haste, smartly cracking his head. Oblivious to pain, he crowed, "Off to Astley's, are we!"

Celia and Celeste winced with identical discomfort, and Allan groaned and said, "Hallo, that must have hurt."

Creighton was benumbed. He grinned and rubbed his head as he sank down next to Margaret, who could not help but fall back from the appalling odor of brandy that hung about his person like an offensive cologne.

"A bump on the head is nothing," he insisted cannily. "I have been at a wedding most of this afternoon, and that is far more painful, let me tell you." He fell loosely against the squabs as the horses were commanded to walk on, his shoulder bumping Margaret's with every cobblestone crossed.

Creighton would have been refused a ride had Lord

Dornton caught a whiff of him. But their chaperon, in a most untimely fashion, had got down from the coach to examine the aft hind leg on one of the wheelers, and chose to ride beside the coachman rather than crowded inside.

Allan tilted his head toward the sound of creaking springs and the mutter of voices over their heads. "My father will throw you out of his coach if he discovers you are foxed," he hissed at his guest with a frown.

"We must be sure to keep the old hound off the scent, then," Creighton suggested, his eyes sparkling dangerously as he put finger to lips.

Celia, who sat immediately opposite Creighton, where she bore the brunt of his brandied breath, moaned and buried her nose in the scented silver pomander dangling from a chain at her throat.

Creighton grinned at her and belched.

"Really, sir! Have you no manners?" she snapped.

Creighton patted his mouth, laughing boisterously, in excellent spirits in more ways than one. "None whatsoever when I have been drinking," he admitted unabashedly. "Have I not just informed you I have been to a wedding? Good friend of mine too, more's the pity. What else does a sane man do on such an occasion, having lost a comrade to such an institution, but drink himself silly? Don't worry, though, my dears. I intend to have a very good time tonight, in celebration of my own freedom from such shackling. I have heard that an entire village goes up in flames tonight. Cannon fire and Chinese rockets suit my mood admirably."

Allan shot Margaret a worried look as Creighton sagged happily against her shoulder. "Here, here, Cray. That is my cousin you are mashing, and not some orange girl."

Margaret shrugged him away, and Creighton shifted heavily. "Oh, I say, no slight intended, Miss Margaret. You look quite the thing tonight. Much prettier than Oscar's bride. Dashed plain woman. I cannot think what induced him to marry her, and so I told him, but he would have her anyway. Brought him more than seven hundred pounds per annum with her dowry, he whispered in my ear." He lowered his own voice theatrically. "Not the type to expect him to give up either mistresses or gambling, he said. She began to look more attractive when I had heard as much."

Celia seemed to feel obliged to fill the awkward silence that followed such an outburst. "I understand we shall see tonight a young woman who stands on a galloping horse wearing shockingly brief and spangled attire." She allowed a trace of sarcasm to voice itself. "I am sure you will enjoy that, Mr. Soames, as much as a burning village."

Creighton laughed appreciatively. "I'm sure I shall." He leaned familiarly close to Margaret, liquor warming his smile, his volume reduced to a low roar. "I have always enjoyed females who dared to be fearless. I hear there is a character tonight called Molly Malony, who dons the uniform of a Highlander so that she might save her young man from certain death at the hands of the enemy. I could not but think of you, Miss Margaret Dornton, when such a character was described. It did seem to me, you know, that history meant to repeat itself, in more ways than one tonight."

"Whatever do you mean?" Celeste asked. When he responded with nothing more than a wink, she asked again, this time directing her query at the rest of their gathered company. "Whatever does he mean by such a remark?"

Margaret exhaled the breath she had been holding as Allan's frightened gaze met hers. Did Creighton mean to break his silence here in the coach, his tongue loosened by liquor? It could not but cross her thoughts that he might at any time, in such a state, blurt out enough to damn her.

She tried to laugh, but the sound did not have any naturalness to it. "I am surprised that I should so fill your thoughts, Mr. Soames," she said softly.

"We must hope history does not too closely repeat itself tonight." Allan was trying hard, too hard perhaps, to steer the conversation away from danger.

"How's that?" Creighton blinked at him owlishly.

Allan plunged on. "We are in the company of Lord Dade tonight at a reenactment of the Battle of Waterloo."

"Ha!" Creighton slapped his knee, gleefully catching on. "If history does repeat itself, we may none of us live to tell the tale afterward," he sputtered. "That's dashed clever, Dornton! Dashed clever."

Margaret thought the remark anything but clever. Surely it was ill-advised in Allan to entrust such an idea to Creighton in his inebriated state. And indeed, Allan was later terribly embarrassed when Creighton made a noisy point of reiterating the jest to the very gentleman who could find little in it to enjoy—Lord Dade himself.

From the outside, Margaret decided, Astley's famous ampitheater looked disappointingly staid. Her uncle's coach approached the three-story building down a cobbled street much like any other in London. The building front was simple, with a Doric roofline and neoclassical windows and doorways. An awning guarded the entrance from the weather, while little more than the single word Astley's at the base of the roofline proved that they were not mistaken in the address.

Margaret was not in the least disappointed to see Lord Dade awaiting their arrival beneath that same awning, looking particularly handsome with his clean-shaven chin, a new blue jacket and more cheer than was typical of him. She was not accustomed to seeing him wear blue. It suited him and yet made her feel a little sad, as though he was in some way a stranger to her—a stranger who would no longer be walking with her of a morning.

"Wallis has gone up to secure our box," he announced as he helped her from the coach, then lowered his voice to say to her most particularly, "I waited to walk you in. I wanted to witness your first impression of Astley's."

"Do you expect my eyes to pop?" Margaret asked.

"Something like." A lopsided smile lifted the corner of Lord Dade's newly exposed mouth in a most attractive fashion. Margaret felt as if she would have to learn all of his expressions anew. Again, the impression that she faced a stranger assailed her. She felt a little lost.

"Our friend Mr. Soames has been to a wedding today," she said as Creighton lurched out of the carriage.

"Bosky is he, and ripe to embarrass us all?"

Margaret was pleased he so readily understood their predicament. She made an effort to shake off her melancholy.

"Yes, and we would all greatly prefer my uncle was not privy to his condition."

"Of course." He smiled and gave her hand a reassuring squeeze. "We shall see if it cannot be managed."

Margaret thought him appropriately gallant in that moment, less the pirate and more the gentleman than ever as he offered to look after Creighton. She was inordinately pleased he had chosen to wait to walk her up. She felt like a lady on his arm, despite the fact he hooked his other arm through Creighton's and was forced to abandon his hold on her more than once that he might steady his inebriated friend. Together the three of them followed the rest of the party of Torntons beneath the awning and through the doors—the knight, his lady, and the court fool.

The smell struck her first, even before she had stepped inside: an exotic mixture of sawdust, horses and oranges. Her nostrils flared in anticipation. This promised to be something quite different, she could tell, despite the added complication of Creighton's drunkenness.

Beyond the doors, a blaze of light and color assaulted her senses. Margaret felt as intoxicated as Creighton for the moment, without benefit of a drop of liquor. She was forced to stop and gape, head swiveling dizzily to take it all in. Four ranks of brightly painted and gilded boxes reached to the high ceiling. In the golden light provided not only by windows in the ceiling but by myriad lamps circling a furiously modern fixture that dangled above the center of a huge ring of pale, raked sawdust, everything glittered.

"Oh, my!" She could not stop a smile of childlike wonder from taking possession of her lips. "This is magical! Grand and glittery and absurdly common all at once."

"Too damned bright in here by far," Creighton complained, shielding his eyes.

Dade ignored him. "The real magic begins, Pearl"—he whispered provocatively in Margaret's ear—"when Astley's trained horses step into the ring." He pointed, and in so doing, his shoulder came in contact with hers. Shivering, Margaret realized there was more than one sort of magic to be found on a night like this.

The stage at the far end of the ring was enormous, three

stories tall, with intriguing levels and platforms of a size big enough to hold a coach and four.

Surrounded by such opulence, Margaret was glad she had donned her favorite gown for the occasion, an attractive confection of satin and velvet in a cheerful golden yellow color that was referred to as primrose. She was glad her bared shoulders were covered by a dark blue, sarcenet-lined merino cloak with honeycombed yellow satin running up each side of the back and across her shoulders and bosom. In anything less she would have faded into insignificance. The style of her cloak had been dubbed the Wellington mantle the previous year. Margaret considered it the perfect attire for a reenactment of Wellington's most famous ordeal. She hoped to catch Lord Dade's eye with such an outfit. She was not disappointed. Every time the viscount turned to look at her, his eyes warmed in the most gratifying manner. Yet his very interest filled her with an unfulfilled sort of sadness. Too soon he meant to absent himself from her life.

"You fairly glitter in this light" was what he leaned down to say to her.

She shivered again, as if she were cold. It was not the temperature that troubled her. Her chill was provoked by the proximity of the tall, dark gentleman beside her in this place that filled her with a sense of imminent change. Margaret felt as if she were caught up in the sleight of hand of some grand magician who meant to dazzle not just her eyes but all of her senses at once.

"This is a glorious place," she said.

Dade smiled, but Soames laughed, rolled his eyes theatrically and said with jaded ennui, "There is no glory here. It is all a glittering sham, but an amusing sham for all that. I hope you do not mind, but I have the distinct feeling that Ev means to give you a tour of the place, and as I've seen it all before, I shall just toddle off and chat with Aurthur Pendley. He has had a set of Waterloo teeth made up especially for the occasion tonight. Do you see him grinning at me? I must go and get a gander at them." With a reeling bow, he did just that.

Beside her, Lord Dade went rigid. The impression was a passing one.

"Come," he said. "We fall behind the others. Watch pockets and purse, Pearl, for if anything is snatched we will never be able to catch the thief in this crush."

It was true. Astley's was an obstacle course. There were so many people milling about in so little space! Margaret had never before encountered such a crowd. There were all different kinds of people bumping elbows, as though someone had scooped up a great handful of folk from the busiest street corner in London and dumped them here.

There was something frightening about such a churning, odiferous crush of humanity. Margaret did not realize her feeling was anything more than excitement until for an instant, due to the rowdiness of the crowd, she was separated from Lord Dade's arm. Fear became a cognitive thing then. And her impending loss seemed larger than ever. Lord Dade seemed to be letting go of her. She was immensely grateful when he battled his way against the press to return to her side.

"Almost lost you." His voice was breathless with the same level of concern she had been feeling in the pit of her stomach. She was pleased he did not want to lose her.

"For now, I am rescued." She tucked her arm in his.

Through the gathering crowd they plunged. The ascent to the box was fascinating. Margaret could not get her fill of looking, even when they settled with the others in the cramped confines of their box. She sat on the edge of her chair, gazing with delight at the crowd. She did not really realize how close the seats in the box were arranged until she leaned back and found herself hip to hip, shoulder to shoulder, elbow to elbow, with Lord Dade, who took out a pair of opera glasses he had rented and handed them to her so that she might continue her peering to greater advantage.

So pleasing was the lovely shivery feeling she got every time she, or the man beside her, moved that her interest in the glittering crowd soon focused itself on but one man. Despite the dull roar of the crowd, Margaret became quite intimate with the unique rustle of fabric that was Lord Dade's coat raking against his starched shirtfront. None of the sumptuously dressed people who passed could divert her attention from the sleeve of blue superfine that occasionally slid against her elbow. Like the ripples in a pond, Evelyn Dade's every move caused an eddying sensation deep within Margaret's chest. Her entire being seemed taut and bursting, like the tender green point of a hyacinth just breaking through the dark surface of the ground. She could feel her blood running hot and fast, the sap in a tree in springtime. Something within her was ready to burst forth, something wonderful, colorful and true. The feeling had something elemental to do with the man beside her. The humming energy between them, which she had felt so many times before, was stronger today, as though Lord Dade's intimate proximity and the buzzing bee-like voice of the crowd somehow intensified its strength.

She looked about her a bit wildly. Were her thoughts writ too plainly on her face? Celia turned to smile at her. Her uncle shared a passing remark. No one seemed to notice the change within her, no one but Lord Dade. He noticed. She was sure of it. The careful way he breathed, the vibrating tension between them whenever they brushed against each other, told her it was so. She was afraid to look directly at the viscount, afraid he would have an immediate awareness of the heated stirring that burned within her veins like too much wine. She was too afraid of her own strange feelings to relax.

Not so the others. Her uncle seemed intent on having a good time. He laughed and pointed and clapped in appreciation as a troupe of clowns, mounted on the tiniest ponies Margaret had ever seen, trotted into the ring. Allan and Wallis were more impressed by the acrobats who tumbled and leapt and walked on wires.

"Bravo!" they shouted after each daring demonstration.

Her sisters exclaimed and gasped, declaring themselves dazzled and amused. Only Margaret and Lord Dade remained silent. Margaret could not help but think that this strange friction between them, this new and bubbling feeling within her veins and in every part of her anatomy that came into glancing contact with the man beside her, was more interesting and vital and glittering than anything that went on in the ring.

Dade watched her. The heated intensity of his gaze warmed her cheek and neck and lip. Nothing in the ring so absorbed him as she did. She burned with the power of this attentive regard, as if each time he looked at her, he reached out with a flaming finger and touched her. She could not, would not, turn to look at him. His pointed concentration imbued within her too much danger, too much rushing life.

The horses, as promised, made an impression from the moment they trotted into the ring. Margaret was momentarily distracted from Lord Dade's focused regard, distracted from the singing heat in her veins. Individually and in ranks, these clever, exquisitely groomed animals cantered into the ring, moving as one with the men and women who nimbly clung to their backs, sitting or standing. Manes and tails floating like silk, haunches gleaming and feet carefully blacked, these creatures seemed to have little in common with the average coach horse. They knelt and bowed, leapt obstacles, even stood upon their hind legs on command. Because Lord Dade had mentioned them specifically, and because Margaret so completely agreed with his assessment of their beauty, she dared at last to share a glance with him. "They are sublime!" she breathed.

Their eyes met, hers glowing with enjoyment and surprise, his unexpectedly open to her, unguarded of their feeling for her. He cared for her! Cared for her opinion. She could see it all in a glance. He found her as wonderful, as beautiful, as moving and awe-inspiring as anything she had just observed. The power of that open admission of his regard for her—indeed, his desire for her—shook Margaret to her toes. For one wildly irrational moment she wanted nothing more than for Evelyn Dade to touch her in some way, that the spell in which his gold-flecked eyes caught her might be broken. She could not move a muscle. It was even difficult to breathe. Deep in the dark centers of his eyes, Dade read her feelings for him as clearly as she read his.

It was her uncle who broke the suspended heartbeat. "Marvelous," he exclaimed, leaning back from the front row. "Isn't this marvelous?"

Lord Dade's devastating eyes released their hold on her. Margaret's paralysis ended.

"Magical," she said softly, the word catching in her throat.

Chapter 14

A CLOSER look at the horses was what the others went seeking when a short intermission was declared before the main event.

"Does everyone wish to come?" Margaret's uncle asked. Dade was surprised to hear Pearl decline. He had been sure she would go where Wallis went.

"I should like to remain here, if you do not mind, Uncle. I do not care to be pushed about by so many people." She slid a swift glance in Dade's direction.

He felt as if his heart had skipped a beat. Such a glance gave him the impression she meant to be alone with him.

Wallis urged her to reconsider. "Oh, but you must come."

Her uncle nodded. "I cannot leave you here by yourself, my dear."

"I mean to stay as well," Dade said calmly, though his blood raced with an unruly desire to shove them all bodily out of the box so that he could be alone with his Pearl.

Lord Dornton agreed to abandon his niece to Lord Dade's care. The two were left to themselves. An orange girl, who sold sweetmeats and fruit from a basket tied to her waist, was the only intruder to bother them. They sat peeling oranges and chatting, with only a hint of the tension between them, which made the Pearl's hands tremble when she took off her gloves, in order that they not be stained by the juice of the fruit she pulled into pieces.

Feeling strangely guilty that he should be trusted so implicitly with the one female that might give him reason to break such a trust, Dade kept an eye on the crowd below as the pungent smell of citrus filled the box and bits of orange peel fell at their feet. Crowds fascinated him. Their reactions to the spectacles they watched fascinated him. That was part of the reason why he had spent so much time watching Pearl's reactions to the horses and clowns and tightrope walkers in the ring. He would have watched her even had he not fallen in love with her. Her reaction, the reaction of the uninitiated, the unspoiled, was at least as edifying as watching the antics of paid performers.

"I hear you no longer go to public executions at Newgate," he heard her say as if from a distance—just as he spotted Creighton and his cronies in the lower ring of seats. Creighton was entertaining his friends with both word and gesture. Dade's eyes slid over them and would have passed on had not something caught and held his attention even as he formulated an answer for her with regard to the executions.

"Yes," he said slowly, distracted. The entire bevy of gentlemen that Creighton stood amongst had begun to look in their direction. Dade got a sinking feeling when so many heads swiveled as one to peer up at him. They laughed, these young men who had never seen war, other than on the stage, especially the one Creighton had identified as Aurthur Pendley. His new Waterloo teeth gleamed in the light as he threw back his head to bray.

Dade could think of only one thing that might so amuse Creighton and his cronies. In his state of inebriation Creighton entertained his friends with a juicy slice of gossip that had something to do either with himself or with the lovely young woman who sat sectioning an orange into her lap beside him. Dade leaned back, his mind alive with the notion that whatever Creighton's companions found amusing, he and Pearl would not find it half so entertaining.

"My lord? Is something wrong? You have the strangest look." Miss Dornton's observant gray eyes fixed on him.

Unwilling to alarm her with his fears, he tried to pick up

the conversation where she had left off. "About Newgate. Your informant is correct," he murmured. "I am no longer fascinated with watching men die. I have found . . . other subjects that intrigue me as much as death ever did." He referred to his fascination for her, of course, but he would never come clean and say as much aloud. Dade thought he wanted Margaret Dornton to fall comfortably into Wallis's arms. Not his own. He was convinced she would be far better off with someone like Wallis.

Her cheeks went pink, as if she read his thoughts and was embarrassed by them. "I am glad to hear you no longer frequent such places," she said, and went on to ask him with her characteristic earnestness, as she concentrated too intently on selecting one of the sections of the orange, "Will you tell me, I wonder. Why did you go to places of death?" She slid a quick glance his way and popped a piece of the fruit in her mouth, as if to stop more questions from tumbling free.

Dade sighed, his thoughts still distracted by Creighton. "You ask a question, Pearl, to which you may find you do not really want to know the answer."

"Perhaps." She swallowed her mouthful, and he found himself quite foolishly marveling over the working of her mouth and throat. "How can one come to understand a thing unless one asks questions?" she asked him.

"And this thing you would understand?"

She pointed a crescent of fruit at him. "Is you, of course, my lord. Do you mind so much that I would try?"

He said nothing for a moment, merely looked at her, committing the way she looked at him in this instant to his memory. He would remember this conversation whenever he smelled oranges. "I do not understand myself."

"Do you feel, then, that no one can?" She bit into another section of orange. Juice dripped from her lips.

He extended to her the use of his handkerchief. Their fingers met in the exchange. She had such a look in her eyes, such a softness to her mouth as a result of that brief encounter of their flesh, that it occurred to him that of all the people who might ask him such a question, perhaps this was the one who would actually listen to his answer.

Her hand and gaze fell away as she daubed her chin.

"The reason I went to executions, Pearl"—he began. Her head rose abruptly. The handkerchief paused in midair—"was because in death I sought the quickness of life, bright and brief, like the pinched-out light of a candle. I went to witness man's reaction to such a snuffing."

"What?" The orange lay forgotten in her lap, a pale sun lying heavily on his handkerchief, crescent moons fanned across the monogrammed square of lawn that protected her golden yellow gown, which sagged into the sweet universe between the tops of her legs.

"You would listen for the last whisper of life, as it slips from a desperate man's lips, before a crowd of callous individuals who have hardened their hearts and souls against the fragile beauty and purpose of being?"

Thc question drew his gaze away from the dangerous curve of her thighs. He looked at her face. It wore a pained look. He had been right to suppose she would not like to hear the answer to her question.

"But sir, surely you will not tell me you actually found the true essence of life in such places?"

"No? And why do you think I would not?"

She continued to regard him with her deep, mcasuring look—a wise gray-eyed stare that captured his imagination far more than any hanging had ever done. The sweet disposition of her mouth as she spoke, her lips, still dewed with the juice of her orange, became an object of desire. He wanted to kiss those lips between each word, to taste the orange flavor of her truth there. He could tell by the tone of her voice that she cared for his well-being and peace of mind as no one else in his acquaintance ever had.

"The sweet breath of existence is what goes on bctween birth and death," she said urgently, echoing the tone of some reverent and kindly old nun. "It is caught up in the small folds of time that pass away with every tick of the clock."

His eyes strayed to the orange caught in the folds of her lap.

She went on, oblivious to his focus. "Life is to be found and experienced in the simplest of moments, pure and perfect moments. It is to be witnessed"—she held out her hand so that it passed through a golden shaft of the lamplit straw dust that floated in the air about them—"in the golden beauty of a dust mote floating in the wind. Life is to be heard in the voice of a crowd." She turned her head to scan the audience around them, and the low roar of its combined voices filled their ears. "Life can be touched in the softness of velvet"—she stroked the sash bound just beneath the fullness of her breast. Dade's imagination played with the image of stroking a very different softness.

He picked up where she had left off, his voice low and slow and suggestive of the lurid thoughts that filled his mind, "It can be tasted . . ."

Oh, how he would like to taste of her, he thought. His mouth echoed the tenor of his thoughts.

"—tasted in the firm . . . wet . . . flesh . . ."

Her eyes widened and her lips parted on a gasp as he reached into her lap for one of the sections of orange still fanned out across his handkerchief. The fruit went into his mouth without his ever finishing the thought.

The silence between them stretched.

"Of an orange?" she ventured, uneasy with the open-ended sentence, her gaze leaping from his lips to her lap and back again.

He smiled and arched an eyebrow as he chewed and thought of other flesh he would like to savor. It had been a long time since such a hunger had teased him, and the desire seemed stronger and sweeter than he remembered perhaps because of that lapse.

She had run out of things to say. Her face was touched by the color of embarrassment. She read some hint of what he was thinking without full knowledge of the subject and reacted with instinctive reserve.

He was staring at her intently, hoping she would look up at him again instead of at the fruit in her lap. "Could it be that sometimes life is caught up in the glowing eyes of someone who voices profound and original thoughts?" He was not disappointed. Her gaze, when she raised it, reflected both the sparkle of the lights in the center of the ring and the turmoil of her thoughts.

A pair of pearl gray eyes widened. She realized he was referring to her and did not know how to respond.

His right hand rose to push a curl away from her cheek. "Is life, then, to be found in a lock of hair, falling just so, on the face of a loved one?"

She did not know where to look. Her hands clutched uneasily at the remains of the orange in her lap, and her voice faltered. "Y-yes, small, simple things."

"Flighty creature, life. A bit like love."

Her gaze flicked his way as she wet her lips, uneasy with this mention of love, uneasy with the touch of his hand on her hair. "I suppose so."

"I have chased it in all the wrong places."

Before she could wipe the stunned look from her face and respond, they were silenced by the return of her sisters and Allan and Wallis.

"Father has gone outside to blow a cloud," Allan said.

"He would not do so within the ampitheater, where there is so much sawdust," Celia explained.

"For fear of fire," Wallis finished the thought.

The mention of fire brought a frown to Margaret Dornton's already troubled countenance and gave Dade cause to search once more the crowd beneath their box for signs of Creighton. The danger of fire was not the only one they faced this evening.

What he saw did not please him. Like waves spreading from a pebble thrown into a pond, ripples of gossip seemed to have spread from the area where Creighton and his fellows had been standing. In an ever widening circle, heads were turning, curious, amused faces lifted to stare, an occasional finger raised to point. They were all of them looking up at the box where he sat with the Dornton party.

Evelyn would have gotten up then to chase down Creighton and shake from him the truth as to what he had gone blabbing about had not the culprit chosen that moment to enter their box and plop himself down on the other side of Margaret.

Chapter 15

THE lights dimmed as Creighton joined them. Margaret looked about for her uncle, still concerned that he would discover Mr. Soames's state of inebriation. Luckily for them all, Lord Dornton was not yet returned from his smoke. Dade, when she turned to glance at him, was studying Creighton.

The main attraction began. A staged village, illuminated only by torches and firelight, was traversed by a woman costumed as a peasant, who related the horrors of her existence to Prussian patrols. The Prussians were largely unsympathetic, but Margaret leaned forward in her seat, moved by the woman's plight, player though she might be, nothing but a fiction on horseback. A group of French farriers struck sparks from the glowing work at their anvils, in time to a carefree refrain, before a bugle announced the entry of Napoleon and his retinue.

"Gomersal," Creighton announced.

"What?" Margaret was distracted.

"Shh!" the others hissed at him.

Mr. Soames felt it necessary to lean very close to her ear to explain. "The young man playing the part of Napoleon. Name's Gomersal, and very like in appearance to the real thing, so I am told."

"Is he like?" Margaret turned to ask of Dade so that

Creighton would let go of her shoulder and breathe his hot, moist, brandied breath someplace other than her ear.

Dade nodded, eyes straying only briefly from the action in the ring. "Prodigiously so," he said softly. "Height, attitude, stance. It is eerie. The horse he rides is the very image of the animal Napoleon favored." He fell silent, his eyes locked on the unfolding action, a man mesmerized.

Margaret, on the other hand, found it difficult to concentrate on anything going on in the ring. Her attention was otherwise occupied. Creighton Soames had grown amorous in his inebriated state. The first nudges of his elbow, shoulder and knee she assumed to be no more than the accidental contact that sometimes occurs when too many people are crammed into too little space. When she had shifted herself out of his way three times, though, and his limbs came again into play with hers, she had to acknowledge that his moves were made with lecherous forethought.

What was she to do under such circumstances? She had no idea. Perhaps saying something brusque and a good shove would serve. Perhaps it would it be better to ignore him. To continue staring at the display in the ring as if there was nothing untoward in a gentleman shamelessly pressing his arm into hers, while his boot dallied with the hem of her skirt, was wearing her nerves raw. She found herself scowling. Margaret did not like to scowl. Celia might have told her how to handle Creighton, but in order to consult her elder sister she must lean over both Creighton and Wallis. That would not do.

Creighton nudged his knee against hers.

Margaret jerked away. She would have liked to gasp along with the crowd as they evidenced genuine concern when a skirmish in the ring resulted in a mounted trooper being dragged out of the arena by a racing horse, his foot theatrically caught up in the stirrup. She could not follow what went on before her very eyes. Her attention was focused, unprovisionally, on the anguish of having her body touched when she possessed not the slightest desire that it should be so assaulted. Her arm where it grazed Creighton's sleeve, her knee too as she pulled away for the second time from his unwanted touch, seemed awkward and weighty. She could not seem to find a position in which Soames could not make himself free with her in some mortifying manner unless she climbed into Lord Dade's lap. It was demeaning. Margaret had always assumed gentlemen would regard her with a respect equal to that which she regarded herself. She had never dreamed that someone might attempt to press unwelcome attentions upon her.

That was not wholly true. She had at one time imagined that Lord Dade, or Captain Dead, as she had thought of him at the time, was the sort of fellow capable of such behavior. Ironically, it was the affable Mr. Soames who made himself a pest. Margaret was daring enough to have tested the boundaries of proper etiquette, and yet she was a novice. She did not know how to combat any real assault on the mores she had spent most of her life learning.

It would not be ladylike to scream, or to strike the man beside her. How could she go about asking for assistance without shaming both herself and those around her? Her uncle returned from his smoke, smelling of cigar, but she could not bring herself to request his assistance as he settled in the row of seats in front of hers. He was sure to realize Creighton was foxed.

Dade had been ready to pounce on Creighton the moment he entered the box, to discover what mischief Soames had been brewing, but Creighton was too drunk to discuss anything rationally. Disgusted, yet willing to wait for Soames to sober up now that the damage was done, he turned his back on Creighton and concentrated on the reenactment. In a strangely removed manner, it allowed Dade to observe a dark piece of his past.

So affected by the drama before him did Dade become that he did not observe the drama unfolding beside him in the dark. Long numb to reaction with regard to the war, it surprised him—shocked him, in fact—that a play concerning death and battle should at last touch the dormant pain within him where executions and dissections had not.

The sounds and smells of battle washed over him with unexpected impact. The clash of swords, the crack of musket ball, the booming of cannon, and over all, the acrid tang of gunpowder hit him directly in the abdomen like a blow. He felt doubled over by it, as flags fluttered and horses charged and uniforms glittered in the artificial light of the arena. Explosions and gunfire sent both horses and riders into mock poses of death—poses painful to witness, far more painful than any hanging at Newgate had proven. This playacting at war was real and surreal and wrenchingly familiar.

So long stoic and cold and calmly emotionless about the war, Dade found his eyes cloudy with tears, his throat tight with an unvoiced cry and his ears ringing oddly—as if to shut out the sounds of men shouting and bayonets clashing, over the constant thunder of galloping hooves as more than two hundred horses took to the ring and stage to recreate the deafening fury of a day of infamy.

As the mock battle raged, Margaret fought her own. She considered her position untenable. Withdrawing her knee from its light contact with Creighton's, she was angered by his continued pursuit of it. She glared at the man, only to have him smile loosely back at her—a gleaming, seductive smile in the half-light that had melted the hearts of many a maid before her. Margaret did not melt. She cracked the bone fan she carried across his knee. He chuckled, as if he had won points in a game she did not know how to play. Catching her fan in one hand, he touched the bare spot between the buttons that fastened her glove to wrist with his other.

With the feeling she fenced with a master and would soon find herself pinked if she did not closely guard her defenses, Margaret pulled away.

Cheers resounded from the audience as some Prussians were rescued from drowning. Margaret was left with the queer feeling that the cheers were meant for Creighton. He was, after all, winning the battle between them.

Dade's hand rose briefly to shut out the sight of the mock battle that raged. He could not guard his eyes forever behind the flat of his palm, though, so he diverted his gaze from the proceedings, concentrating instead on the fair curve of feminine cheekbone beside him. It seemed odd to Dade that while horses charged and fell, Miss Margaret Dornton could murmur something to Creighton Soames that made him chuckle richly with appreciation. In that lighthearted exchange Dade realized just how vast the chasm yawned between his perception of battle and theirs. What did innocence know of death and anguish and dying? Nothing. The innocent could not truly comprehend and still remain innocent. He, having steeped himself in awareness and worldly knowledge, could never again return to innocence. He might approximate the behavior of one unjaded by reality, but innocence, pure, blind, unknowing innocence, was never to be his again.

Margaret decided to ignore Creighton. Withdrawing as far from him as she could, she pointedly turned her face away from his and concentrated on the drama that went on in the ring. Ignoring Creighton proved a problem. He took her silence as some form of encouragement. Folding his arms, he discreetly began to prod her arm with her stolen fan, while his boot tip sought out her slipper.

Before her eyes, Blucher's horse was shot out from under him, while a throng of uniformed horse and foot fought over a fabricated bridge that connected two parts of the stage. Certainly, she thought, Blucher's predicament was no more perilous than her own.

A cheer sounded from the crowd as a familiar flag rippled in the breeze of the passage of men and horses. Wellington's troops were reviewed immediately before charging into an armed confrontation with a French division. Rifles cracked, cannon boomed, men pitched from the backs of rearing animals. The Duke of Brunswick, played by the actor Ducrow, died very movingly on horseback.

And yet Margaret saw little and enjoyed less. She burned with humiliation that she sat, completely ignored, beside the only man whose caress she might have allowed under cover of darkness, while his inebriated and unwelcome friend annoyed her with what she deemed completely inappropriate contact. She kicked Creighton's leg, only to find that Soames expected such tactics. He trapped her foot by nonchalantly crossing his boots at the ankle, catching her slipper between flexed calves.

"Stop that!" She hissed, stamping her free foot rather ineffectually against the leather of his boot. Creighton found her efforts amusing. With a suggestive wink he reached down to stroke her trapped ankle.

Beside her, Dade shifted in his seat. "Excuse me," he murmured, his voice gruff. Clearing his throat with what sounded like disgust, he stood abruptly and left the box as the booming, cracking, flashing thunder of the horse play reached a crescendo.

A mock village caught fire. Costumed peasants ran for their lives, against a backdrop of Highlanders being gunned down in a field of corn. The action focused on two who could not run. A woman with a babe in arms was trapped in one of the burning facades. Her screams sent a frisson of terror racing down Margaret's spine. The mother and babe were in danger of being consumed by the fire! The image struck at the core of Margaret's deepest fears.

"No!" she whispered, one hand pressed to her mouth, the other clutching the flat of her stomach.

Beside her, Creighton released his hold on her foot and leaned over to leer in her face.

Two Prussian soldiers raced to the rescue, only to be turned back by the imagined heat from red silk flames.

"No! No!" No other thought could fit itself into Margaret's consumed mind. "No, no, no," she whispered as the flames licked higher. Tears slipped down her cheeks.

Creighton caught some essence of the power of her reaction to the scene. He backed away from touching her, flicking uneasy, clouded glances from her face to what went on in the ring. "It's only make-believe," he said.

A horseman raced onto the scene, charging the animal right up to the the smoking doorway. With a flurry of his cloak Napoleon himself plunged into the flames and carried the woman and child to safety. The audience applauded enthusiastically. Margaret could not be soothed by the happy outcome of this staged production. There had been no valiant, caped horseman to come charging to the rescue when her baby brother had been threatened by flames. The pain of it was shockingly fresh for something that had taken place so very long ago. Margaret tried to breathe through the ache in her chest, but when the rescued woman held up the babe that Napoleon might kiss it, she could not go on watching. Turning her back on a horror she preferred not to relive, Margaret made her way to the back of the box.

Old images, ugly images, images far more moving than anything she might witness on a stage, flooded her mind. With a clarity that astounded her, they washed out of the deep recesses of her memory with such vividness that she clutched the wall by the arch that led out of the box, knees gone watery, her ears still ringing with the screams of the woman so recently rescued. Stuffing a handkerchief that tasted faintly of orange in her mouth so that none might hear her, she began to shake with stifled sobs.

In the shadows of the archway, she froze thus, hand to mouth, her accelerated heartbeat thrumming loud in her ears as her tear-swollen eyes settled on Lord Dade, who paced toward her along the gallery that led to the stairs. Light and then shadow passed over his face as he passed the lamps on the wall, obscuring what message she might have read in his dark eyes. A lock of hair had fallen across his high forehead. He made no move to push it away. His hand rose instead to pass in an agitated manner over his mouth and chin, as though in search of the missing mustache and beard. When his hand fell away, his mouth seemed changed. His entire expression as he drew near was possessed by a bleakness she was not accustomed to.

Margaret could not bring herself to face anyone, not even Lord Dade, who probably understood better than any what she was going through. It looked as if he meant to reenter the box. Pulling the handkerchief from her mouth she made ready to return to her chair. Chin up, she thought, chin up! Perhaps no one would notice her swollen eyes.

But Lord Dade stopped outside the archway. With a heavy sigh he leaned against the wall, no more than an arm's length from where Margaret stood watching.

She held her breath and waited.

The tightness in Dade's jaw dissolved for the briefest instant. His features presented a picture of anguish. His posture was affected by an attitude of distress: eyes squeezed shut, head thrown forward, back arched. His throat spasmed, but no sound escaped. His whole body sagged. It looked as if he might slide down the wall given no more than a feather's push. There was in his expression the look of a man who has been kicked in his most vulnerable parts.

Never before had Margaret seen anyone in such anguish fight so hard to suppress all sounds of distress. His hands, white-knuckled, were balled into fists that he pressed into the wall. So exactly did the features before her mirror her own anguish that she could only stand and stare as a tide of pain washed through her answering heart.

A second gentleman appeared in the light of the wall sconce, come to the gallery from one of the adjoining boxes, a tortoise-shell cigar case in his one good hand. The other was missing, all the way up to the elbow.

Dade's posture underwent an immediate transformation. In the blink of an eye he pulled himself together and away from the wall.

"Captain Dade?" the newcomer said, his voice almost obliterated by the noise from the ring behind her, and yet Margaret heard enough to know he called Dade, not Dead.

"Lieutenant Boggs?"

"Yes, sir, though I'm no more a lieutenant these days then you are a captain. Damned difficult thing to watch, this reenactment. Don't you agree?"

The sleek seal brown head nodded. "I suppose we saw too much of the real thing to take pleasure in the imitation of such a moment."

"Saw and heard, tasted and smelled, sir." The lieutenant waved the case in his hand. "I took up this infernal habit to remove the memory of those tastes and smells. My wife hates the things."

"Do you dream, Boggs?" Dade asked in a low voice.

"Aye," Boggs laughed. "Another thing my wife puts up with, God bless her. I wake her now and again, flailing about, or letting loose with an occasional shout. I dream I've still got my hand, sir," Boggs admitted brokenly. "Every night, the same dream. I see it all again, up to the very moment when the hand was lost. I keep thinking, as I'm dreaming, that if I can but wake myself up before it is gone, I shall have the thing back again. Stupid really, but it is a living bit of hell. Not only do I lose the thing, but I must go on reliving the instant it was lost over and over again."

"We're all of us walking around in a bit of a nightmare, sleeping or waking," Dade said softly. Margaret closed her eyes against the wave of pain and understanding she suffered for these men and all those like them who had survived the war. Her own problems with Creighton seemed very small. Even the death of her brother seemed insignificant by comparison. They were dubious heroes all, she decided.

Chapter 16

"MAGGS. Your cloak."

It was Celia who nudged her shoulder, Celia whose soft voice reminded Margaret that she should not stand in the dark, eavesdropping on Lord Dade's conversation.

"Oh?" She turned to take the Wellington. In the ring and on the stage the battle escalated. Napoleon rode through his troops as they fell amid a volley of brilliant, smoking, shrieking Roman candles.

"Are we leaving?" she asked. It did not make sense, but everyone in their box had risen. All of them were donning hats, gloves, cloaks and reticules. "The performance is not finished." It had, in fact, reached spectacular zenith.

Celia looked worried. "I know. It is all on account of what some orange girl said to Uncle."

"An orange girl?"

"Yes, she leaned in over the partition to the box next door, whispered something to Uncle, even though he had told her twice he was not in the least interested in any of her goods. He looked quite shaken for a moment, and then asked me if I would mind changing seats with Allan. I complied. He whispered something in Allan's ear that made our poor cousin go white as a sheet. Then they were both asking me if I knew where you might be." Her gaze slid awkwardly toward the noisy, smoke-darkened ring. "I saw you get up. It was the fire that bothered you, wasn't it?"

Margaret nodded. Chin up, she thought. No more tears.

Her sister tucked her arm around her waist. "It bothered me too," she said with so much understanding that Margaret offered no resistance whatsoever to being led out of the box and onto the landing, where Lord Dade and his friend stood watching them, curiosity alive in their eyes.

"Is that the one called Pearl?" the one-armed man whispered to Lord Dade just loud enough that she heard him.

Margaret was shocked. This fellow, whom she had never met, knew her as Pearl?

"Is everything all right?" Lord Dade asked. There was something about the way he looked at her that made Margaret sure he had overheard her conversation with her sister.

"It would seem we are leaving," she said calmly.

"I see," his gaze moved past her to her uncle.

"Lord Dade," her uncle said with a serious look and a tone that was more proper than polite, "you do not mind seeing to Mr. Soames's getting home, do you? I do not care to have him casting up accounts in my carriage."

Dade nodded.

"Oh, yes, and would you do me the honor of meeting me for breakfast at my club? There is something I would like very much to discuss with you." Margaret thought her uncle looked quite perturbed. What might an orange girl say to upset him so?

"Boodles at eight, then?" Dade directed a last look at Margaret and they were off, the evening foreshortened, and only God, her uncle and an orange girl knew the reason.

The expression Margaret's uncle turned upon her as soon as the door to the carriage had enclosed the Dornton sisters and their cousin gave her the distinct feeling their leaving had something to do with her.

"I do not think you will be pleased when you hear the question that has been put to me by none other than an orange girl, Margaret," he said heavily.

"What is that?" she asked with a sinking feeling.

"She asked which of the young ladies was called Pearl."

Margaret looked at him dumbfounded, never anticipating what was to follow. "Why should an orange girl care what I am called?"

Her uncle's expression darkened. When Margaret looked at Allan for some hint of what had so upset her uncle, she found she had become an object of concern, even pity.

"She then asked me if it was true that you liked to dress in men's clothing"—her uncle's voice was gruff—"and whether it was true you frequented fencing salons often in such a state. She knew for a fact that you had leapt between two of your lovers before they killed each other with swords on one such occasion. She even dared to insinuate that I might be one of those lovers, for she had heard they were both in the box with you!"

Margaret blinked. At the root of this twisted growth of gossip was a seed of truth. What had blossomed from it, however, was almost comical in its error. She might have laughed had not her uncle looked so forbidding.

"Wherever did she hear such a Banbury tale?" Allan interrupted.

Her uncle's gaze traveled angrily from her face to Allan's. "Apparently the story was circulating widely tonight. I can only wish that I had heard some hint of the truth that lies at the bottom of such nonsense before all of London heard it. My guess is that you are the mysterious female who broke up Allan's sword fight with Lord Dade. Am I right?"

Margaret bit her bottom lip and nodded.

Celia and Celeste drew identical breath. Her uncle made a disgusted noise in the back of his throat. "You have deceived me, Margaret, in keeping this from me. Allan as well. I am gravely disappointed in the both of you!"

There was no room for argument.

As it happened, there was no arguing either on the following morning, when Dade met Lord Dornton at his club. Dornton began with the irrefutable statement that he was gravely disappointed in Lord Dade. He then very clearly, quietly, and ever so politely forbade Lord Dade from further contact with his nieces.

As a result of this unhappy breakfast, Dade went immediately to pay a call on Mr. Creighton Soames. He was informed at the door that Mr. Soames was still abed.

"Well, it is high time he got up." Dade strode past Creighton's astonished manservant.

It turned out, Creighton was up, risen in dire haste to cast up his accounts in a slop bucket placed beside the bed for that very purpose. He sagged against the washstand that occupied one corner of his room in a spoiled nightshirt, splashing water onto his face and mouth. He groaned and almost lost elbow's purchase on the marble top of the washstand when Dade knocked briskly on his chamber door.

"Creighton!"

"Oh God, Dade!" he winced. "You need not knock. Just come in quietly, if you will."

"You are looking a trifle out of curl this morning." Dade bit out the words as he pragmatically resisted slamming his fist into Creighton's perfect Grecian nose.

Creighton's shoulders rose around his ears. He turned a pained, bloodshot look on Dade, pushed himself up off the washstand and clapped his hands to his ears. "Don't shout," he croaked, face, hair and hands dripping. "Don't say a word . . ." He freed one guarded ear to reach unsuccessfully for the folded linen that was meant to dry his face, knocked it to the floor, waved at it in disgust and staggered back to his bed, where he sat down heavily and used the edge of his pillowcase for a towel. "My head cannot stand another peal rung over it this morning," he rasped. "Be a good sport and come back when I am completely sober."

"Another peal?"

Creighton winced and pulled the pillow over the top of his head, muffling his ears. "Yes, you have been preceded this dreadful morning by both Mr. Eckhart and Mr. Dornton."

"And what did Wallis and Allan have to say?"

Creighton sank back in the mattress, the pillow still cradling his head. "They both came at the crack of dawn, in a terrific state of agitation for such an early hour, one right after the other." He moaned into the pillow. "Rattled me off without mercy at the top of their lungs, both of them. I've a splitting head as a result."

"You've a splitting head on account of all the brandy you

guzzled yesterday, and you have yet to reveal what it was that Wallis and Allan wanted."

"Wanted? To pile guilt and recriminations upon my already miserable head. What else? Is that not why you came?" He moaned into the pillow again.

"Of course. But I hate to be redundant. Tell me what they chewed you over for, and if they have covered all of the necessary ground, I will leave you in peace. If not, you will hear my bit too." Revolted by the awful smell in the room, Dade crossed to the window, threw back the drapes and lifted the window sash.

"Argh!" Creighton drew the bedcovers over his face, on top of the already clutched pillow. "Must you?"

"Yes, it reeks of vomit in here."

Dade kindly recovered the window most of the way and placed a chair in the fresh draft of the breeze that occasionally parted the drapes. "Indulge me, Cray. What have Wallis and Allan said to you? You see, if anything pertinent has been left out of the little scolding they have given you, I intend to follow up in terms you will not forget."

Creighton gave a muffled moan and pushed the covers off his head. "All of it?" His bloodshot eyes peered warily at Dade from around the pillow.

"Every word," Dade said softly.

"You cannot be serious," Creighton squawked.

"The sooner you begin, the sooner you will be rid of me," Dade said calmly. Taking out his pocket watch, he checked the time.

"Oh, all right," Creighton sighed gustily. Arranging the pillow behind his head instead of on top of it, he stared at the ceiling and began to recite in as bland a monotone as he could muster, "Allan said I was an unbelievably uncouth and totty-headed clunch who did not know any better than to get himself drunk as a wheelbarrow. Wallis said I better belonged under a table in a sluicery than in a box with polite company. He called me a cow-hearted, hen-witted, loose fish of a maw worm—"

Dade interrupted. "Dispense with the bestial comparisons. It sounds as if you have been adequately insulted."

Creighton nodded, muttering, "I had no idea those nice young men were schooled in such language, but they managed to come up with several epitaphs I had never heard before."

"Get on with it," Dade said. "What else?"

Creighton rolled his eyes moodily at the ceiling. "You know what they were on about."

"Tell me." Dade was relentless.

"My loose tongue. Appears it was well oiled yesterday. I told them both I hadn't the foggiest idea to what they referred. Wallis looked like he meant to hit me. Can you picture it? He said I had ruined weeks worth of effort on their part and yours. Said never to show my face anywhere near the Dorntons again. Said that it should not prove too difficult a task, even for me, seeing as the girls were all packing to leave London in disgrace and would be hibernating in the country because of me. Said that since he meant to marry one of the sisters, I was to be cut from his list of friends and acquaintances and would I do him the honor of refraining from addressing him in public. Dornton said much the same."

There was regret in Creighton's delivery of this portion of the conversation, but Dade's interest had fixed itself on Wallis's declaration with regard to marriage. He meant to marry a Dornton, did he?

"Wallis means to save one of the Dorntons from ruin?" He had to be certain.

"Yes. That comes as no real surprise. I've seen just such an end approaching for weeks now."

"Have you indeed?" Dade's voice was faint. The stench in the room was beginning to overpower his patience. "I have not been so observant," he said tersely.

Creighton leaned up out of the bed to sip from a glass of rhubarb on the table beside it. He made a face and sank back against the pillows. "Well, I was bloody well thrilled to hear him say as much, as you may well imagine. I should not have cared to feel obliged to offer for the girl myself for no more reason than a loose tongue."

Dade was not listening. He was peering through the drapes at the hazy brown pall of coal soot that clouded the view of London's rooftops. His hopes had just fallen under an equally ugly pall. He shook himself, but the dark cloud was not to be flung off so easily. "You said the Horntons meant to return to the country?"

"Tomorrow, according to Allan."

"So soon?" Evelyn twitched the drapes back into place over the ugly view. "Well, then, I've no more time to waste in your company, have I, Creighton?" He made for the door.

Creighton sat up in the bed. "No lecture, Ev? I say, that's bloody decent of you."

"Decent, Mr. Soames?" Dade paused in the doorway to spit the words out between clenched teeth. "You've no real notion of the meaning of the word."

Chapter 17

"YOU must return to your parents." Lord Dornton made his decree from his chair by the fire in the drawing room that evening, when he had heard the whole story of the fencing match from Margaret and Allan. "In fact, it would be best if all of my nieces returned to the care of their mother."

"But, Father!" Allan objected.

"Silence!" Lord Dornton thundered. "This is not a matter open to negotiation."

Margaret looked at her aunt for reaction.

Charlotte Dornton's hands fluttered as her son opened his mouth again. "No, Allan," she said softly, "you must not argue. I am sure your father knows what is best. I shall personally hate to see the girls go, but I must support your father's decision. You do understand, Margaret?"

Margaret nodded, her heart like a lump of lead in her throat. This was her fault, entirely her fault.

Her aunt struggled to remain cheerful. "Now, do not be downhearted. We've one evening's entertainment left."

Her uncle's severity was unrelieved. "It would be wise to avoid public gatherings, where this dreadful wave of gossip will take the shine off of any pleasure to be had."

Her aunt quietly disagreed. "I have decided on an evening at Vauxhall, watching the fireworks!"

Margaret's uncle frowned. "You would go to so public a place after last night's fiasco?"

His wife nodded emphatically. "Yes. You must not object, Harold. I would not have the girls go away thinking themselves completely unpresentable. I mean, in this small way, to exhibit my love and support for them."

"This is foolishness!" Lord Dornton warned her.

Dade went straight from Creighton to call on Allan, chancing on him in the narrow lane where Mr. Dornton took bachelor's lodgings.

"Dornton!" Dade shouted to the driver of the passing carriage even as it rounded the corner. The horses were pulled in. Allan greeted him with a concerned expression and the roving glance of someone who feared being caught engaged in illegal activity.

"My lord," he said, and with great difficulty at last met Dade's eye. "I am dreadfully sorry the way things have worked out. My father—"

Dade held up a hand. "Most unfortunate, I agree, but not so much for us as it is for your cousins. I understand they mean to remove to the country tomorrow?"

"Yes. Father thought it best."

"And Wallis goes with them?"

"Yes, sir. I go too. Father will be glad to see the backside of me." He laughed uneasily. "I beg your pardon for his inability to recognize you are in no way to be blamed for Margaret's escapades."

Dade licked his lips and clutched the side of the carriage with undue pressure. "Yes, I should like to part with all of your family on better terms, but most of all your cousin Margaret. Will you pass that on to her?"

Allan nodded. "Of course. I wish I could do more."

Dade backed away from the carriage with the strangely unbalanced feeling that he was losing something vital. With a sinking sensation the old darkness welled up within him, surged over him. Life was bolting out from beneath him, and there was nothing he could do to stop it. His voice was uncertain as he managed the niceties, saying, "Safe journey,

Dornton. I hope we may encounter each other at some future date under happier circumstances."

He would have walked away without the slightest hope of encountering Miss Margaret Dornton before she left for the country had not Allan pulled his carriage up beside him, shouting, "Sir! My lord! You might be . . . I mean . . ." He seemed not to know exactly how to relay what he had to say.

Dade pushed the darkness from his thoughts and grasped at this pale ray of hope. "What? Out with it, Dornton!"

Allan grinned at him. "We intend to go out tonight, all of us except Father. One last hurrah, you see, to view fireworks at Vauxhall."

Dade smiled, a surge of hope rising in his chest like a sparkling Roman candle. "I've a sudden desire to see a few sparklers myself," he said.

"Indeed, sir." Allan chuckled. "I thought you might."

To Vauxhall the Dornton sisters went, in the company of their aunt and cousin. The party was subdued. They did all that one was expected to do in the Gardens. A prettily painted supper box was obtained near the shade of the Grove, and while Wallis and Allan bespoke their repast, the girls strolled with their aunt along the Grand Walk's awning-covered colonnade, examining a variety of paintings that were on exhibit. They were in turn examined by many of their peers. Any number of snubs were endured with straight backs and lifted chins, including one from Lady Sarah Jersey herself, whom they encountered in the Hermit's Walk on their way to view the transparency of the hermit and his hut. It occurred to Margaret they would soon be hermits themselves if everyone continued to turn nose up at them.

Returning to their box, they choked down expensive slices of ham and glasses of wine and endured an orchestral arrangement of Handel's work while a wave of whispers and turning heads spoiled both appetite and music. When, at nine, the clang of a bell signaled that it was time to gather to watch the cascade of a waterfall in a beautifully painted mountain scene that for fifteen minutes foamed over a miller's wheel, Aunt Charlotte, her face pink with embarrassment, made a painful point of approaching all of her friends and acquaintances in order that her nieces might be seen to have some contacts remaining in polite society. Aunt Charlotte was forcibly cheerful for the entire quarter of an hour. Margaret found her brittle smile and ebullient conversation excruciating to watch.

As they returned to their box for the remainder of the orchestral performance, Celia hissed into Margaret's ear, "This is quite possibly the worst evening I have ever experienced, thank you very much."

Hearing the exchange, Celeste caught up to her at the table to say, "Don't mind Celia. She is just unhappy to be leaving London in disgrace, without a single offer. Mama will not be pleased to see us return without prospects."

Margaret knew her mother would not be pleased. She was not particularly happy about the situation herself. Chastened by the lecture she had received the night before, and the knowledge that her uncle had breakfasted with Lord Dade that morning with the sole purpose of informing him he was no longer welcome company, Margaret empathized quite genuinely with her sisters. She found it difficult to smile this evening, difficult to imagine their return to Sherborne in shame. How would she go about explaining their unexpected expulsion from her uncle's house? Would she ever see Lord Dade again?

Only Allan seemed at his ease, despite his father's disappointment with his behavior. He even went so far as to pull Margaret aside at one point to whisper, with a conspiratorial grin, "When the fireworks start, you must offer to go with me to fetch refreshments."

Margaret regarded his mischievous expression with mistrust. "Why? What devilment are you up to? I would rather watch fireworks than carry jugs of arrack through a crowd of people who have nothing better to do than stare."

He arched his eyebrows at her with a secretive smile. "You will regret it mightily if you do not do as I ask."

Won over by her curiosity, Margaret followed him in one direction along the Grand Walkway while her aunt and sisters went the other. With a quick look over his shoulder, Allan avoided the most direct route to the kiosks where wine and arrack might be purchased. He set off down a pathway Margaret had been warned against taking—Lover's Walkway.

Margaret protested as she scurried after her cousin. "Aunt Charlotte would be furious if she found me here. What mischief do you mean in leading me down this path?"

Allan shrugged and steered her hastily away from a row of bushes whence moaning sounds emanated. "This is rather risky, but it was the only place I could think of that my mother would never look for us—where you might, if only for a moment, have privacy."

"But why should I require—" Margaret froze in midstride.

A man stood silhouetted in front of them, his back to what little light there was along this tree-lined walk, and at his feet sat a dog. The dog was Hero.

"Lord Dade!" she breathed.

"None other," Allan laughed, vastly pleased with her reaction. Margaret had eyes only for Evelyn Dade.

"I have come to wish you well, Pearl."

Margaret was touched. The viscount cared enough to come and wish her good-bye on the sly despite her uncle's edict.

She had begun to believe she was never to see Dade or Hero again. Despite this gentleman's supposed reputation and the name of the lane in which they stood, Margaret plunged breathlessly toward him. She would like to have thrown herself against Dade's chest, but restrained the impulse and crouched down to clasp Hero instead.

"I am so very glad to see you," she said. As quickly as she had bent to hug the dog, she stood again to gaze at its master, cheeks flushed. "I cannot think of anyone I would rather encounter at this moment. Allan said I would regret it if I did not come with him, didn't you, Allan? I had no idea. I thought it was something to do with fireworks."

As if her words had set them free, the first of the evening's fireworks exploded with a cracking boom above their heads. "And see, they have begun." She pointed, and followed the sparkling path of a blue-flamed rocket as it shot into the heavens, where it exploded, showering her awestruck expression with blue light. "Oh! Are they not like wildflowers blowing across the sky, spilling bright seeds to earth?"

She had little notion how mysterious, how beautiful her face became in such a light, or how strange her companion found it that a creature as fine as she was thrilled to run into him in the darkness of the notorious Lover's Walkway.

Dade was shaken. He was shaken by the sound of the fireworks, which was too much like gunfire and equally shaken by Margaret Dornton—by her words, her perfume in the evening breeze, by the very look of her. The fireworks reminded him not of flowers but of her. Margaret Dornton was to him a brilliant and enchanting burst of light in the midst of his darkness. She awakened in him the seeds of hope and happiness and awe—the fireworks of the soul. He could not dismiss the notion that they stood in Lover's Walkway and that there was nothing more naturally done here than making love to this woman he was losing, who of all women he would most like to take into his arms.

She turned to say something directly to Allan, but her cousin, deepening the charged danger of the moment, was already striding away from them.

"Oh, dear!" she said artlessly. "I do not think Allan's leaving us alone together can be at all judicious given my current circumstances. What if we should be seen?"

Dade tucked her arm in his and drew her into the shadows of an overhanging tree. Deeper still, into his arms, she was pulled. When she might have objected he said gently, "Here in the shadows anyone who sees us will immediately assume we are but two lovers come for a private tête-à-tête, just as they have. A blind eye will be turned in the hopes that we will honor them with similar courtesy."

"Oh!" Her breast rose and fell a little faster as his hand slipped comfortably around her waist. Her eyes, round and big and touched with what looked like anticipation, shone in the darkness. "Will they really?"

"Yes. You are wise to be careful about whom you chose to walk with here, Pearl." He warned himself as much as he warned her. He willed his hands to be still, willed his thoughts to remain trustworthy and pure. He brought forth the image of Wallis Eckhart, whom he loved like a brother and whom he had begun to envy like an enemy. He brought forth too the image of Creighton Soames as an example to himself of what he would not do here in the dark. "It is to be no more than expected that someone would read your willingness to tread Lover's Walkway as an open invitation for forward behavior."

She laughed, a sound warm and sunny and completely beguiling as darkness surrounded them.

"Do you not consider my being left here alone with you an open invitation?"

Dade searched the darkness for some clue to her expression. Her words were provocative.

"Why is it that men have such an interest in taking advantage of the very women they find attractive? Such action would seem to be in direct contradiction to the respect one naturally offers an object of admiration." She asked her question in all seriousness, innocent of how ridiculous such a query sounded.

He was amazed and amused. "Have you never enjoyed the words, or touch, or kiss of any man? I cannot think you would ask such a question if you had."

"But you are wrong, sir! I have been wooed by words, and warmed by no more than a touch. I even came close to kissing once. Yet still I am confused."

The darkness was Dade's enemy. He could not read her expression for its cloaking, and in this instant it would have been particularly valuable to read the message of her features. "Who has dared to almost kiss the shining pearl?" he asked in a deceptively mild voice. He would have the blackguard's head on a pike! "Is it Creighton who has done such a poor job of it, to leave the job unfinished?"

Her voice warbled a little with uncertainty. "Mr. Soames? How absurd! If I chose to allow such liberties, it would not be with someone like Creighton Soames."

"Who, then?" he said gruffly, leaning closer so that he could see what was to be seen of her expression in the brief interludes when the sky lit up. "I shall set Hero on the rogue. Do not tell me Wallis—"

"No, no," she laughed, her voice throaty—seductive without intent to seduce. "I wonder if I should not feel insulted, sir, that you do not remember. The culprit is none other than yourself. You were delirious with fever at the time, and mistook me for someone in your dreams."

It was not a dream. Her golden head had lain upon his pillow! Dade was speechless. "I beg your pardon," he said.

"What? Do you not believe me, or did you mean to apologize for—what was it you said?—leaving the job unfinished?"

"Neither. I beg pardon for making such a muddle of your first kiss that you were left wondering what to make of them. You must not judge me, or kisses, based on that fevered exchange."

Her chuckle was utterly delicious in the darkness. "I don't. But neither can I judge based on prior experience. My knowledge is limited to good-bye kisses."

"I understand you are to leave London?" he said, his lips itching with the desire to offer her just such a kiss, but was restrained again by his respect for Wallis.

She searched his face as intently as he examined hers as another shower of celestial light bathed her troubled features. "Unfortunately, it is so. I feel as if I owe a great many people apologies for my scandalous behavior—especially you."

"Me?"

"Yes. My crude attempts to be heroic have at last caught up with me. I am dreadfully sorry my uncle assumed you were involved."

He sighed and pushed away the thought of good-bye kisses. "No matter. In arranging to meet you in Lover's Walkway, I have far surpassed any ills you may be responsible for. Your uncle would have my head."

"He would, wouldn't he?" she mused uneasily.

"Yes, but I care less for Lord Dornton's opinion than I do for that of his niece."

She seemed very pleased he should say so. "Have no fear, then. To me, you shall always be the hero who saved me from the jaws of a mad dog."

The heavens shed sudden sparkling light on her, and he reached out in the burst of light to push a strand of hair off her forehead, relishing the silken warmth of flesh and hair against his fingertip. In this instance, he was the mad dog she needed saving from. He ached for her: arms, chest and loins.

His voice was thick with repressed desire when he said, "You must get it through that naive little head of yours that I am not a hero." His voice shook. This evidence of her effect on him made him long to shake her, to touch her, to kiss her. He wanted to flog himself for the profane thoughts that roamed through his head as he stared down into the innocent, shining eyes that would seem to see him, in the brief bursts of illumination, not for who he was but for who she imagined him to be.

"I am not a hero." His voice was gruff. "There are very few of them in this world, Pearl. Most of us are just men, trying to get through life the best way we know how. Most of us, like Creighton, would take advantage of your innocence, given half a chance. We would steal something precious and irredeemable from you."

"Do not say so," she cried, her voice husky as she turned away from him, pulling free from his hold on her. "You are nothing like Creighton."

He could not resist reaching out to capture her elbow. "I will say it and you must hear me, or you come to ruin. It is a fantasy, this land of heroes you put your trust in. It is a sham. I am no hero. The name of Captain Dead would seem far more appropriate. You see, it is true that I led my men into death for no more reason than the lack of proper equipment that I should have fought harder to obtain. We required curb chains for the horses. It was hopeless to try to hold them in the heat of battle without them. I was naive to agree to our position. That naivete cost many lives."

She took his hand in hers. "That's why you could not watch the reenactment of the battle at Astley's, isn't it? I do understand, you know . . . in a way . . ."

He pulled away from her touch. "How can you?" His voice was harsh. "You have no idea the feelings that rage within me." His hand passed over his mouth, as though to stop more angry words leaping from his tongue. "Perhaps it is best you go to the country," he said tersely.

* * *

Best? she wanted to shout at him. Are words the *best you have to offer me*? Words that would tear her esteem for him into shreds of disillusionment? She wanted more in this wonderful opportunity of darkness. She wanted some evidence of his feeling for her, some expression of his friendship, of his sorrow they must part, of—dare she wish for it—passion. She could not bear it if the best he could come up with was *Perhaps it is best*.

She wished he would hold her, touch her, try to kiss her: anything but stand before her regretting the past and insisting he was not a hero. How could it be best she go out of his life and thoughts and sway? She had begun to hope he loved her, to believe he might offer for her as he had once before, only this time with some evidence of love.

A carmine rocket creased the sky. Margaret wished she could put some of the sparkle that lit the night into the blank darkness of his eyes. She wanted to shock him in some way, as she had once shocked him by dressing up in her cousin's clothes and leaping between raised blades. She felt too a despair that after all this time she had not reached him, had not touched his soul and changed it in the way his presence, his company, the promise of something wonderful between them, had touched hers.

Some hint of her longing must have exhibited itself in her expression, for when next the sky shed light on them, he said, "You have the strangest look in your eyes. What wildness is it you are considering, Pearl?"

Pearl's eyes blazed with reflected light from the Roman candles that lit the sky. There was something dangerous in such a light. It drew Dade too much, and he would not be drawn. He was still convinced that this sweet pearl of innocence before him was meant for some gentleman simpler than he, simpler and wiser and as innocent as she. He was still convinced that Wallis was the perfect match for Pearl.

"If you are so firm in your conviction that there is nothing in the least heroic in you, and that it is best we never see each other again, then I would ask that you do not call me Pearl," she flung at him, pulling her arm from his grasp.

Her vitriolic outburst stunned him. "But what has one to do with the other?"

She paced away from the tree that embraced them and back again, her arms and hands agitated. "I simply will not have it."

He shook his head, surprised and confused. Such logic was anything but simple. "I am sorry, Miss Dornton, if you find my words in some way offensive. It was not my objective to bother you. I did but mean to please you in wishing you godspeed this evening."

"Why should it please you to say good-bye?" she demanded heatedly, no longer controlling the fire of rage and hurt that burned within. "I was under the impression, mistaken though it may be, that you and I—that we shared a regard for each other . . . that you had some feeling for me." The words seemed torn from her throat. "I feel positively dreadful that I shall never see you again. I dared hope you might feel equally dreadful." A strangled laugh burst from her throat, as if she found her own words both strange and amusing.

"Shh-shh, sweet Pearl." His words only made her shake her head.

"You must not call me that," she insisted, wrapping her arms around herself.

"All right. I will not call you Pearl anymore if it grieves you. It is not out of any desire to pain you that I came tonight."

"No desire to pain me? No desire to trouble me? What was your desire, then, in arranging this meeting, my lord? You tell me too plainly what you do not desire without ever explaining what you do."

His eyes probed the darkness in disbelief. Did she truly have no inkling of his feelings for her, of the heat which burned quietly within him, like a charge that must soon explode? Her silhouette was supple and lithe as a sapling as she paced away from him. He wanted more than anything to trace it with his hands. Her own hands, unable to settle themselves in her agitation, fluttered like moths above the pale gleam of her breasts, which tried his resolve by taunting him from a fashionably low neckline.

"What is it you want?" she insisted again. "Do you want me to despise you as others do? Shall I see only that which is imperfect within your mind and heart and soul rather than concentrate on what is good and right and heroic in you? You have been a hero to me, my white knight. Please do not try to convince me otherwise. You saved me from a mad dog and did your utmost to save me from my own folly and from the advances of Creighton Soames."

"The only one your white knight would seem incapable of saving you from, my dear Pearl," he rasped, "is me." He pulled her into his arms with gentle urgency, succeeding in the very endeavor he had foiled in Creighton Soames. Without another word, without another thought of Wallis, he lowered his lips to hers.

Margaret did not in the least resist Lord Dade's advances. She had, in fact, been hoping he might kiss her, might in some way indicate his recognition of the seriousness of their parting. Tilting up her face, she put forth her lips in the manner in which she was accustomed to kissing friends and relatives. What followed, however, was not at all what she was accustomed to, or even what she had imagined—and Margaret had imagined kissing this man many times, since they had come so close to it on two occasions.

Evelyn Dade's lips descended lightly, a warm, glancing contact that seemed to bounce away as quickly as it came. Before she could begin to draw away with a faint feeling of disappointment, Margaret was caught completely off guard by the intensity of his second kiss. His hands slid firmly around her waist and pulled her close. This meeting of their mouths was awkward, uncertain and a little off center. Rather than pull away in disgust at her ineptitude, however, he sought out her lips from a different angle, with the slightest adjustment in the positioning of his head, and drew her even more intimately against the hard resistance of his chest and stomach by gliding one hand down the the middle of her back as the other hand ran up. She could feel the rise and fall of his chest against her breast. Startled by the magic of his touch, her mouth opened to his as he let out a little sigh and darted his tongue, quick and wet and surprising, across her trembling lips.

The sky lit up as their mouths careened together once again, and just like the Chinese torch above their heads, something exploded inside Margaret, showering her with the sensation of light, heat and color. Her mouth melted into his, hot, wet and searching.

These kisses were not at all like those one expected from a relative. These kisses affected her from the lifting hair at the nape of her neck to the tingling of her toes. Her lips were incredibly sensitive, almost tender, under the onslaught of his. There was something predatory and primal and not at all polite about his kiss, and about the unexpectedly demanding pressure of his palms as he pulled her so close she thought he meant, by some magic, to make her disappear within him. The undeniable need of those demanding hands sent waves of unexpected feeling shooting up her spine and then down again, until it felt as if he touched her as much within as without. His lips sought out the softness of her neck. His thumb came up to trace the edge of her jawbone while his fingers dipped down, stroking the hollow of her throat, tracing the edge of her bodice. Margaret moaned. The heat of his hands, the heat of his lips, the aching heat that grew between her legs, struck at the very heart of Margaret's understanding of what love was. It consumed her.

Relishing the liquid taste of her own mouth, relishing the almost liquid heat of her own body, Margaret was convinced that something so powerful, so all encompassing, so sensually assaulting that it left her weak in the knees and brought every cell of her body into an acute state of awareness, must be dangerous and sinful. The very air, as fireworks continued to explode above them, seemed to carry a whiff of brimstone. If this was sin, she abandoned herself to it. Her mouth sought his with a passion she had not known she possessed. Her hands wrapped themselves around his neck as her back arched under the guiding pressure of his hands. The aching heat between her legs reached explosive proportions. She wanted, without knowing how, to relieve that ache. She wanted his hands to continue roving and his lips to go on seeking. She wanted, she wanted, she wanted. It was at the zenith of her surrender, when his tongue darted out to wetly probe her lips and she moaned in delight as his hand slid beyond the edge of her bodice to stroke one hard and aching nipple, that heaven interceded on her soul's behalf with an explosion that rocked the very ground beneath their feet.

Chapter 18

THEY fell away from each other in dismay.

Lord Dade's face seemed lit by an unholy fire as he cried out, "Dear God," and bolted toward the sound.

Margaret, far less quick to recover from the assault on her senses, swayed, and then staggered after him, toward the source of the explosion instead of away, as everyone else seemed to be headed, their eyes wide and mouths open in fear. Into an acrid cloud of smoke she went, Dade's dark, flapping cloak in front her only source of direction.

They came, one after the other, to the end of the dark pathway. Ahead of them, beyond the last of the overshadowing trees and shrubbery, stretched a clear swath of grass, where two men with torches had been setting off the fireworks.

There were voices around them, disembodied voices in the pall of smoke.

"Gunpowder," one voice wheezed in agitation. "It was the gunpowder went up."

"Is anyone hurt?" Dade asked. She could not mistake his voice despite the fact she could no longer see him. He was one of a half dozen dark shapes whose movements made the smoke eddy and swirl. The nose-biting smell dizzied Margaret. Courage, she chided herself. Have a little courage.

"You there. You must go for a doctor." It was Dade's voice, calm and decisive.

"His hand. Poor Ted's hand is an awful mess," someone else said hysterically. "Poor bastard's done for if we cannot stop the bleeding."

"I'll fetch a physician" came a cry.

The smoke cleared. Dazed, Margaret brushed past the man who meant to fetch the doctor, stopping only when she reached Lord Dade's crouched figure. He was kneeling on a patch of blackened grass with two other men nearby, one kneeling as he did, the other sprawled on the ground.

"Oh, my!" Margaret whispered, feeling faint. Where the prone man's hand should have been there was blood, only blood. She had seen injuries before, but nothing like this. Blood spattered the man's shirt, blood stained the grass, blood colored Lord Dade's vest and hands and shirtsleeve.

"Ted. Don't give up, old boy." Blood again, on the man who knelt next to Dade. Chin up, she thought, chin up!

"Is he dead?" she asked weakly, her head whirling.

Dade did not so much as look up at her. He slid a knife from his boot, took up the unspeakably bloody stump of what had once been a hand with a gentleness that made her eyes tear, and began to cut away the man's sleeve. "I require your petticoat, Pearl," he said matter-of-factly.

"My petticoat?" The world was spinning, and he asked for her petticoat? She looked away from the blood and the wretched figure who had generated so much of it. The air was too thick. She must move away in order to breathe.

"Quickly," Dade barked. "Else this man bleeds to death for the sake of your modesty."

Numb, Margaret raised her skirt, exposing an expanse of starched white muslin, and fumbled about until she had her tapes unlaced. The petticoat dropped to the grass with no more than a wriggle of her hips. She twitched her skirts modestly back into place in the face of any number of uneasy onlookers who had gathered around the spectacle they made.

"Here." She bundled up the petticoat and held it out to Dade, but he paid her no mind, busy as he was shouting orders at a man across from them.

". . . in the torch," he was saying, "until it is red hot. We must cauterize the wound, else he'll bleed to death right here between us."

"Tear it into strips, my dear." It was a woman's voice, a lady by her tone and diction.

Margaret jerked her head around, the petticoat still wadded in her hands. It was Lady Jersey who addressed her with the bracing and very practical instruction. The same Sarah Jersey who had denied the Dorntons entry to Almack's. Her presence and the unruffled suggestion vaguely irritated Margaret. She grasped her fluttering petticoat with new purpose and ripped along a seam. The Jersey, or Queen Sarah, nodded with unmistakable approval.

"Excellent! Give me half to tear and we shall finish the work in a trice."

Margaret had no desire for Lady Jersey's approval, but she readily complied. Despite the difficulties this woman had brought her and her sisters in the past, Margaret took strength from her self-assured approach.

"You are the Dornton gel, are you not? The one everyone calls the Pearl?" Lady Jersey enunciated clearly, with the same vigorous energy with which she went about tearing the petticoat into bandages.

Margaret focused her concentration on the neat strips she ripped—anything but the man on the ground, the man with the crimson stump where hand and fingers should have been. "I am." She nodded grimly. Be brave! The words kept running through her head. Her mother voiced them. Be brave. Have courage. Keep your chin up. The words echoed from her childhood. She had been very young when they were first directed her way.

"Well, my dear, I had been informed you were tantamount to the sort of heroine one might encounter in a gothic novel." Lady Jersey interrupted her thoughts. "I understand you make a habit of dashing into the midst of all sorts of danger. It seems only appropriate I should discover you in the midst of yet another harrowing adventure!"

Margaret stiffened. "I would not call this man's misfortune an adventure at all, my lady," she said tartly, tearing the petticoat with renewed energy.

She turned to hand a stack of linen strips to Dade, but

she reckoned without the sight of the bloody stump, without the sight of the heated blade blackened by the smoke of the torch. Her anger dissolved instantly, her stomach threatened to turn. Her knees got all wavery.

"You must not faint, Pearl," Lord Dade insisted almost harshly, with a glance that swiftly assessed her state of mind. "I warn you, I cannot leave this fellow to catch you. Come! Have courage. Hold the poor fellow's arm while we do the nasty business of cauterizing his wound. Distract him if you can. Talk to him." His lips lifted in a tight smile that never quite reached his eyes. "Perhaps he plays chess too."

Margaret nodded, took a deep breath, clenched her lower lip between her teeth, and took hold of the bloody arm just below the leather lacing that Dade had tied above the elbow to slow the gushing blood. Have courage. The poor man was unconscious. His lips had a bluish tinge. Be brave! She did not see what good talking to him would do, but talk she did, for no more reason than because Evelyn Dade had asked her to. Chin up, Margaret.

Her grip was firm and her lips moving in a spate of cheerful conversation as the glowing knife was pressed to the bloody stump. She talked and talked, even as she heard the faint sizzle of burning flesh. She continued to babble as a spiral of smoke rose from the edge of the knife blade. It was the awful smell of scorched flesh—a smell one could never forget once it had been encountered—that overwhelmed her. The anguished cry of the injured man, as pain jogged him out of his faint, made her lean close to him and whisper weakly, "Have courage, sir. You are going to be fine."

That was the last thing she remembered. She came to, stretched out on the grass, Wallis fanning her face, while her sisters patted her wrists and cheek and called to her. "Margaret. Maggie. Maggs. Wake up, my love," said Celeste. The expression on her face as it swam into view was very gentle and concerned.

"However have you managed to make a friend of the great Lady Jersey in the midst of all this mayhem?" It was Celia who asked. "Wake up." She rattled Margaret's hands urgently. "Come, Maggs. You must tell us. You are all over blood and your hair smells of smoke. You must tell us what has happened. We are all agog. The Jersey said you played a part in saving a man's life. Whatever did she mean?"

"Leave your sister be." Aunt Charlotte hovered in the background, wringing her hands. "Wallis. You are a great strapping young man. You must carry her to our carriage. We shall have the doctor in to see her. Anyone can see the girl is completely overwrought."

Dade saw Wallis carrying the burden he would himself have enjoyed bearing out of Vauxhall Gardens while he saw to it that an unconscious man was carried away to the hospital. Lady Jersey stood beside him as the Dornton party passed them, strips of Pearl's petticoat still clutched fast in her hand. "Will he survive, do you think?" she asked.

Dade shrugged, his attention returned to the poor man who had been lifted into the back of a cart. "There's no way of knowing. I have seen men survive worse."

"A remarkable young woman, your Miss Dornton." Sarah Jersey handed him a pale, fluttering handful of muslin.

"I shall miss her." Dade tucked the raw-edged bits of fabric, all that was left to him of Pearl, in his pocket.

"Miss her? She is going somewhere?"

The wagon rumbled away with the injured man and his mate.

"To the country." Dade swallowed hard. "Town life has been hard on her and her sisters."

"What a pity. She will be lauded in the morning papers as a heroine for what she just did. I have always fancied numbering a true heroine among my acquaintances."

Dade transferred his attention from the receding figures to the bit of cloth beneath his fingers. "Then it is best, I am sure, that she return to the country. The Misses Dornton have been the focus of lurid stories far too much of late as it is."

Lady Jersey's face was a picture of concern. "A pity, that," she said softly.

Dade looked down at the bloody mess of his shirt. He wiped his hands on the tattered linen rags, and wondered if a bit of muslin might serve to bind up a broken heart. His was most certainly torn asunder tonight.

Chapter 19

EVELYN Dade went the following day to the hospital where the unfortunate injured man was being cared for, to see how he got on. He took with him his old military mate, the one-armed Mr. Boggs. Boggs had arrived on his doorstep, newspaper in his one good hand, volunteering succor and sound council for the victim from Vauxhall. Dade was pleased to accept his assistance.

"Someone told me I had been rescued by none other than the notorious Captain Dead!" Ted Peeples chuckled weakly from his hospital bed when introductions had been made.

"I say—" Boggs began to object.

Dade silenced him with a shake of his head. "I am called that by some," he admitted. "I hope you are not concerned for your health as a result?"

"I'm not one as puts much stock in such nonsense," Peeples said comfortably. "The way I hears it, I would have been cocking up me toes now if not for your intervention. I told the fellow who was filling me ear that I reckoned you to be a turncoat if it was indeed Dead who kept me alive."

Dade smiled appreciatively. "A turncoat, you say?"

"Well, yes, bit of a joke that. Thought it might lighten the mood. I must say, I'm very pleased to meet you, my lord, no matter what it is you are called. I hope you will not refuse to shake the one good hand I've left to me." He thrust forward the appendage in question.

Dade's smile broadened as he grasped Peeples' hand. Before the man could launch into more expressions of gratitude, he introduced Mr. Boggs. The two men naturally fell into discussion on how one managed with only one hand.

Dade left them and dropped in at his club, where he read at leisure the article that Lady Jersey had predicted would appear with regard to the happenings at Vauxhall. It declared Dade a hero and Miss Margaret Dornton an angel of mercy. Evelyn set aside the account with a sigh. He was pleased to have saved a man's life, but his chest was bound up by guilt in his having fallen slave to cravings of the flesh where Pearl was concerned. He had long ago decided she was best cherished by Wallis. He remained firm in that resolve, but there was a terrible melancholy that came with knowing that he might never hold the warm and willing young woman, delicately scented with jasmine and her desire for him, within his arms again.

It would have been easy for Captain Dead to return to his former bad habits, so melancholy was his spirit, but such a course of action never crossed his mind. Fortunately, in an effort to distract his thoughts from stolen kisses and moonlight on golden hair, he began to frequent not cockfights and executions but, for the first time since his return from Waterloo, the club in Albermarle Street that catered exclusively to his fellow officers. There, over glasses of wine and platters of rare beefsteak, he spoke at length with others who had lived through the battle at Waterloo. The brief but telling disclosures of these men helped him to understand better the darkness that had become so much a part of himself, the darkness that so deeply scarred his soul.

In dribs and drabs, they commiserated over friends and acquaintances lost on the battlefield, or on the long, thirsty road away from it. Countless brave lads wounded in the heat of battle had survived the ordeal of a bumpy wagon ride only to be butchered in a surgeon's tent.

Brave boys, brave men, brave horses, they spoke of them all. The mistaken charge of the Scots Greys and the Royal Blues was recounted in detail. The invincible strength of the infantry squares marveled over. When the tales grew too lurid or morose, a laugh was sure to be had in merely a mention of the rocket corps. A good head shaking always followed any discussion of the wives and lovers who had followed their men onto the battlefield only to die.

When cups and bottles began to pile up on the table like dead soldiers, the survivors even spoke in sad, hushed voices about the aftermath of war: the dreadful looting and outright murder of the fallen, the lack of water and medical facilities, the scandalous abandonment of the wounded by their officers on the long, crowded road away from the battlefield. There were heartrending accounts of beloved but broken horses trying valiantly to rise despite missing limbs; tragic accounts of half-dead men left to bandage their own wounds and fight off looters who thought nothing of finishing off the fallen for no more than a water flask or the buttons off a coat. Every survivor Dade spoke to carried with him the dark dreams of the dead—nightmares of bodies and blood and bayonets—dreams rooted in the concern that had one acted differently in some small but important manner, there might be one more survivor sitting at table recounting tales of the day they had almost died.

Dade immersed himself in these discussions. As he talked and listened while others unburdened their souls of the intensely affecting moments that changed a man, his thoughts flicked back to something Margaret Dornton had long ago suggested: "It is a good thing to share one's grief and horror and pain." She was absolutely right. There was a feeling of reunion within him, a reunion with his fellow man. It was good to know he was not alone in his thoughts and fears, not alone in his moments of quandary as to whether he had done his best in the given circumstances.

There came several turning points: a day when he had talked and listened enough; a morning when the nightmares did not wake him drenched in sweat; a day when he insisted Gimble dispose of his old uniforms; a day when he sat at his secretary and wrote letters to the families of the fallen in his regiment. Dade felt free to call on old friends with whom he had lost touch. He began to accept an occasional invitation to balls or soirees. And yet for all his renewed social activity and the burgeoning success of his career contacts, Evelyn Dade suffered pangs of deep, biting loneliness. He missed Wallis's good-natured companionship. He missed Creighton Soames's brash bravado. He missed the morning walks in St. James's with two fiesty whippets teasing Hero's tail. Most of all, he missed Pearl. No matter how many balls he attended, no matter that sweet-faced young women began to flock about him, due to Lady Sarah Jersey's touting him as a remarkable catch, Dade could not dispel the feeling that in Pearl's absence something vital and necessary to his happiness was missing. There came a day too when he decided it was time he saw to the business of his inheritance and the distribution of his brother's personal effects. He struck out for the country home he would always associate with Gavin. There, he went through desks and packed up or gave away belongings. He talked with managers and solicitors and bookkeepers until his mind whirled. In the process he gained a new appreciation for just what it was Gavin had done while he was off trying to get himself killed.

A wrenching business, this tidying up after the dead. It could not but remind him of how sweet life was, how brief. He thought often of Pearl, especially when among his brother's effects he found a chessboard and its men, a pretty thing, the pieces hand-carved and masterfully inlaid with glossy bits of mother of pearl. He wished Margaret Dornton might have known Gavin, and Gavin the Pearl. It seemed no more than natural to pack the chessboard and its pieces into a crate and direct it to Miss Margaret Dornton. There was much Dade would have liked to write to her. Yet he feared words would betray his feelings. No more note was enclosed than his name, and the penned remark that he hoped all of the chess pieces would survive their journey intact.

Wallis would be the one to play the game out with her. He was sure it must be so. It would be Wallis in whom she would confide and Wallis she would grow to love. She was ripe for love. The heat of her lips had told him as much. Sweet, honeyed, virgin kisses, uncertain and hesitant at first, fervent and eager given the slightest encouragement. She had pressed herself quite willingly against him on that fateful night at Vauxhall. She would, he was sure, learn to press herself as willingly on Wallis. He tried to avoid such thoughts, but not a day, not an hour, passed when he did not think of her, when he did not want her. In trying to push his desire aside, it became all the more persistent.

"The sun was never appreciated as much until it came on to rain." Wasn't that what she had once said? She was a wise young thing. The light and joy and life he had felt in her presence was never as obvious to him as now that she was no longer to be seen. Far better, he tried to convince himself, that Margaret Dornton should fall in love with Wallis, so like her in sensibility and temperament, than one as different as he.

Lord Dade returned to London more exhausted than when he had left. In a melancholy mood he visited all the places he and Margaret Dornton had frequented. He sought memories of her just as he had gone seeking memories of the Battle of Waterloo, just as he had gone seeking memories of Gavin. There was no denying it. He chased after a better understanding of her as fervently as he had once chased after an understanding of death. To St. James's Church he went, to the Elgin marbles and Astley's and Vauxhall. No place was her absence more noted than in St. James's Park. Dade expected to see her there. He thought at times that her dogs would come running across the grass to worry Hero's tail, that he would hear her clear voice calling them. "Lads! Here, lads."

She was to be seen and heard only in the memories he carried in his head, memories that grew soft and vague with the passage of time. It was hard to believe that something soft could so sharply pain his heart. It ached with a yearning for her sweet lightness, for another of her wise gray looks. In her absence the sun seemed less intense, colors less vibrant. The birds no longer sang as sweetly. The bloom was off the jonquils and hyacinths that had flourished while Pearl traversed these pathways. Of the flowers that had smiled upon her, only the sweet white periwinkles still lifted pale faces to the sun.

And yet as Dade looked upon the things that had stirred the heart and soul of his beloved Pearl, there was a quickening come to his blood. His eyes viewed the world with fresh appreciation. Though she was many miles away and destined for the arms of another man, Pearl walked with him still. A piece of her joy had become his.

He longed to see the light glinting in her hair, to hear her voice as she identified flowers and birds, trees and ferns in three different languages, each word spoken with perfect inflection. He longed to have a pair of ears so ready to listen, a pair of eyes that looked so deep into his soul, a mouth so ready to laugh at his magic. How he missed her. How he wanted her! To a man who had gone so long feeling nothing at all, the pain of their separation was almost exquisite in its intensity.

With loss and longing to stoke the fires of his vigor and ambition, Dade plunged into the world of ambassadors, diplomats and peacekeepers and found himself a niche in the process. He moved with renewed purpose, circulating among men of influence, wealth and power. Yet no matter how hard he worked, no matter how successful his endeavors, there was, deep within him, a sense of unfulfilled longing, a hollow emptiness that nothing satisfied or filled. He thought of Pearl in such moments. He thought of their walks in the park and the depth of their conversations together. He knew, now that she was gone from him, that he loved her: body, heart, intellect and spirit. He admitted as much and yet could not convince himself he deserved her affections in return. Conflicted, and lonelier than he had been in a long time, despite the crowds he immersed himself in, he applied himself ardently to his work.

"Maggie, my dear." Mrs. Dornton placed a cool palm against her daughter's forehead. "Do you feel all right? You do not look at all rested."

Margaret shook her head so her mother's hand would fall away. What a fraud she was, to worry her parent so. "There is nothing . . . I'm fine," she said lamely as she stared out of the window, thinking of London—not so much the city as the man she left behind there. She was not fine. Miserable, worrying images kept repeating in her head, just as they had when she was a child.

"Are you still troubled by the fact that your uncle sent

you early home from London? Do you still suffer those awful nightmares, my dear, about the man who lost his hand?"

The nightmares were part of it.

Margaret sighed. "On occasion," she admitted.

"Well, that explains it, then, for this is the third time you have declined to visit someone who has been injured in the neighborhood since your return from London."

Margaret could tell her mother nothing. Sharing the dreams that disturbed her sleep would only trouble her parent anew with the old sadness of Todd's death. Not a word must pass her lips about the endless nightmares. The dreams revolved around Lord Dade. In one he swept her into his arms only to be cut down by the blade of a swordsman. In another he rose, half-conscious from the midst of a sickbed covered in leeches, shouting the name of his brother. There was a dream in which she and Dade, carved from marble and both missing bits of their hands and feet, reached out to each other without ever touching.

The dream that troubled her the most, however, was in Vauxhall as fireworks lit the sky above their heads. Always, there was the heated embrace, interrupted at its most passionate moment by an earthshaking explosion. She was lost then in a thick fog of smoke. Sometimes a baby's cry cut through the smoke. Sometimes she saw blood, everywhere blood. Sometimes she could smell the awful odor of burning flesh. She usually woke then, to the still darkness of her room, unutterably saddened by what had become of her baby brother, wondering what had become of the poor man in the Gardens and the man who had saved him. She would have liked to have unburdened her heart in the comforting circle of her mother's arms, but could not. Would not. Too well had she learned the lesson of Creighton Soames's example. A loose tongue was a weapon that brought pain to many. If she explained the dreams that woke her in an icy sweat, there were those around her whose happiness would be as affected as her own. Her parents, her sisters, her cousin and aunt and uncle, all of them played parts in the drama of her dreamland. Lord Dade especially would surely suffer some backlash did she make free with what concerned her.

How did one explain away a kiss in the arms of a gentleman her parents had never met? How did one explain nightmares about a man with a blown-off hand, blown into bits that spattered her with blood, a blown-off stump of an arm that had bled and bled as she held it steady while someone seared the flesh in order to stop the river of blood? Her part in helping an injured man was no secret. She had read the newspaper account of the incident. Her aunt had written her parents some version of the events. Yet the web of truth and half-truth had grown complicated. The connection between past and present was too difficult to explain. She kept her little secrets, and yet was weary of subterfuge. It did not suit her personality to bear alone the weight of such happenings.

There was a part of her that wondered if the dreams, if the very event involving the explosion, had not been some sort of divine intervention, stopping her from shamelessly throwing herself at Lord Dade. She had been ready to go with him anywhere, to allow his hands, his lips, to do with her what they would. Her entire body had seemed lit by a fire with his kisses. Was such a fire unholy? Certainly the melting thoughts she had every time she remembered those kisses had to be a wicked thing.

"You look a trifle feverish, my dear," her mother said. "Or are you merely disenchanted with the country now that you have tasted of the fruits of a city like London?"

Margaret dragged her attention back to her mother. "Disenchanted? Never that. I am quite relieved to be once again in the peace of the countryside, untroubled by the gossip and game playing one finds so common in the city."

"Then what is it, love? You have not been at all yourself since you have come back to us."

"Have I not?"

"No." Her mother's expression was so sweet, so loving, it almost triggered tears. "Your lovely smile is so rarely to be seen, I have half convinced myself you are in a pet because your sisters are so happily engaged with Mr. Eckhart and your cousin Allan, from whose company you appear to remove yourself more often than not. Has this something to do with this Lord Dade your aunt has written to tell me of?"

Margaret turned from her mother's discerning gaze, unwilling to let her know how close she came to the truth. She was nothing but happy for her sisters, but the company they kept reminded her of who was missing among their number. She would have liked to discuss with Dade her bad dreams and sense of malaise. If anyone might understand, he would. She was sure of it. And yet in all the time they had been separated, he had made no effort to put pen to paper to dash off a note to her.

"I grew to care for him, Mother, more than anyone I have ever met. Knowing that I may never see him again leaves me melancholy." She sighed, and forced herself to smile. "Never fear. This mood of mine shall pass."

Her mother cupped a palm against her cheek. "All of my girls have been similarly affected by this trip to London. Too soon I shall find you have flown the nest. I am sorry your first love was not well chosen, my dear, but take cheer. Most ills will be mended if you but give them sufficient time to recover." Her eyes clouded, and though she said nothing to the effect, Margaret knew her mother was thinking of the chick that was already flown, never to return.

"Busy yourself with what makes you happy, Margaret, and your melancholy cannot help but improve."

That afternoon, two things occurred that promised to improve Margaret's mood immensely. Wallis Eckhart formally asked Margaret's father for his daughter's hand, and a package arrived from Lord Dade.

A brief note and a beautiful chess set were enclosed.

Chapter 20

It was in St. James's Park, some six months after the Dorntons had left London, that the past and Lord Dade's carefully harbored feelings for Pearl caught up to him, in the form of Wallis Eckhart.

"Congratulations on your recent appointment, my lord," the young man said, coming up beside him as he watched the feeding of the canal's captive pelicans. "I understand you leave us for the continent soon."

Dade did not need to turn to know who addressed him. He would have recognized that voice anywhere. "Wallis! Are you returned from the country?" He turned with subdued joy to face his friend. "However did you come to hear of my appointment? I have only just gotten the news myself."

Wallis grinned sheepishly. "Well, sir, I have been to your town house to talk to Gimble, and thence to your office, where he said you would be, but a Mr. Hughs . . . ?"

Dade nodded. "My secretary."

"—told me I would most likely find you here."

"Yes, I come here often." Dade looked his young friend up and down. Wallis seemed more mature for his absence, more confident. "Does it surprise you? A glimpse of greenery and a bit of sun on my face clarifies my thinking somehow."

"You are very changed, sir, since first we walked together in this very park."

Dade smiled. "I am pleased you should think so. I have long since decided that it is this park and the people who walked here with me that are responsible for that change. You too are changed, Wallis."

"Am I, sir?" The young man's smile approached the ridiculous, so deep was his satisfaction.

"Yes. You look well pleased with yourself," Dade said with a sense of forboding.

"I am pleased," Wallis laughed. "I bring such splendid news—my heart, you see, has wings."

Dade's own heart felt as if it were made of lead. "You speak with the ebullience of a man in love, Wallis. Are we soon to hear wedding bells, perchance?"

"Is it writ so plain on my face?" Wallis laughed.

Dade felt as if the boy had cheerfully delivered him a kick to the stomach. "Yes. When is the ceremony? Am I correct in assuming the fortunate young woman who will have you for husband is none other than Miss Dornton?"

A seed of hope remained alive within Dade's heart until Wallis plucked it out with a nod. "Who else have I been mooning over these many months? I am the most fortunate of fellows that she should find something to love in me."

Beyond that, Dade heard not a word. His ears stopped listening, so filled were they with disappointment. He nodded and smiled. He promised to do his best to get away for the wedding, which was to be held in Dorset rather than London out of consideration for the bride's family. But all the while his ears were deafened by the shout that rose from both heart and soul, *"No, no, no!"* The word became an internal litany. He smiled and nodded when he wanted more than anything to bury his head in his hands and wail. *"No! You may not have her. I will not allow you to take what I have offered up to you so freely. No, I will not allow that she is forever lost to me, and by my own hand."*

Not a word passed his lips.

Wallis blathered on, as blind to his disappointment as he was deaf to the young man's joy. When Dade was alone again, he dragged himself through the day in a state of shock, mortally wounded and yet unable to stem the life's blood that poured from his soul with every passing hour. His heart ached. His head pounded. He was quite without appetite, and yet he would not allow it was anything more than indigestion. He could not acknowledge that his body was thrown into as much a state of shock as his mind. It was not until he sat staring into the painted distance of the walkers in the park that Pearl had picked out for his sitting room that a pain very similar to that he had experienced when told Gavin had died hit Dade so hard in the gut that he doubled over. Covering up his mouth with shaking hand, he choked back a cry.

Hero, who sat at his feet whenever he took a chair, lifted a wet nose to comfort him in his distress. A high-pitched keening sound broke from the dog's throat. With a shuddering sigh Dade raised his head. "It's all right, boy." His voice shook with uncertainty. The thin whining sound still leaked from Hero's throat. Dade sniffed and reached out with both hands to cup the wolfhound's head. His voice grew stronger. "All will be fine. You'll see."

In many ways everything did seem to be all right. Dade buried himself in preparing for his work in France, impressing both himself and his associates with the capacity of his memory, the value of his knowledge of languages and his tact in dealing with sticky situations. He was forced to remember Wallis's wedding only when a written invitation arrived reminding him both of the impending date and his obligation to pick out a gift for the couple. He could not bring himself to so much as glance at the creamy card that reiterated what he had no desire to acknowledge. He handed it to Gimble, unopened. "You will be so good as to mark this engagement on my calendar," he recommended.

Gimble neatly penned in the date. Eckhart Wedding, his calendar proclaimed. Every time he saw the markings, Dade thought long and hard and balefully about his folly in forcing Wallis and Pearl always in proximity of each other. He had gotten what he wanted, only to find it was quite contrary to his desires after all.

They had been bound to form an affection. He had said as much to Pearl's uncle. They were the perfect couple, and yet he could not be happy in their agreement on the matter. He could not be happy, either, with the beautiful set of embossed silver bowls he picked out for them when he visited a jeweler. They were, after all, a gift intended to bless a union he privately cursed, a shining symbol of an opportunity lost to him forever.

As the cursed bowls were wrapped up for him, he stared sightlessly at a glass case filled with pocket watches.

"Is there anything else you wished to look at?" The clerk who was waiting on him took his cue from the direction of his gaze. "A watch, perhaps, or an hourglass?"

Dade focused in a distracted manner on the huge hourglass in the center of the case. The clerk, anxious to make another sale, turned it so that the sand from one gleaming glass globe sifted into the other. Was his life like the hourglass, swiftly spilling away time? Was opportunity sliding through his hands like loose sand? "A watch? No." Dade could hear the curt displeasure in his voice. He carefully modulated his tone. "I am interested . . . in pearls."

The clerk was happy to oblige him with a display of every pearl in the place. Dade had come with no intention of purchasing pearls. And yet he lingered over the cases, deciding at last on a lady's gold filigree bracelet ornamented by two entwined filigree hearts whose centers were highlighted by the pale luster of perfectly matched pearls. As he addressed the cards that went with each package, the silver bowl to the happy couple and the bracelet to Pearl alone, he admitted to himself that he had played with Fate, pushing it inexorably to this miserable, unthinkable conclusion. He would test Fate again in sending the gift of pearls. If they provoked some sort of reaction, perhaps the wedding would not take place after all. If he was destined to be heartbroken, then so be it. He would not go to the wedding. Expensive gifts would arrive in his stead. He hoped both Wallis and Pearl would forgive him the slight. He hoped Pearl would wear his gift of pearls.

The gifts, when they arrived at theDerntons' comfortable home in Sherborne, caused a bit of a stir. The silver bowls were universally admired. The bracelet addressed to Pearl raised eyebrows and drew remarks from everyone who gathered in the main drawing room to see the parcels unpacked.

"Lord Dade has not forgotten us entirely, it would seem." Allan winked at Margaret suggestively. "First a chessboard. Now silver and pearls. What next, cousin? The offering of a hand perhaps?"

Margaret blushed furiously, which change in color her mother noted. "I would hear more of this Lord Dade," she said.

"Oh, but Mama, we told you all about him," Celia protested. "When we first returned from London."

"Yes, you did, my dears," her mother said calmly as Margaret held the bracelet to the light and slipped it onto her wrist, "with at least one major oversight. You failed to mention that our Margaret had fallen in love with the man."

"Mama!" Celia and Celeste complained in unison.

"But she isn't—wasn't—couldn't be," Celia carried her protest further. "Not Captain Dead!"

"Are you in love with him?" Celeste asked in wonder.

Unable to deal with uncomfortably personal questions and the sight of what Dade had sent her all at once, Margaret made a muffled, throaty choking sound from behind the hand she held to her mouth. Clutching the beautiful bracelet to her heart, she rushed from the drawing room to her private chambers. Falling face first across the bed, she sobbed and choked and laughed out her happiness and misery in muffled fashion.

Of course she loved him. How could they be so stupid—so blind? The bracelet glistened in the light from her window, a testimony to her almost extinguished hope that he returned the feeling. Two hearts entwined. Surely there was some significance to such a choice in motif? Margaret's fingers shook as she traced the outline of each filigree heart. Surely this was more than just a remembrance?

Her mother knocked upon her door. "Margaret. Are you all right? May I come in?"

Margaret wiped her tears away on the counterpane. "Yes, Mama. The door is open."

Her mother pushed open the door and came to sit beside her on the bed. "May I see the bracelet, my dear?"

Margaret held forth her arm. "Isn't it beautiful, Mother? You will not make me return it to him, will you?"

Her mother took up her hand and examined the bracelet from every angle with care. "It is lovely, my dear. As is the sudden transformation in your expression on receiving it. Is this Lord Dade in love with you, perhaps, as much as you are in love with him? Is this gentleman's absence the reason you have been withdrawn and mopish since your return from London? Did you think perhaps he had forgotten you?"

A tear slipped down Margaret's cheek. "Oh, Mother. How did you know? It made me perfectly miserable to think that I might never see him again, that he might not care for me as much as I do for him. He was so very interested in matching me up with Wallis. Time after time he said he thought we made the perfect couple." Her hand flew to her mouth. *But then he kissed me,* she thought.

Her mother patted her arm. "And now that Wallis is to be married, he has sent you this lovely bracelet. Surely that is a sign of some significance?"

Margaret had been inclined to think so herself. To hear her mother echo the thought was immensely comforting. "Do you think so? I hope with all my heart you may be right."

Her mother got up. "Well, we must pray he makes it to the wedding, for surely all your questions with regard to his feelings for you, and yours for him, must be answered then."

"Do you mean, sir, to go to Mr. Eckhart's wedding?" Gimble stood before Dade's desk asking the very question Dade had asked himself at least twenty times in the past four days. He put down his pen and looked up at his trusted valet's very neutral expression.

"I have not yet made up my mind," he admitted.

Gimble nodded. "Shall I pack a bag, sir? In case you decide at the last minute to go?"

Dade sighed. He was, he thought, resolved to stay true to his initial intention. He would not go to Wallis's wedding. The day approached. The time in which he must set out if he meant to go came nigh to waning. His head and heart warred with indecision.

He picked up his quill again. "That would be most considerate, Gimble."

The packed bag turned out to be both considerate and wise. At the last possible moment, Dade decided to attend the wedding, not because he wished to see Pearl taken from him forever, but because it was his last opportunity to stop this nightmare of his own making. He could not live with himself, could not confidently pack up his things for the trip to France, without knowing if things might have ended differently had he only made a push to change them. He grabbed up the waiting bag, mounted his fastest horse and loped out of London with the same gritty determination and sense of duty that had enabled him to march into battle. He had a mind to putting a halt to the joining of two people he cared for more than himself, if only long enough to declare his true feelings to Pearl.

He made excellent time out of London, through Surrey and into Hampshire, where he stopped the night. Rising eagerly before the sun did, Dade got on with his journey, determined to arrive before the ceremony, in good time to insist upon a moment alone with the bride.

The image of sand in an hourglass sifting swiftly away played strongly in his mind with every beat of the horse's hooves. He believed the clock beaten only when he had arranged for a fresh mount in Salisbury and set out along Cranborne Chase for Blackmoor Vale, where Sherborne was. He was ahead of schedule. He would arrive in plenty of time to arrange a private tête-à-tête with Pearl. He was imagining a happy outcome to that very conversation when the horse he was riding threw a shoe.

Chapter 21

THERE was not a fresh horse to be had in Milborne Port, the milling village in Blackmoor Vale into which Dade and the horse limped, hot, dusty and footsore. The animal had lost a shoe on the long, empty stretch of wooded road between the village and the last town he had clattered through on the western bank of the river Stour. Dade felt as if he had been walking for hours. The sands of time were wasting. To be told there was not a fresh horse to be had sank his spirits.

"A blacksmith?" he inquired. "Have you a blacksmith?"

But of course they had a blacksmith. The smithy was no more than a short walk. A walk again! More time slipping away from him. Dade set out for the smith's.

"Aye, the horse can be reshod right away," the blacksmith agreed, skeptically surveying the sorry condition of his dust-coated person. "For a price."

Dade flashed a coin. "It's vital you work fast."

The blacksmith set to with a will. As the shoe was banged into shape and plunged into a barrel of water, Dade paced like a nervous cat. The hot, metallic smell of the smithy reminded him of Vauxhall, of burning kisses beneath a glittering sky. With every ringing blow of hammer and iron, his mind rang with concern for the delay. Too late, too late, too late, the sand sifted through his fingers no matter how tightly he clenched them. *Pearl, do not hurry into marriage:*

the words turned over and over in his mind. How could he have left something so important, so vital to his happiness, to Fate and the mistiming of a lost shoe?

The last of the nails hammered home, Dade was on the road again, the horse goaded into a gallop, thundering out a tattoo with which he would erase delay and doubts, with which he hoped to catch up to lost time—lost opportunity. The horse was lathered and blown by the time they clattered into Sherborne, a pretty town of curving streets and houses built of a local stone that glowed golden in the midday sun. Could it be that here, among these warm, mellow houses, his heart would be broken forever?

Dade feared it was so, for though the horse was winded and his own chest heaving, the bells began to ring before he reached the chapel where the wedding was to take place. Too late! Too late! They sang. He came too late!

Quickly, still covered in road dust, he slid from the saddle and sprinted to the door of the chapel. In he burst, temporarily blinded by the sudden change of light.

He came too late! The bride and groom were making their way out of that very door, surrounded by the wedding party. He and Wallis collided head on.

"Dade!" Wallis said, grabbing him, his eyes gleaming with pleasure, his mouth hitched up in a lively smile. "You made it after all. We had quite given up on you. All except Margaret, of course. She was convinced you would come."

Dade backed against the heavy door he had just entered, in need of support. His breath was unsteady, his eyes affected not so much by the gloom in the church as by the gloom in his heart. They were all there: Pearl, all in white sarcenet, worked flounces and scalloped lace, her fair hair upswept in a circlet of orange blossoms. Her sisters wore white as well, with matching hairpieces. Wallis, Allan, Lord and Lady Dornton—all in wedding finery, looked utterly pleased with themselves and the occasion. He had failed. He had come too late. The two were wed. Pearl was lost to him.

"I fear I come too late," he said, closing his eyes in his distress and in the hope that he might see a way through this catastrophe a little better when he opened them.

"Not too late to be the first to kiss the bride," Wallis protested.

Dade opened up his eyes again as the shy bride was thrust into his arms, her fair, flower-decked head tipped down so that Dade could not read what she might be feeling in this moment.

"The new Mrs. Eckhart. Isn't she beautiful?" It was Allan who spoke.

"As always," Dade managed to reply, though it felt as if a crushing weight were loaded on his chest in the form of this delicately orange-scented female. Oranges brought to mind the night at Astley's.

He prepared himself for the worst. He prepared himself for the last kiss he might share with the woman he loved, prepared himself as well for the expression with which she must meet such a kiss. What he was not prepared for was discovering that the face that tilted shyly up to accept his salute was not Pearl's at all. It was Margaret's sister Celeste that Wallis had wed!

So relieved was Dade that he kissed the blushing bride with more fervor than might be considered proper. She pulled away with a throaty laugh.

"Sir! I am a married woman."

"And the sweeter be your kisses for it," Dade laughed. His elation knew no bounds as he allowed the married couple to pass and fell in step beside Margaret.

"Pearl. I have missed you," he said in a voice meant only for her ears, bending close to the orange-blossomed head as they passed out of the chapel and into the sunlight.

"Have you, sir?" She looked up at him, against the glare of the sun. Her eyes had a distant, shuttered look. For an instant he thought he saw a flicker of relief, of desire, of joy in her gaze, but before he could make certain she lowered her lashes, hiding her thoughts and feelings from him. Her mouth was tight, he thought, almost forbidding, as she held up her hand. The bracelet he had sent circled her wrist. "I had begun to think myself forgotten when this came." She spoke with a forced lightness that was not genuine enough to loosen the bound look of her mouth.

"Forgotten? By no means." He took her hand, but the

tension between them heightened as she pulled away before he could raise it to his lips.

"No." Her voice was low, her eyes bright and wounded. The tendrils of hair which hung down on brow and temple whipped about in a breeze, which seemed to personify the agitation of her temper. "You must not kiss me. You turned my life, my emotions, my very perspective upside down with past kisses and then chose to ignore me. I cannot allow my heart to suffer so again."

Before he could even begin to explain himself to her, she slipped away from him, losing herself in the throng that poured out of the church to congratulate the newlyweds.

Shocked, Dade stood motionless in the eddying rush of people, the sun warm on his dusty shoulders, the breeze tugging his sweated hair. In all the miles traversed, he had never imagined meeting with such a cold reception. For the first time Evelyn Dade realized just how deeply his months of silence had injured this young woman. He should have known Margaret Dornton would respond in this fashion, should have prepared himself. He had, after all, cut her off almost completely since the awful incident in Vauxhall, since he had taken her in his arms and claimed her mouth with his own. But he was not prepared. To be met by anger and biting chill when his own emotions had reached a flame took him aback. He knew he must do or say something to set things right between the two of them, but how to go about it in this press of people stretched his imagination.

He began in the only way he could think of, introducing himself, in all his road dust, to Margaret's parents. He struck up conversation too with Allan and Celia. It occurred to him he might need the support of allies in order to secure a moment alone with Margaret. He did his best to live down the cold greetings received from Margaret's Aunt Charlotte and Uncle Harold. That Margaret herself echoed their frosty politeness struck him afresh.

It was the new and glowing bride, Celeste, who unwittingly offered him an opportunity to melt the growing chill between he and Pearl. She leaned down from the carriage that was to take the newlyweds away to whisper something in her mother's ear.

"Excellent idea!" Margaret's mother agreed. When the happy couple had pulled away in a shower of rice, she turned to her youngest and said, loud enough that Dade might hear, "Will you be so good, Margaret, as to take the flowers which decorated the chapel and dress the family graves?"

"Yes, of course, Mama," Margaret agreed with a quick, stricken look in Dade's direction.

Mrs. Dornton turned her attention to Dade when he made a move to follow her daughter. "Lord Dade," she said politely, looking him straight in the eye with a gaze almost as gray as her daughters. "Would you mind assisting Margaret with the flowers in the chapel?" Margaret's aunt tapped her rather urgently on the shoulder, her eyes fixed on Dade. Mrs. Dornton turned briefly to remark to her sister-in-law that she would attend to her in a moment. Facing Dade again, she said sweetly, "Will you see to it that Margaret returns safely home to us when she is done? I do not care for her to walk about the countryside without proper escort."

The urgent tapping on her shoulder increased its tempo.

"In a minute, my dear." Mrs. Dornton took her sister-in-law's insistent fingers in her own and patted them, as she might a recalcitrant child's. There was something in the wise, knowing look she bent on Dade that gave him the feeling her remarks to him were not idly made.

"I am honored to be so entrusted," he said.

She smiled. In smiling, the resemblance to her daughters was remarkably pronounced. "I am pleased you chose to attend the wedding today, my lord. My family has told me enough of you to make me wish to know you better. We must find an opportunity to chat before your return to London." She paused, brow arched suggestively, her eyes bright with unspoken questions. "We might speak of mad dogs and fencing matches and the fireworks at Vauxhall Gardens, perhaps?"

Dade flushed like a schoolboy. "I would be pleased." He sketched a bow. "I shall be honored to answer any and all questions to your satisfaction, madam. I hope . . ." he paused, wondering if she guessed at the significance of his desire, "I cherish the hope that you and your husband will find time for a private word with me."

Mrs. Dornton tilted her head. Her smile brightened knowingly. "You may depend upon it, my lord." She spoke with such conviction that Lord Dade knew he was not likely to be met with astonishment in requesting Margaret's hand.

With heightened optimism he took his leave of Mrs. Dornton and set off after her daughter.

Like a pale jewel in the golden light that mellowed the interior of the chapel, Pearl stood by the altar, gathering an armload of the fresh flowers that had adorned the wedding ceremony. Her billowing dress, the ashen gold of her hair, the circlet of pale orange blossoms and the cascade of blooms in her arms, all were gilded by the light that poured through jewel-bright windows. Dade paused. This vision of beauty had nearly slipped his grasp.

The very idea that Pearl might now be riding away from him, clasped in the arms of another man, chilled him. Thanksgiving lifted his heart. His gaze rose for a moment to the exquisite, fan-vaulted ceiling of the chapel. One could feel God's hand at work in such a moment, in such a place. Evelyn Dade, who had looked so intently into the face of death in the past years, ever questioning the means and methods of God's connection in such events, bowed his head. Lips moving silently, he thanked the one whose house he entered, for providing him with renewed hope and purpose, and for the blessing that Pearl might yet be his.

"Who is there?" his beloved called, unable to discern his identity in the shadows where he stood.

"Pearl," he said. "I have come to share your burden."

"Lord Dade?" she said uncertainly as he advanced on her. Again he saw an uncertain flicker in her eyes, as if she was pleased he had followed her here but was determined to hide her pleasure. "I do not think I should be alone with you."

"Your mother sent me," he said to ease her mind. "Shall I take these baskets?"

"My mother?" She considered the concept with confusion. Brow clearing, she said, "Oh, but sir, Mother's mind is full of weddings. She must have the mistaken impression . . ." She paused awkwardly as he stepped close enough to take an armload of what she carried.

His hand touched hers.

Her eyes widened. Her gaze fell uncertainly. Clutching the blooms to her bosom like a shield, she pulled stiffly away from him.

"You are afraid she might have the wrong impression? The impression that she may soon have another wedding to plan?" Like a shadow he moved with her, insistent in his intention to relieve her both of her burden and of her disgust of him. "I have reason to hope such an impression is no mistake." Gently he reached out to her.

"Oh?" Her back was stiffer than ever.

"Yes." He stared unblinkingly into the wary gray of her look, willing that some sense of his love might witness itself to her in his gaze.

"Oh!" Her tone changed, her eyes slanting away from his, her back suddenly gone soft. As though the weight of the flowers was too much for her, she thrust them at him. He was not yet forgiven, however. Her chin was defensively high. The brittle sparkle in her gray eyes struck like a knife to his heart. "How could you kiss me as you did and then simply let me go?" She set off briskly between the pews, her voice echoing hollowly from stone wall to vaulted ceiling. "Did you, like Creighton, think me ripe for seduction?"

"Pearl, you know that is not why I kissed you." He started after her, his voice large as it reverberated in the space that separated them. "I set out to save you from seduction, from Creighton. He vowed to win your innocence from the moment he laid eyes on you."

"Save me?" she scoffed. With a mocking curtsy she held open the door so that he might pass into the graveyard. "Do not tell me you meant to play the hero?" Her sarcasm was so unusual it wounded him. "You, who made a point to tell me that is not your role?"

He squinted in the light as he came level with her in the doorway. "I am, my sweet Pearl, no more and no less than what you make of me."

She frowned, the look in her eyes still unyielding as she closed the door behind them.

He began to say what he had been rehearsing on the way to Sherborne. The words did not come easy. "I failed to recognize what it was I had in your regard, Pearl, in your belief that within me there was a spark of heroism. Only when you were gone from me did I understand how dear was the prize I lost in you."

She regarded him carefully for a moment. Her lips had a wistful look. "One never does appreciate the sun until it rains." Her voice was so low he almost did not hear.

"Exactly," he breathed, relieved she understood.

She was softening to him. He could hear it in her voice. She took a handful of the flowers from his grasp, refusing to look up at him. "This way," she said.

He followed her as she made a path between graying headstones.

As she bent to her task, she said softly, with a pained edge to each word that twisted at his heart, "I thought we were of like mind. I thought I understood exactly what your thoughts and feelings for me were. Many have been the times"—she looked up sadly—"that I wished you here, beside me, ready to listen, as you appear to be ready to listen now." He felt pinned beneath the weight of the flowers. He wanted to kiss the sting from her words, not stand helpless while she reminded him of how wounded she was. "I knew that you, of all people, would understand the disturbed state of my emotions, the unruly tenor of my thoughts. But now that you are here, I cannot be happy for wondering why you did not reach out to me while my heart was breaking."

He winced. Dare he drop the flowers and grab her up in his arms? He restrained himself, reaching out to her with his words. "Pearl, I do apologize. I beg you will forgive me my negligence. I was standing on the edge of my own personal precipice at the time. So precarious was my position that I was convinced that had I reached out to you, I would have fallen and taken you over the edge with me. I got it into my muddled head that Wallis—"

She sighed impatiently. "Wallis again?" She relieved him of another handful of flowers, her mouth set.

"Yes. Hear me!" His voice cracked with emotion.

She looked up from the grave she bent over, shading her eyes to see him more clearly.

"I thought he loved you. Not your sister."

A light dawned in the gray eyes. She straightened, flowers still clutched in her hands.

On he plunged. "I thought you had begun to love him too. He seemed the perfect match for you—so worthy, so full of hope and light and life, where I was anything but."

She pursed the lips he would have liked nothing more than to press to his, and bent again to arrange the blossoms in her hand upon the bleak mound of the grave of an ancestor. "You place me on a pedestal, sir. I am undeserving of so high a perch."

Hopeful, he advanced on her, his arms no longer hampered by too great an abundance of flowers. She ducked her head, took up another handful of blooms and moved on to the next of the graves to be brightened.

"I saw the two of you together, as easy in each other's company as any two people can be." He pressed his point as ardently as he pressed orange blossoms and roses to his chest. "I imagined that what I witnessed was the love between a man and a woman and not just that of dear friends. When you left London in Wallis's care, I was relieved. My desire for you could no longer be denied, yet, I would not take you from the arms of a better man."

Her brow furrowed with concern as she took yet another bunch of flowers from his grasp and looked up at him through her lashes. "You believed Wallis somehow more worthy of my love than you?"

"Exactly!" He gazed at her intently, willing her to understand, willing her to lift her face that he might bend and kiss her lips.

"Go on," she encouraged as she stared at the pocket of his vest.

An unexpected warmth in the depths of her voice gave him the impetus to continue. "It came to my attention that Wallis meant to offer for one of the Miss Darntons—that he meant to follow you here, into the country. I imagined he came to see you. It never crossed my mind that he might be drawn to any other Miss Dornton. I came here today in the belief that you were the woman he meant to wed."

Her eyes flew wide. Her gaze rose to meet his. "No!" she gasped.

"Yes. I came to see you one last time. I could not stay away any longer. I could not keep silent. It was my intention to stop the wedding if need be, in order to tell you as much."

For the first time since he had come to Sherborne, Miss Margaret Dornton allowed the hint of a smile to touch her lips. "You looked so very strange when you came into the chapel." The wise look of understanding he had so missed flickered in her eyes.

"Yes! I realized I was losing you forever, to the worthy gentleman I had done my utmost to thrust upon you. I was miserable in my imagined success." He closed his eyes and bent his head to the flowers he clasped.

Margaret went into his arms then, much to his surprised gratification and the detriment of the flowers he had been holding. She flung herself into his arms and sighed with relief as he pulled her tightly to his chest, sank his face into her hair and nuzzled his nose against the velvet softness of her earlobe.

"Dear God!" he sighed. "I thought I had lost you."

Margaret buried her face in the wonder of Evelyn Dade's embrace. A few hot tears of relief and release wet the willing handkerchief that was his shirtfront, but it was not long she allowed herself such an indulgence. With a strange, choking sound, she began to laugh, her tear-streaked face rising from his chest. Dade dashed all traces of moisture from her cheeks with gentle fingers.

"Pearl, my love, you laugh and cry at the same time," he said so gently her tears flowed a little faster.

She touched his lips with her fingertips, a movement that closed his eyes and released from deep within the heart of him a shudder. He kissed her teasing hand, kissed fingertips, knuckles, palm and wrist.

Her hand felt a separate thing for such kisses, a separate and cherished entity regarded with jealousy and longing by every other inch of her flesh.

She sighed. "Do you know I did fear for some time after you first kissed me at Vauxhall that God had in some way voiced his displeasure with the explosion of gunpowder."

"No!"

"Shhh!" She touched his lips again with two fingers, hungry for their velvet warmth, hopeful he might yet touch these lips to her own. "Yes," she insisted as memories of noise and smoke and the smell of burning flesh assailed her in a wave. "Is that what battle is like? All noisy explosion and smoke and screams and everywhere blood?"

The gold-flecked eyes searched hers, as if to verify her true desire to hear his answer. "Yes," he said sadly. "Hour upon hour. Day after day. It is a beastly business."

"I'm sorry."

He frowned. "What have you to be sorry for?"

"I did not understand what it means to be a hero."

He shrugged and shook his head. "I did not understand myself when I bought my colors."

"Why did you not explain?"

"One cannot, you know." They were silent a moment together, pondering the truth of what he said. "Have you been able to explain all of your feelings in connection with the goings-on at Vauxhall?"

Her expression saddened. "No. Not even to those who act as if they truly wish to know." Her gaze drifted along the row of headstones. "My thoughts were too frightening—too raw and ugly to make for polite conversation."

"Do you wish to speak of it now?" he asked softly, his desire to hear her simple and honest and profoundly moving.

Her eyes went misty, so gently did he ask. She found it difficult to do more than nod. "Come." She gathered up his hand and a few of the flowers that had fallen to the ground. "There is one grave yet to honor."

Clutching the solid, square warmth of his hand as though it were a lifeline, she led him to a very small headstone. On its shoulders sat an angel clasping a lamb.

"This is where my little brother rests." She was surprised by the sudden warble in her voice. Her mouth twisted as she tried to control her emotion. "He died when I was three. I—" She bit down on her trembling lower lip, unable to go on. There were things she meant to say that she had never put into words. Faced with the opportunity to do just that, she found herself stymied.

"You witnessed his death," he said flatly.

She was surprised he knew as much.

"Allan told me."

She nodded, her eyes fogged with unshed tears.

He touched her shoulder. "Are you troubled by dark dreams, Pearl? Do you suffer from a numbness, a feeling of disconnection, a sense of melancholy when others are happiest? Are you bothered by simple, trivial things?"

As though the combination of his words and touch released all traces of her rigid control, she sagged against him and her tears brimmed over. "Yes. How did you know?"

"We have both lost brothers, you know," he said, drawing her deeper into the comfort of his embrace. "It is only natural that you should think of yours again now that the memory of his pain and suffering has been thrust so graphically under your nose. You once told me that it was not good to hold our miseries inside, to bear them alone. You were right, you know. It helps to talk to someone who understands. Perhaps you could tell me about him."

She sobbed a little.

He waited with infinite patience.

At last she took a deep breath and told him what she remembered of the events that had led to her brother's death and of the nightmares that troubled her sleep. She mentioned her sensitivity to loud noises and the smell of fire. She told him haltingly of how much the horrors of childhood had been revived both by the enactment at Astley's and by the incident in Vauxhall.

He listened, responding now and again with gestures and nods and an occasional timely word or thought that expressed his perfect understanding. She was touched by his gentle empathy, a quality she had never appreciated in him before. He listened. Such listening was a gift beyond measure.

She fell silent at last, with nothing more to say. Wordless, he drew her more tightly into his arms, kissed her chastely on the forehead and fell to stroking the line of her back between the shoulder blades. As though she had come home, Margaret nestled contentedly against his chest. After an interlude of comfortable silence and the pleasant rhythm of his hand, she said softly, "Thank you for listening. My heart does not ache so much when you hold me and listen."

He tightened his hold. "I know," he said softly, his breath humid in her hair. He kissed the crown of her head.

"Thank you for coming here today." She tilted her face up to his. His gaze passed over her lips with a look of longing, but he refrained from kissing her. She dipped her chin, unsure of his reason for resisting the draw between them. "Will you tell me about Gavin and Waterloo?"

He considered her request as he continued to look down on the crown of her head. He cleared his throat uneasily. She lifted her gaze to study the shadows that flitted across his expression. There was a look in his eyes that she had seen only briefly in the past. It was a warm and open expression of his love for her, a beautifully stirring connection he was willing, even desperate, to make. With their eyes locked together in such an expression, she was not at all surprised that he opened his mouth and began to talk, painting a vivid picture of his brother, and a less colorful one of a small part of what he had witnessed in battle. His voice was flatly matter-of-fact, the picture an ugly one, but in every instance he mentioned there was some subtle connection to her own traumatic experiences, some thread of understanding that bound them together in a way they had never before connected.

He talked, his words a river of sound and thought and feeling that swept her along without any threat of drowning, for he seemed to require no help in expressing what he had seen, how it had affected him and what he had recently done to come to a better understanding of his experiences. She listened until there was nothing more to be said. A silence engulfed them, heavy and full and completely comfortable. She bent her head to rest on his chest. As she listened to the heartbeat beneath her ear and savored the warmth of the rise and fall beneath her cheek, he stroked the silk of her hair beneath gentle hand and leaned now and again over the crown of her head and kissed her hair. It was a perfect moment, a fragile moment, a moment of unadulterated bliss.

She nestled closer and, wrapping her arms around him, sighed, "I would not let this moment end."

His hand cupped warmly the back of her head. Leaning into the bowl of his hand, she smiled up at him. Cradling her head, his thumbs stroking just behind her ears, he leaned forward to kiss her, his eyes searching hers for her reaction to such an advance.

She closed her eyes. This was the moment she had been waiting for and wanting ever since he had first kissed her at Vauxhall. Her hands bound him tightly to her, while her mouth yielded to the soft search of his lips. He responded with a long, hard, urgent kiss of such desperation that it knocked her unsteady. In this meeting of their mouths was the same engulfing desperation she had witnessed in the expression of the man whose hand had been so terribly injured that he thought he must die. It was the desperation that came with the fear of losing something quite precious. The grasping, groping intensity of that kiss told her more clearly than any number of words that this man had been desperately afraid he might lose her.

She recognized the feeling to be read in his kiss as clearly as it was expressed in her own seeking mouth. She could not get enough verification from his hands and arms, from his very lips, that he meant to hold onto her this time, and never try to give her up to some other, more deserving soul. There was a shuddering, clutching, bruising magnitude to their coming together.

His hands roved over her back and sides, sought out the most sensitive spots on her neck, her throat, her earlobes. One hand slid up her ribs to cup her breast. She moaned in delight. This was another moment she had hungrily awaited.

Her moan seemed to startle him. Inhaling heavily, he pulled away. "I do apologize," he hastened to assure her. "I should not take such liberties, I know, but I have missed you mightily, my breath of sunshine, my sweet and shining Pearl." His laughing mouth sought hers again, repeatedly. In between kisses he said, "We must talk to your father."

She laughed, and pressed herself against him quite brazenly and encouraged his hand to cup her breast once more. "Yes, my dear, brave hero. But not just yet. I would not have you continue to rescue me—not from your love."

Author's Note

At the bloody battle of Waterloo, it is said that two things resulted in the annihilation of several regiments of British Horse: the absence of curb chains and the presence of the rocket corp. The absence of curb chains for the mounts of the Household, 1st Royals, Scots Greys and Inniskillings cavalry divisions made them much harder to control in the fierce hail of grapeshot and musket ball amid the noise of cannonfire. Curb chains are small metal chains that pass beneath a horse's chin, attaching to the bridal on either side. Considered hard on a horse's mouth for normal riding, in circumstances such as battle where extra control was imperative, the chains exert a painful pressure on the animals chin, rendering them more receptive to commands from the rider. Added to the normally fearful conditions of battle, Wellington carried with him a very modern and secret weapon, the rocket corp. An inexact science at best, the smoking, hissing, spitting rockets were hard to control and largely ineffective other than at making a great noise and demoralizing the enemy. The careening rockets succeeded in terrifying the English almost as much as the French. It certainly terrified the horses.

The result was chaos. Halfway through the day, a number of regiments that had been ordered to remain in a position at the rear of a cavalry charge into the thick of the French position, defending the retreat of the regiments who went ahead, were swept by their uncontrollable mounts into a mad dash that carried them into a barrage of fire from Bachelu's infantry. With no safe retreat, they were finished by Martique's lancers.

Wellington was so infuriated by this senseless destruction of his heavy cavalry, despite his overall victory, that he set out the events that had taken place in a written text *(Instructions to Officers Commanding Brigades of Cavalry in the Army of Occupation)* as an example of what not to do.

When the bloody battle of Waterloo was over and the field littered with bodies of the dead and dying—as had been the habit in the American Civil War—the corpses were plundered of all valuables. Teeth were part of that plunder. Tooth drawers extracted what amounted to barrels full of teeth for dentists who put together false sets of what came to be known as "Waterloo" teeth.